The Pilot

By

James R. Nelson

Chapter 1

"WHAT DO YOU mean he tried to kill himself?" April Stoughton shouted into the phone.

"Well, I really don't think he was serious," her mother said, trying to calm her. "At least, I hope not! I came home from grocery shopping, and I found him passed out on the living room floor. He knew I was only going to be out of the house for about an hour. There were pill bottles all around him."

April gasped. "That sounds serious enough to me! What did you do?"

"I dialed 9-1-1. The EMT's got here in a few minutes. They took him to the hospital and pumped his stomach."

"I thought he was doing better," April said.

"That's what Doctor Craig indicated. I thought so too. Anyway, I have an idea I want to run by you," Margaret said.

"Um, okay. What?"

"I think Eddy needs a change of pace. A new environment. Something new to focus on."

April had a feeling of what was coming next. "And...?"

"Ah, I thought it would do him good if he could come and stay with you for a while."

April paused. She thought about how much she wanted to share. "You know Dennis only got home two months ago."

"I know, I know. But Eddy and Dennis always hit it off. I thought it might be good for your brother to spend some time with him."

April thought carefully. "Mom, you know there's a transition time when they come back from Afghanistan. I'm...I'm not sure we're ready for company."

There was a pause. "Is there a problem? Does he have...that PFD?"

"It's PTSD, Mother. And, I don't know. He won't talk about it, but I know he's been through a lot. That I do know. I'm not sure company would be the best thing for us right now."

"Think about Bobby. He loves his Uncle Eddy. I think it would do Eddy a lot of good to spend some time with Bobby; and if Dennis is having some issues, maybe he could talk to him about them. They get along so well."

April bit her lip. "I...I've got to think about it. How long were you thinking?"

"Oh, I don't know. Maybe a few weeks. Just a few weeks. Enough time for him to quit dwelling on living at home with his mother. I know that's bothering him." She paused. "And, September can be so nice in Chicago. I'd hate to think of him being cooped up in this house all fall. We both know what the winter's going to be like."

"But I thought he was getting better?" April asked.

"He is. But it's a slow process. He actually got a job for a while a few months ago."

"He did?" April said sounding surprised. "Why didn't you tell me?"

"Well, I was going to see how long it lasted before I mentioned it. He...he was only there a few days. The pressure got to him, and he had to give it up."

"What was he doing?"

"He was helping the produce manager over at Pete's Groceries."

"What pressure was there with that job?" April asked.

"Oh, you know, dealing with the public. Eddy's been home so much. That's why I think it would be a good idea for him to come and visit you for a few weeks."

April paused. "Okay, Mom. Let me ask Dennis. If Dennis is okay with it, I'll let you know."

"Okay, dear. Say hello to that handsome grandson of mine."

"I will. Bye, Mother."

Three hundred and eighty-one miles due north, Wilfred Fredericks stood on the third story widow's walk of his old Victorian house and gazed out over Lake Superior. He was still in shock. It had only been a few weeks since a freak Great Lakes storm had sunk his fishing boat, the *Pere Marquette*. The whole crew was lost. Five local men. Their ages ranged from 23 to 47. Only three bodies had been recovered.

While storms weren't rare on the Great Lakes, most occurred between November and March. This storm developed from nowhere. There was no warning. Wilfred had worked the shortwave radio from his office and listened as thirty-foot waves pummeled the boat to pieces.

He turned around and walked down the steps that led to his bedroom. His old German shepherd, Fritz, was waiting for him at the bottom. A narrow wrought-iron circular stairway went up to the widow's walk. Fritz had no problem navigating the closed staircase that led from the first floor to the second, but he never worked up the courage to navigate the open circular staircase that lead up to the roof.

Wilfred sat down at his desk and picked up a small calendar with September 8th circled in red. That was the day of the accident. Next to where the calendar had been, Wilfred noticed a chipped blue plate covered with a large piece of homemade apple pie. He smiled as he pictured Ruth stealthily placing it there while he was up gazing out at Lake Superior. Ruth had been his housekeeper for fourteen years, ever since he had hired her husband, Robert Halstead, to be his full time handyman.

The house had been built by his grandfather, Clarence Fredericks, in 1891. It was a large Victorian dwelling with a kitchen, dining room, parlor, two bathrooms, and a library downstairs. Upstairs were eight bedrooms. Four large ones were located at each corner of the house with four smaller ones nestled in between. Two more bathrooms were upstairs, and there was a sunroom in the back of the house that was used during three of the four seasons.

The house sat on top of an eighty foot cliff at the end of Peninsula Point Road on a spit of land that jutted out into Lake Superior. A large, black wrought-iron fence with pointed spikes surrounded the house and unmistakably sent out a message which boldly stated, keep out! This is private property! The house was a landmark for local fishermen since it stood out in such stark contrast to the surrounding swath of dark green pine forests. On a clear day, men a mile from the shore could spot it.

It was the perfect place for his grandfather to start his fishing business. The house was built on twenty acres of land sixteen miles northwest of Marquette, Michigan. A quarter mile from the house, at the bottom of the cliff, was a small fish processing plant and a fifty foot dock. Both had been abandoned for many years.

His grandfather had moved from the rich waters of Nova Scotia hoping to start his own fishing business. Wilfred liked to tell people that his grandfather had been run out of the area by a group of the town's jealous husbands, but that bit of colorful rumor had never been substantiated.

Wilfred's father, Alfred, took over the operation in 1917 and ran it until 1967 when he passed away at the age of seventy-seven. During the fourth year of Wilfred's tenure, he bought a second boat and worked two crews for the next thirty-five years. When Wilfred was twenty-three, he met Frances Stevens. She was the most beautiful girl he had ever seen. They were married two years later. She was the daughter of the ore dock master in Marquette. She and her family had moved to Upper Michigan from Detroit when she was eleven.

In March of 1976 they lost the twins, a boy and a girl. Both of them fell through the ice down by the fish house dock. Frances never got over it, and the harsh winters and bitter isolation living far out on the peninsula didn't help matters. Her mental health slowly deteriorated, and Wilfred's heart was broken four years later when Francis was committed to a mental hospital downstate.

They had spent so many wonderful evenings standing on the widow's walk, hand in hand, gazing over the wild and beautiful Lake Superior.

Thirteen years ago, fishing declined on all of the Great Lakes, so the processing plant was closed and Wilfred sold the second boat. Then, two weeks ago, everything changed. His fishing business was finished, and so was his income. He knew he was too old to start over and, he knew fishing on the Great Lakes was a cyclical thing. Some years were good and some were bad. The last three years had been bad. Because of it, he was two years behind on his county property taxes. He knew he had to have a meeting with the bank to see if they would give him a loan. Since he now had no income, it would have to be secured by his property value. He knew he didn't have much more time to pay off his delinquent bill.

Wilfred put the calendar down, glanced at the clock, and descended the stairs towards the dining room. As he entered, he saw that Robert was already sitting at the table. Wilfred could smell a beef roast cooking in the oven. Ruth walked in with a large bowl of boiled potatoes and cooked carrots. She headed back to the kitchen and returned with the meat steaming on a platter. As Wilfred sat down, he could feel tension in the room.

"I found where the cold air was comin' in from the library," Robert said. "Had to caulk around the windows on the north side."

"Good," Wilfred said. "What about the other windows? How'd they look?"

"I checked them all. Only ones that seemed a problem were the ones to the north. They get quite a beating from the wind and rain off the lake."

Ruth picked up the bowl of potatoes and handed it to Wilfred. He took one and passed it over to Robert. "You know I'm going to try and set up that meeting down at the bank."

Robert didn't look up from his plate. "I know."

Wilfred took a sip of coffee. "If they don't come up with something, I think I can only hang on to the place for a couple more months. That's what Norm Flath told me down at the tax office. He said he's delayed it about as long as he can." He glanced quickly over at Ruth. She didn't say anything.

"Let's hope it goes good," Robert said.

Wilfred ate quickly and pushed himself away from the table. "I hope you don't mind, but I'm going to head up to my room. Thanks for taking care of those windows."

"You're welcome. Get some rest. You look tired. I'll see you in the morning."

After Wilfred left, Robert helped his wife clear off the table. Once the dishes were washed, they retreated to their room on the second floor. They had divided one of the large bedrooms in the front of the house into a tiny bedroom and small living area. The room had a hot plate, small refrigerator, and a television set. Ruth was brewing a pot of tea. She drank it every night to help her sleep. "Have you heard from your sister?" Ruth asked.

"No."

"Do you want to call her again tonight?"

Robert picked up a magazine. "No. I told you I don't want to move back to Grand Rapids. I'm not going back downstate. Twenty years was enough. My roots are here."

"I know, I know. When I go down to Ann Arbor to see my sister, I can't wait to get back up here. Too bad good jobs are so hard to find around here. I'm just scared, I guess."

"I know. Fourteen years is a long time. We've got it good here. We're not getting rich, but Wilfred treats us right, and we sure don't have a lot of stress like your sister does."

"What are we going to do if that loan doesn't come through?"

Robert rubbed the two day stubble on his chin. "I think it will. Hell, the man's lived here his whole life."

Ruth raised her eyebrows. "I'm not so sure that's going to mean much. His business is gone. What's he going to use to pay back the loan?"

Robert flipped through a few pages of his magazine. "I don't know. And, you know what? I'm done wasting my time worrying about this again tonight."

Ruth didn't respond. She knew he wasn't going to talk about it anymore. She knew how he felt. She had been born in Green Bay, Wisconsin, but had moved up to the Upper Peninsula when her father was transferred to K.I. Sawyer Air Force Base when she was three. Her father had been a career airman. It was sad when the base shut down. It had taken a heavy toll on the area's economy. That was just one more reason jobs were so hard to find.

Like her husband, she was very comfortable with where her life was. It took a little getting used to at first, living so far from town. The isolated feeling of living on Peninsula Point without any neighbors. It took her even more time to get used to the house. Even from the beginning when they first moved in, she thought the place smelled musty. Things got better when she started opening the windows every spring. Her husband thought the storm windows had probably been on for the last ten years. It had taken a lot of work to get them off. Then there were the cobwebs. Living alone for so long, it was apparent that Wilfred had never given the place a good cleaning. And the dark wood. It seemed to absorb even the brightest sunlight. It had been tough that first year.

She had never gotten used to the sounds. At first Robert just laughed at her as if she were crazy. But she heard things. She felt things. Women were more sensitive than men. The cold drafts in the library. The sadness that would come over her when she walked into that back bedroom. Things like that. Things she thought she would get used to, but never did.

She glanced at the clock, picked up the remote, and turned the television on. She flipped through the channels until she found her show, *America's Most Haunted Locations.*

Robert said, "Can you turn it down a little?"

She turned the volume down and settled into the faded love seat.

"I should email them about this place."

Robert looked up. "What?"

"I should let this show know about this place. How creepy it is."

"This place? What's so creepy about this place?"

Ruth got up and poured herself a cup of tea. "What's wrong with you? You never listen! We've talked about this plenty of times."

"Ah, no. You've talked about this plenty of times. Every time you bring it up, I tell you you're crazy."

"I know. But one of these days...."

"Ruth, you keep talking about noises. This house is over a hundred years old. It creaks and groans all the time. Especially when we get those big winds off the lake. That's what old houses do."

"What about the cold spots when I walk into some of those rooms?"

Robert laughed. "Like the library? Didn't you hear me tell Wilfred I fixed the caulking around some of the windows today? Guess what? I felt a cold spot, too. But, I bet they're gone now."

Ruth ignored him. "How could there not be spirits in this old place. I can just imagine what Wilfred's grandmother looked like hanging from the railing."

"That's your problem. You imagine."

"I told you I think I've seen her a few times."

"I know you did. If you don't believe in that stuff, you don't see anything. Like me. I've lived here as long as you, and I've never seen anything"

"You should have been with me that night a few weeks ago. I couldn't sleep. I went down to the kitchen for a glass of milk. When I walked back to the stairway, I could see her hanging down from the railing."

"Oh, come on, Ruth. What did she look like? It was a shadow."

"It...she was transparent. She was just hanging there by a rope. Slowly twisting around in an eerie breeze. I took one look and ran back to the parlor. I spent the rest of the night terrified down there. I finally fell asleep around four o'clock and you didn't even know I was gone."

"Like I said, that's your problem." He shook his head.

"What's my problem?"

"Your imagination. Your overactive imagination. All the old houses around here had people dying in them. That's how they did it back then. People didn't

11

run to hospitals or emergency rooms when they got sick. They stayed home. And, that's where they died."

"It's a little different when you kill yourself. And then the twins. How sad. I can just imagine how horrible...."

"See. There you go again with your imagination. They fell through the ice. It happens every winter. We're surrounded by water. Every year someone falls through."

"That's another thing. When I go into the old nursery to dust, I always get a cold, clammy feeling. I've heard things in there."

"I have too," Robert said. "There's bats in the walls up there. Is that what you hear?"

"No. Little voices talking. Sometimes I hear them singing. Some days I can't even clean in there. I just have to get out."

"Do you see them, too?" Robert asked with a big grin.

"Now, you're just making fun of me," she said. "What about when things move around? We put things down and find them in a completely different place. It happens a lot."

Robert laughed again. "And, that would be Wilfred. Goodness, the man's in his seventies. I hate to admit it, but I think he's slipping a little. With all that's happened this year, I can see it's taken a toll on him."

"Laugh all you want. I bet that TV show pays good money when they use somebody's house. Since you don't seem to be doing much about our situation, maybe I should write to them and tell them about this place."

"And if they were interested? Good luck explaining to Wilfred that a bunch of strangers from Hollywood are going to be taking over his house. I want to be around when you tell him that!"

Ruth took another sip of her tea. "All this talking and now I've gone and missed half of my show."

Chapter 2

"UNCLE EDDY! UNCLE EDDY!" Bobby screamed when he saw April's brother step off the train at Union Station. Eddy walked over, set down his suitcase, picked up Bobby, and held him high in the air. "You've grown like a weed! How old are you now?"

"I'm ten!" Bobby shouted.

"Ten years old! That's a great age to be," Eddy said, giving him another push towards the sky.

Eddy put him down and turned to April. "Thanks for letting me stay with you. It's great getting out of Fond du Lac." He looked around. "Where's Dennis?" He saw April's smile disappear.

"Um, he wanted to come. He really did. But...he doesn't like crowds. He told us to hurry home because he can't wait to see you."

"Oh, okay." That didn't sound like the Dennis he knew, but he thought it would be best not to push the issue.

During the ride back to the apartment, Eddy quietly asked, "How's Dennis doing? I've seen on TV that a lot of servicemen are having a rough time of it when they get back."

April glanced at the back seat and saw that Bobby was engrossed in one of his many video games. "I…it's too early to tell, I guess. But, Dennis *is different*, that's for sure."

"What do you mean, *different*?"

"Remember how outgoing he used to be? The life of the party."

"Yeah."

"Well, he's not like that anymore. He's very…I don't know, quiet, I guess. He doesn't talk much, and he likes to spend a lot of time alone."

Eddy shook his head. "That is a change." He laughed. "Sounds more like me than Dennis."

April smiled. "Speaking of you, how are you doing?"

Eddy shifted in his seat. "Oh, I'm…I'm doing better, I guess. I had a rough patch there for a while."

Tears welled up in April's eyes. "How could you…do you know how much…?"

Eddy reached over and patted her on the shoulder. "I know…I know…it was a stupid thing to do."

As they pulled up to the apartment, April said, "Dennis is anxious to see you. I'm hoping you can help him out. Maybe he can make you feel better, too."

Eddy pulled his suitcase from the back of the SUV, and as they approached the apartment, Dennis walked out and shook Eddy's hand. "Hello, Eddy! It's been too long. Nice to see you."

Dennis directed Eddy to the guest room, and April started putting food out on the table.

During dinner, April made sure the conversation was kept light, especially with Bobby listening attentively to everything. She turned to Eddy, "I almost forgot. I ran into an old friend of yours a few days ago."

"You did? Who's that?"

"Joel Radke."

Eddy looked surprised. "Joel? How's he doing?"

"He seems to be doing just fine. He graduated from the University of Wisconsin and took a job in finance. He's moved to Chicago. He's got an office down on Wabash Avenue. I told him you were coming, and he said he'd love to see you while you're here."

Eddy frowned. "Um, oh he did? I don't know. Maybe I...."

April cut him short. "Now Eddy, mother wanted you to come stay with us so you could get out of your rut. I think it would be nice to see Joel and catch up with him. He said he could come over around two o'clock tomorrow. I told him that would be fine."

"It won't take him very long to catch up with me. One sentence will just about cover it. I still live at home with my mother."

"Don't be foolish. Joel doesn't care about that. You guys were close in junior high. I think it's nice that he wants to see you again."

Eddy didn't reply. He glanced over at Dennis and noticed that he didn't seem to be paying any attention to the conversation. Dennis had his head down, and he was concentrating on cutting his meat. It dawned on Eddy that Dennis hadn't spoken at all during the meal.

April decided it would be best to change the subject. She asked a few questions about their mother and inquired about some of the neighbors. After dinner, Dennis said he was tired. He got up from the table and disappeared into the bedroom.

Bobby asked Eddy to play some of his video games with him. After picking up the dishes, April grabbed a book and sat next to the guys as they worked their controllers and bantered back and forth. At nine o'clock she made Bobby go to bed. She grabbed two beers from the fridge and handed one to Eddy. "What do you think of Dennis?"

Eddy took a sip and thought for a while. "Like you said in the car, he seems like a different person. Something's bothering him. Is he getting any help from the V.A.?"

"Yes. He signed up for counseling after I got on his case, but I don't see anything changing. He's really got me worried." She took a sip from her drink. "Don't say anything to Mom. She's got enough to worry about." Immediately she regretted what she had said.

Eddy looked over at her and smiled. "You got that right!"

"I'm sorry, Eddy. It's just that with Dennis coming back...."

"Don't worry. We both know what the situation is. Look, maybe I can talk to him tomorrow. We were close. You know....before he went overseas."

"I'd like that. He needs to be around someone who knew what he was like before."

They talked for two more hours, and then April glanced at the clock. "Oh, it's ten after eleven. I need to get to bed. I have to catch the "L" tomorrow morning at seven." She got up, walked over and gave him a hug. "I'm glad you're here. Is there anything you need in your room? An extra blanket?"

"No, no. I'm okay. You still working down in the Loop?"

April sighed. "Yes."

Eddy shook his head. "I don't know how you do it. All those people!"

Joe Casperson slammed the receiver down and let out a string of obscenities. "That bitch won't let me talk to the old bastard."

His wife looked over at him. "You keep up that harassment, you'll find yourself right back in jail. All she's gotta do is call the cops. They'd love to haul your ass back there. I can't believe you didn't get arrested when they run you off his place last week. They could have picked you up for trespassing. You should thank your lucky stars old Wilfred didn't call the cops on you. You should know how probation works by now."

Joe sneered at her. "Just listen to yourself. Tony's gone because of that asshole."

"I know, Joe. And there's nothing you can do to change things."

"But we made a promise to your sister. We promised we'd watch out for him."

Madge wiped a tear from her eye. "She went so fast."

Joe walked to the refrigerator and pulled out a beer. "And Tony sat right here at this table and told us how pissed off he was that old man Fredericks kept sending them out no matter what the weather." He took a swig. "I swear, he knew this was going to happen. He kept bitching about how that boat was falling apart. How Wilfred never put no money into it." He ran his fingers through his hair. "I should have gone over there and checked it out. I...I can't believe he's gone. And them poor other guys. Needlessly. Just so Fredericks could sell more fish."

Madge pulled a cigarette out of his pack and lit it. "Nobody should have gone out that day. I know Svenson pulled all their boats. Nobody else was out there but Fredericks. Somebody should sue him and sue him good."

Joe gave her a weak smile. "Maybe that's why he won't take my call. He thinks we're gonna sue his ass."

"Why are you calling him anyway?"

"To tell him what I think of him. Tell him everybody knows what he done."

His wife looked at him through a cloud of blue smoke. "You don't think he knows? His boat's gone. He's out of business."

"He knows, but he don't care. I gotta make this right for Tony."

She frowned. "How are you going to do that? Tony's dead."

"I don't know. But I gotta do something."

Chapter 3

IT WAS APPARENT that the meeting didn't go well. Brad Feldman's secretary, Roxanne Deloria, watched as he stomped passed her desk, walked into his office, and slammed the door. The door hit with such force that the picture of him with the studio head, Irving Smaltzman, came crashing down onto the floor right next to her.

Roxanne had worked for Brad for three years. Brad was forty-six years old when she had met him during her interview. She found him very attractive and outgoing. He stood about six feet tall with black hair that was graying at the temples. Compared to other television producers she had worked for, she found that he was quite genuine. Not so full of himself.

She walked over, gently picked up the larger pieces of glass from the broken picture frame, and tossed them into her waste basket. She knew that under these circumstances, it would be best to let him cool off by himself for at least half an hour.

Thirty-five minutes later, his door opened. Brad walked over to her desk and sat down. She waited for him to talk first.

"That damned Irving wants to cancel the show. Say's it's getting stale."

She thought for a moment. "Well, it's been on for four years. That's a long time for a cable channel."

"It's been on for four years because people love it. Our ratings have been going up, up, up."

She knew the ratings had started to decline this last season, but she didn't say anything because she knew Brad knew it, too."

"So, it's over?" she asked.

"Just about. He said if we could freshen it up and reduce the production costs, he'd consider another season."

"That's good. Do you have anything in mind?"

"I do. I was thinking about what the best way to cut costs would be."

"The travel?"

"You got it! Sending our crews all over the country is costing us a fortune. We feature four different haunted houses per episode. That's where the money goes. What if we found one great place and filmed the whole season there?"

Roxanne smiled. "I love it! That would give the show a whole new slant and Irving would be thrilled. He's always sending me nasty emails about hotel and meal expenses. Great idea!"

"We'll have to find a new place and shoot a pilot. We could do it in about ten days. Then show Irving and see what he thinks."

"Do you have any place in mind?" Roxanne asked.

"People send me emails just about every day with suggestions. We've got to come up with a place. Can you take a look at some of them and grab the best twenty for me to review?"

Roxanne turned to her computer. "Sure, when do you want them?"

"Let's meet tomorrow around eleven o'clock. Would that give you enough time?"

"I think so."

Brad stood up. "Good, I'm headed over to the Frolic Room. I need a drink."

She looked surprised. "The Frolic Room! On Hollywood Boulevard?"

"Yes."

"Did you know that that was the last place...."

"The Black Dahlia was seen alive," he interrupted. "Yes, I do know that. Hey, if that place was good enough for Elizabeth Short, it's good enough for me."

"Don't end up like her. Dead and mutilated a block away. We've got enough legends around here. We don't need another one."

The next morning, Brad's head felt like it was twice its size. Even the smell of coffee, a fragrance he normally loved, was enough to almost trigger an episode of the dry heaves. He stood in the shower for twenty minutes and let steaming hot water pour over him. He thought this part of his life was behind him. After all, he had been married seven years and had two kids. It had been such a shock when they moved out. That first night when he came home to an empty house, he thought they had been robbed. Then, he found the note.

He knew things had not been going great for about the last year, but he blamed that on his hectic travel schedule. He remembered how she had given him those ultimatums. First, he had never thought they were actually ultimatums and secondly, there was really nothing he could do about it. The job dictated that he travel every week. She didn't seem to mind the money he was pulling in.

Brad stumbled out of the shower, dried off, and hurriedly got dressed.

When he walked into the office, Roxanne looked up and did a double take. "Oh, so it's Mr. Black Dahlia. Looks like someone did a number on you."

"He did. Felipe, the bartender. He should have cut me off way before he did."

"Tell me you didn't drive home from there," Roxanne said, with a look of concern.

"No, they called a cab. That's how I got here today. You're going to have to drive me over there at lunch so I can pick up my car."

"Great! Maybe we can have a triple martini lunch, like they did in *Madmen*!"

Brad rolled his eyes. Just the thought of more alcohol was enough to make him sick. "Stop! I'm going to my office. Wake me up when you've finished that house list."

At eleven fifteen, Roxanne knocked softly on his door and pushed it open. He was sleeping with his head on the desk. She walked over, pulled out a chair, and coughed discreetly. He rolled open one eye and slowly sat up.

"I know it's none of my business," she said, "But, you really need to get back with your wife. This new single life is going to put you in an early grave."

He sat up and slowly massaged his temples. "Tell me about it. It's not that I haven't been trying. Most of the time she won't even take my calls."

"Keep trying. You need to get back to a stable life." She was about to say, "You're getting too old for this," but changed her mind.

He headed towards the door. "I need to wash my face. I'll be right back."

When Brad returned, he looked a little more awake. "Before we look at the houses, I want you to write down this name."

She flipped open her notebook. "Okay."

"Doctor Hilton."

"Who's he?" Roxanne asked.

"He's not a he. He's a she."

"Oh, sorry. Who's she?"

"Someone I completely forgot about. But, last night at the bar, I was talking with some of my friends about how we could change the show, and one of them started talking about her. She was all the rage in...I'm not sure, the late sixties or mid-seventies, I think. When he mentioned her name, I sort of remembered her. That was before my time, but I've seen her on reruns of some of those old talk shows.

She was quite the character. She taught parapsychology at Duke for a while. See if you can find her."

Roxanne thought for a moment. "If she was popular in the sixties she's probably dead by now."

"I hope not. Just see if you can find her."

"What's her first name?"

Brad thought for a moment. "Claudia, Carol…I don't remember. Something like that. Everyone called her Doctor Hilton." He turned to the folder she had placed on his desk. "Okay, what have you got?"

"I went over everything you sent me. The folder is really thick. I reread all of the possibilities and pulled the top ten. I thought we'd start with those. If you don't like any of them, I've got a hundred more we can look at. I can't believe there are so many haunted houses out there."

"I bet ninety-nine percent of them are just people looking to make a buck. Probably nothing's ever happened in most of them. Do you have them in order from best to worst?"

"I do!"

Brad smiled. "I know how you work. Okay, let's start with number ten and work our way up."

An hour later, they were both standing up at Brad's desk surrounded by papers. "Looks like we're down to two. Which one do you like the best?"

She pointed to a paper and said, "I like this one."

He smiled and looked over at her. "Why?"

"How can you not like it? It's in New Orleans! The place looks very southern gothic. I like the moss hanging from the trees and the old wrought-iron on the balconies. I don't know, it just looks haunted to me."

Brad nodded. "I agree with everything you said. It looks perfect, but one thing bothers me."

"What's that?"

"New Orleans has been done to death. It's what people expect. They've seen countless shows about hauntings in New Orleans. It's old. Remember, Irving said he wanted something fresh."

"Okay, I can't argue that." She picked up the last paper. "To tell you the truth, I don't even know where this house is."

He glanced over the page. "It's in Michigan."

"Let's look it up," she said, sitting down at his computer. "Hmm, are you sure it's in Michigan? Looks like it should be part of Wisconsin. Let's look at the satellite view."

Roxanne bent down and looked at the computer screen. "Are you kidding? Looks like there's a bunch of nothing there. Look at all the trees! There's nothing but woods!" She turned to him. "I don't know. Looks kind of remote, doesn't it?"

Brad looked excited. "Yes! It's different. It looks wild and isolated just like Mrs. Halstead's email said. But think about it. An old lady who hung herself. She says she sees her hanging from the staircase sometimes late at night. Those noises they hear and the things moving from place to place."

"And don't forget about the two kids that drowned," Roxanne added.

"Oh, yeah. Sounds pretty interesting. Send her an email and let's see what happens."

April was in a marketing meeting when the woman who shared her cubicle, Karen Alabaster, burst into the conference room and told her there was some kind of emergency, and she had to call her husband right away.

April quickly walked over to her desk, pulled out her cell phone, and dialed her husband. "You've got to come home right away!" Dennis was screaming in the phone. "No, wait. Meet me at the hospital. You've got to meet me at... at St. Lukes!"

April had never heard terror in his voice like that before. "What's wrong?"

"It's...it's..." Dennis stammered.

"What! What is it? Is it Eddy? Did he try something again?"

"No. It's Bobby. He's hurt."

"Hurt? What happened? Was he on his bicycle?"

"He's...he's been shot!"

A wave of numbness washed over her. "Shot! He's been shot? Where...what...what happened? Is he okay?"

"He...he found my gun somehow. No, it's pretty bad. Get a cab. Meet me at St. Lukes. You need to get over there now!" The phone went dead.

Karen, sitting across from her, saw the fear in her face and then saw her go white. "April! What is it?"

"I've got to leave! It's Bobby. He's...he's been shot!"

"Shot? What happened?"

"I don't know. I need to get a cab. St. Lukes. I have to get to the hospital."

The woman jumped up. "My car's in the parking garage. I'll take you. Come on. Run out and grab an elevator. I'll tell Mr. Marshall we're leaving."

Twenty minutes later, as April and Karen rushed into the waiting room; April knew it was too late. Eddy was sitting on a chair with his head buried in his hands. A doctor and a policeman were talking to Dennis. April started to scream.

Chapter 4

WILFRED STEPPED OUT of the bank manager's third-floor office and walked over to the window. He gazed out over Marquette's Lower Harbor. He was surprised to see that a layer of ice was already forming on the water. This was the earliest he could remember this happening. Usually, it was mid-December when the water started freezing, not the middle of November.

He knew the early ice was a forewarning that the coming winter was going to be long and hard. The perfect winter to follow a disastrous fall. He walked over to the elevator and pushed a button. *What am I going to do now?* The bank had turned him down for a loan. He got into his truck and drove back towards Big Bay Road.

Robert was in the garage when Wilfred pulled up. As soon as he stepped out of the car, Robert knew how the meeting went. Suddenly a rush of guilt hit him. Why hadn't he taken the initiative and tried to find a new job? He knew his love of the Upper Peninsula had blinded him to reality. Wilfred's family had lived here for over one hundred years; it didn't seem possible that something could change and, all of a sudden, he'd be forced off his own land.

Stooped over and looking ten years older, Wilfred slowly shuffled up to him. "I'm sorry, Robert, but it looks like it's all over. Them sons-a-bitches wouldn't give me any money."

Robert put his arm around the old man. "I'm sorry. What are you going to do?"

"I'll have to put the place up for sale. Pay off the taxes and find a new place to live. That is if they don't foreclose on me first. Maybe I'll get me one of them apartments in Marquette."

Robert knew that if he did that, he'd probably be dead in six months. This house and land meant everything to him. He loved the wildness of the big Superior storms blowing on shore. The roar of the waves you could hear no matter where you were in the house. The woods being alive with lightning bugs and trilliums in the spring and the deathly quiet and complete isolation ten feet of snow and minus twenty degrees could bring in the winter. Town life would be the end of Wilfred. There was no doubt about that.

"How long do you want us to stay?" Robert asked.

Wilfred stared down at the garage floor. "Um, geeze, I don't know. Maybe the first of the year...February?"

"Okay," he replied. "I'll go tell Ruth." He walked back to the house. The reality of the situation, of actually hearing a date from Wilfred, hit him hard. He made his way up the front porch steps, walked into the living room, and headed back to the kitchen.

Ruth was standing at the counter, pouring herself a cup of coffee when he came in. "What's wrong with you? Looks like now you've seen a ghost!" She took another look at her husband. "Are you okay?"

"Sit down. We've got to talk." He poured himself a cup and then pulled out a kitchen chair across from her. "I just talked to Wilfred. He got bad news at the bank. Looks like we'll be out of here by January or February. Maybe I better give my sister another call."

She set her coffee down on the table. She thought about saying something like "I told you so," but from the look on Robert's face, she decided to keep quiet. After a few moments, she said, "That's probably a good idea." They sat in silence for several minutes. Finally, Ruth said, "You're not going to believe this."

Robert looked up. "What?"

"I heard from those people with the haunted house show."

"You did? When?"

"About three days ago. They're interested in the house."

Robert straightened up in his chair. "Why didn't you say anything?"

"Because you made me feel kind of stupid when you laughed and said you wanted to be there when I told Wilfred about all those Hollywood people coming on the property."

"How much do they want to pay?"

"I really don't know. I never emailed them back," Ruth replied.

"What! Are you kidding? This could be our answer!"

"What about Wilfred?"

"I bet he'd agree to just about anything about now. Especially if it meant keeping the place. Run upstairs and email them back. See if you can find out how much money they have in mind."

"Are you going to tell him about it?"

Robert thought for a moment. "Not yet. I don't want to give him false hope. Maybe they only give you a few bucks. Come on, go send them an email."

As she headed for the stairs, Robert yelled from the kitchen, "Don't tell them about the tax problem!"

Nicole Peterson, a graduate student at Western Michigan University, opened the door to a small office and started coughing. She waved a handful of papers in front of her face and stood in the doorway.

Doctor Louise Hilton looked up from her desk. "What's wrong? Are you catching a cold?"

Nicole's eyes started to sting and water. She slowly stepped into the room and continued fanning the pages. "The smoke! My goodness, I can hardly see you. How do you get away with smoking in here? I thought the government outlawed that years ago."

"My dear Nicole. The government was never formed to turn this country into a nanny state. If Western wants to bury me down in the bowels of Sangren Hall, in an office the size of a broom closet, the least they can do is let me enjoy the one remaining bad habit I have left."

Nicole smiled. "Oh, so you quit drinking?"

Doctor Hilton shook her head. "The impertinence of today's youth. Gin is a tonic for the soul, not a bad habit. Did you finish grading those papers?"

Nicole glanced at a sticky note that was attached to the first paper in her stack. "Yep. All finished. Five A's, nine B's, twelve C's and 4 D's. Nobody flunked." Nicole reached across the desk and handed her the stack.

Doctor Hilton pushed her wheelchair a few inches closer to the desk and took the papers. "I swear, if I gain one more pound, I'm going to have to demand a bigger office. It takes me half an hour just to maneuver this damn chair behind my desk."

The phone rang. When the Doctor picked it up, Nicole propped the door open, pulled over the one remaining chair into the doorway, and took a deep breath of stale hallway air. She pulled a book out of her backpack and flipped it open.

Doctor Hilton said, "Good morning. Doctor Hilton speaking." She heard a young woman on the phone.

"Good morning, Doctor. My name is Roxanne Deloria. I'm calling on behalf of Brad Feldman. He produces the *America's Most Haunted Locations* show. I was wondering if I could have a few moments of your time."

Doctor Hilton glanced at a small clock on her desk. "I'm afraid I'm not interested, Ms.... What did you say your name was?"

"Deloria. Roxanne Deloria."

"I have no interest in any of those ridiculous reality shows."

"We don't either, Doctor Hilton. In fact, we think they're ruining television, and we can't wait until the reality fad fades away. Our show is more like a documentary."

"I wouldn't know, Mrs Deloria. I don't watch much television."

"The reason I'm calling, Doctor Hilton, is that we're changing the format for next season's show. We understand that you did some breakthrough research in parapsychology at Duke back in the early seventies." Roxanne waited for a reply.

After a long pause Doctor Hilton responded, "Yes, I did."

"Mr. Feldman would like to discuss a project with you. A project where you could continue your research. Funding would be available."

"I don't wish to be rude, Mrs. Deloria, but I'm no longer involved in the field of parapsychology. My research ended in 1977. Currently I'm teaching a sociology class at the university in Kalamazoo. Thank you for your interest, but..."

Roxanne interrupted. "Oh, you're welcome, Doctor. By the way, it's Ms. Deloria, but before you hang up, let me leave my number...just in case you have a question. Our office number is (424) 321-9806."

Doctor Hilton reached for a pencil and scribbled down the number. Not that she intended to call it, but more as a polite gesture. She started to end the call with "Thank you for calling," but she thought it would be foolish to thank somebody for wasting her time. Instead, she said, "Okay, Good-bye."

Nicole looked up from her book. "That sounded interesting."

"Another waste of time. Every few years I get a call like that."

"It sounded like it was someone from a TV show."

"It was. Something called *America's Most Haunted Locations* or some nonsense like that."

Nicole set down her book. "Really! Are you kidding? I love that show!"

The Doctor glanced at her over her thick reading glasses. "Don't tell me you watch that reality stuff." She stubbed out her cigarette and pulled out another one from the pack on her desk.

Nicole gave her a sheepish look. "I really don't. This show is so much better. It tries to be more factual. A bunch of my friends watch it every week. It's really kind of interesting."

"Believe me, I'm sure it can't compare to the research we were doing in the seventies."

Nicole pulled her chair closer to Doctor Hilton's desk. "You worked with the famous J. R. Rhone, didn't you?"

Doctor Hilton looked surprised. "Why, yes. How in the world did you know that?"

Nicole laughed. "When I got assigned to you, I did some research. It looked fascinating. What happened? What made you quit?"

She leaned back in her wheelchair and let out a long sigh. "If you must know, I think we were making too much progress."

36

"Too much progress? That's why you stopped?"

She shook her head. "No. I think what we were doing put a scare into the people above us. They were shocked at some of the things we were discovering, some of the people we had found. It got to be too much. They wouldn't believe what we were telling them. They couldn't believe what our experiments were showing."

Nicole hesitated and then said, "I thought I read there were some problems with how the experiments were conducted."

The Doctor removed her glasses and set them on her desk. "Don't believe everything you read. They discredited Doctor Rhone. Said his assistants were cheating with the Zener cards. Said the people he was testing could see the cards reflected in his glasses or his eyeballs. All a bunch of bunk. Many of the people we tested were in another building. We put them in the library and we were in a lab a hundred feet away."

"What are Zener Cards?"

"That's what we used to test our candidates. They came in a deck of twenty-five. There are five different shapes. Five of each in the deck. The deck gets shuffled, and we test our subjects to see if they can predict which card will be turned over next." Doctor Hilton started coughing. After almost a minute, Nicole asked, "Can I get you a glass of water?"

The Doctor waved her hand. "No...I'll be okay. Sorry." She tossed a tissue she had pulled from her purse into the wastebasket. "You're working on your Master's degree. Let me see how good you are at math. If you used a Zener deck, what percent of correct predictions do you think anyone off the street should be able to guess correctly?"

Nicole thought for a moment. "Twenty five cards, five shapes...ah, I'd say...twenty percent."

"Exactly!" Doctor Hilton said. "One in five. But, would you believe we had a few people who could consistently get thirty and forty percent correct? Once I had someone get twenty of twenty-five. You should have seen Doctor Rhone's face when he saw those results!"

"That's amazing," Nicole said.

"That's when the false accusations started. Since they couldn't explain what was happening, they started spreading rumors."

"What did you do?" Nicole asked.

"What could we do? We were furious. We tried to keep on going, but when the accusations kept coming, Duke stopped the funding and everything fell apart. My colleagues scattered, the gifted people we had discovered moved on." She paused. "Some really amazing people. Most were very reluctant to work with us in the first place. When they were called out as cheats and frauds; that gave them a good reason to disappear back into obscurity."

"That's a shame!" Nicole said.

Doctor Hilton blew out a long stream of smoke. "These people had powers that easily could ruin their lives. The abilities they had were not supposed to exist. At least according to modern twentieth-century intellectualism. As the word got out, some of the people we were working with started getting backlash from people around them." The doctor thought for a moment. "Maybe it was for the better that our funding got pulled."

Nicole sat transfixed. "That sounds so exciting. Don't you miss it?"

Doctor Hilton stubbed out her cigarette. "I kept my own research going for over ten years. Quietly, on the side. If I read something or saw some story on television, I'd try to reach out to the people involved. Many were just plain fakers or people with psychological problems; but every now and then, probably about twice a year, I'd discover someone who clearly experienced something completely beyond our current reality."

"What happened after ten years? Why did you stop?"

"The media mostly. And the times. The media really killed things. They loved to label those people as crackpots. The tabloids didn't help, either. Finally, interest in parapsychology faded. The media went on to focus on different things." She laughed. "Things like UFO's."

Nicole frowned. "That's too bad."

Doctor Hilton reached for her coffee. "I did miss it for several years. But, life goes on. You get busy with trying to make a living." She took a sip. "But I've added to my files. Whenever I see an article about somebody who's had a paranormal experience, I cut it out and add it to my collection."

"Oh, I'd love to take a look at that someday!" Nicole said.

Doctor Hilton coughed again. "What's it like outside? It was snowing pretty hard when I got here at seven."

"Nothing's changed. I think we got six inches already. Thank goodness I don't have any classes today."

The doctor threw her cigarettes into her purse. "I'm headed home. With this weather, if I don't get out of here now, I'll never make it."

Nicole tossed her book into her backpack. "What do you want to take with you?"

The doctor pointed to a stack of books. Nicole grabbed them, and they made their way down a long corridor to one of the elevators. Once outdoors, she helped Doctor Hilton fold up her wheelchair and get behind the driver's seat of her SUV.

"Thank you," Doctor Hilton said. "See you tomorrow morning. Weather permitting."

She had a small cottage just outside of South Haven. It was almost an hour's drive, but most weeks she only had to go into work three days. Luckily, even though it was snowing quite heavily, it wasn't blowing much. As she pulled into her driveway, she noticed it had recently been plowed. Her closest neighbor, about a quarter of a mile away, was retired, and he loved to plow snow. She gave him a fifth of Jack Daniels every year for his service.

Once inside, she made a fire in the fireplace, heated up a pot of chili, sat down at her desk, and started thumbing through one of the books she had taken with her. She was teaching a freshman sociology class, and the head of the department had asked her to review the book as a possible replacement for the text they were currently using.

It was hard to concentrate. She kept thinking about the phone call she had received and the discussion she had had with Nicole about her work at Duke. It had been over thirty years since she had thought about her research.

She wheeled herself into a spare bedroom that had long ago been made unusable because of all the junk she had accumulated. She rolled her chair over to an old wooden filing cabinet and pulled out the third drawer.

She thumbed through about twenty manila folders, stained yellow with age. She grabbed several and returned to her desk. She spread them out in alphabetical order, Bishop, Bingham, Bowers, Reynolds, Stoughton, Taylor, and Weymouth. She picked up the first one and started reading.

Robert walked into the kitchen as Ruth was scrambling eggs. "Have you heard from the show yet? It's been two days."

She turned away from the stove. "Nothing. I checked last night right before we went to bed."

"Maybe you should call them?"

"Do we really want to sound that desperate?" she asked.

Robert poured himself a cup of coffee. "At this point, we are desperate. I'm desperate not to have to find another job and move."

"Okay. Once I'm finished with breakfast, I'll run up and give them a call. I'm pretty sure there's a phone number somewhere in the email." She looked at him. "Don't worry, I won't sound that frantic."

He smiled. "You just knew I was going to say that, didn't you."

He grabbed some plates and silverware and walked out to the dining room and set the table. Ruth was right behind him with bacon, scrambled eggs, and toast. Robert looked at his watch. "It's eight-thirty. Wilfred should be here by now."

"Maybe he slept in. Could you run up and get him?"

He walked down the hallway to the staircase. As he got to the top, he noticed the door to Wilfred's bedroom was open. He stuck his head inside and looked around. The room was empty. He climbed up the narrow circular stairway that led to the widow's walk and pushed open the door. A cold, biting wind hit him as soon as the door opened. He saw Wilfred bundled up in a jacket. He turned when he heard the door open.

"Morning," Robert yelled against the wind.

Wilfred waved and turned back to the water. Robert stepped next to him and stared out over Lake Superior. He had a feeling Wilfred was trying to absorb as much of the lake view as he could before it was time to leave. He kept quiet, not wanting to disturb the old man's meditation. Finally, Wilfred turned towards the door. "About time for breakfast, I suppose."

Robert followed him down the spiral staircase. When they got back to the bedroom, he could see Wilfred had started to pack up some of his books into cardboard boxes. Robert said, "Yes, Ruth's got everything out on the table. Do you want me to help you with some of this packing after breakfast?"

Wilfred shook his head. "No. Maybe this afternoon you can start going through some of the tools in the garage. I'm going to have to sell as much as I can. I don't imagine those apartments in town can hold very much."

Robert just nodded. They ate breakfast in near total silence. Other than a pass this or pass that, there wasn't much of the normal day-to-day conversation. When he was finished eating, Wilfred pushed himself up from the table. "Excellent as usual, Ruth. I'm...I'm going to miss...."

"Now, now, Wilfred. Let's not go there. At least not yet." She grabbed the empty egg bowl and headed towards the kitchen. Halfway back, she stopped to wipe her eyes with her apron.

Chapter 5

APRIL SAT ON her bed and watched through her window as her mother walked out the back door and waved at the neighbor lady, Marge Kulick, who was standing across the alley. As the two women approached each other, Marge glanced up at the window and April quickly ducked behind the curtain.

Even though it was snowing lightly and the temperature was only thirty one degrees, April's mother never missed her daily walk. For the last few years, she was always accompanied by Mrs. Kulick, who had moved to Fond du Lac from Milwaukee after she retired from teaching grade school.

April turned from the window. It had been over two months since Bobby died. It felt a little strange - comforting, but strange - to return to the house she had grown up in after so many years. The shock of losing her son, the strain of the child services investigation, the police threatening to bring charges against her husband, plus the issues Dennis had been having integrating back to civilian life - all combined to be too much for April to handle. She had to get out of that house.

She blamed Dennis for Bobby's death. When she left, she explained to him that this really wasn't a separation; she just needed to get out of Chicago for a while. He claimed he understood, but she knew he didn't.

She felt bad leaving him, but she had started to get worried even before the accident. His distance and sullenness had frightened her. He would snap at her when she tried to get him to talk. She stayed at the house for almost a week after the funeral. She started to feel as if she was drowning. She felt she needed a safe place to stay and to try and get a handle on everything that had happened. Actually, it had been her mother's idea to come back home, and April had jumped on it.

She heard the bedroom door next to hers open. There was a soft knock on her door. "Come in."

Eddy stuck his head into the room, "Where's Mom going?"

April gave him a puzzled look. "On her walk with Mrs. Kulick. Like she does every day."

"But it's only ten o'clock."

"I guess they decided to go an hour early. Maybe because of the snow. It's supposed to pick up later this afternoon." She saw there were dark circles under his eyes. "You look tired. Did you get any sleep last night?"

"A little. Those damn nightmares." He combed his hair with his fingers. "I think you should stay here. It's nice having you back home again."

She smiled. "Thanks, Eddy. But, I have to get on with things. Being able to come home was a life saver. When I think of going back to the house...."

"Sell it!" Eddy said. "Why would you even want to go back there?"

"We'll see. It's not only my decision."

Eddy squinted and started rubbing his temples.

"Another headache?"

"A leftover from last night's. I'm hoping it will be gone in a few hours."

"What about your medicine?" April asked.

"Sometimes it works and sometimes it doesn't. Lately, it seems like it hasn't been helping much."

She walked over and put her arms around him. "I'm sorry. It seems like your headaches have been getting worse since I've been here. I really need to get myself together. It's just that...I don't know, I just don't feel like I'm ready to go back and ...."

He hugged her back. "Not many people have been through what you have. Just give it time."

She let go of him and took a step back. "It's been two months already!"

He thought for a while. "That's not very long."

She closed her eyes. "I know."

"What about Dennis?" Eddy asked.

"He's finally getting some counseling. They haven't decided yet if they're going to file charges about the gun."

Eddy turned and stepped back into the hallway. "I hope they don't."

The roads were clear when Doctor Hilton drove back to Kalamazoo. The snow had stopped overnight, and the sky was a perfect winter blue with no clouds on the horizon. The sun made the snow banks sparkle. Next to her on the seat was the stack of folders she had dug out the night before. She had only been able to read through a few of them, but doing so had energized her in a way that she hadn't felt in years. Reading the case studies and seeing her notes brought back memories of the passion she had felt at the time. Back then, she never woke up with the dread of having to go to work as she felt now. Her research had been exciting and groundbreaking. Not the drudgery of teaching the same thing over and over. Freshman sociology wasn't exactly rocket science.

She was running a little late because she had stayed up so long reading her files. The three gin martinis hadn't helped things, either.

Nicole noticed a change as soon as Doctor Hilton wheeled herself into the office. Nicole glanced at the clock. "I'm glad to see you. I was worried when I beat you here. That never happens! I had visions of you spending the night in the van, buried in a ditch somewhere. Did you make it home okay?"

Doctor Hilton pushed herself behind her desk and tossed the folders down. "It was fine. M-43 was drifting outside of Bangor, like it always does. Once I got past that, it was okay."

Nicole noticed energy in the doctor's voice that she hadn't heard before. She pointed to the stack of folders. "What's that?"

Doctor Hilton turned and smiled. "That's part of my old research. Thanks to you and all your questions yesterday, I dug them up. That's why I'm late this morning. I started reading some of them last night and I couldn't stop."

Nicole's face lit up. "Really! I can't wait to hear about them!" She looked at the clock. "Oh, I'm almost late for Professor van Deventer's class!"

After Nicole left her office, Doctor Hilton lit a cigarette and reviewed her notes for the class she was going to teach at ten o'clock. She found it hard to concentrate because she had taught the same entry level class for over ten years. Trying to work up some excitement to teach was completely impossible. She had to keep reminding herself that even though the material was old and boring to her, it was all new to her students. She wondered how many more years she would be able to get motivated and still be able to drag herself into the classroom.

She glanced down at the folders she had been reading the night before and then looked over at the clock. *No*, she thought. *If I start reading another one, I'll forget all about time and miss my class.* She rummaged through the papers on her desk and found the phone number the woman from California had given her. She picked up the scrap of paper, and on an impulse, dialed the phone. When she heard an answering machine, Doctor Hilton remembered that it was much too early for anyone to be in the office since they were on California time. She hesitated for a second and then spoke into the phone, "Yes, this is Doctor Hilton. Mrs. Deloria called me yesterday. I've been thinking about what she said, and I would like to hear more about this project. Please call me back. You've got my number."

Roxanne was surprised when she listened to the message from Doctor Hilton. She picked up the receiver and was about to call her back but then hesitated and put the phone down. It would probably be better if Brad returned her call. She remembered how excited he was when she told him she had located her, and then, how disappointed he was when she told him it didn't seem that the Doctor was interested.

Half an hour later, Brad stumbled into the office. His suit was rumpled, and it looked like he hadn't shaved or even combed his hair.

Roxanne gave him the once-over look. "More frolicking in the Frolic Room?"

"How'd you know?"

She picked up her legal pad. "Because a Tiffany Torrance called swearing you were putting her in your next pilot."

Brad made a face. "Oh, her."

"Did you even make it home this time?" She looked him over. "Or have you come straight from the bar?"

"I collapsed on the couch sometime early this morning. My back's killing me."

"That place must be something. I'll have to give it a try some night," Roxanne said.

From the tone of her voice, Brad knew she was needling him. "Yeah, I think you'd like it," he lied. "Beats going home to an empty house."

She glanced down at her notepad. "Guess who left us a message?"

A look of panic crossed Brad's face. "Not Irving, I hope."

"No, that doctor lady of yours."

"Doctor Hilton?"

"Yes. She said she wants to know more about your offer." She ripped off the paper with Doctor Hilton's number and handed it to him.

"Great!" Brad said. "I'll give her a call right after I have a cup of coffee."

An hour later, Brad came bounding out of his office. "That went well!"

Roxanne turned in her chair. "Tell me about it."

"Doctor Hilton said your call got her thinking about her old research again. She said she would like to review some of her files and invite a few of the most promising candidates to join us for a week. Only one problem."

"What's that?" Roxanne asked with a worried look.

"We'll have to move fast. She can only do this in January!"

Roxane looked stunned. "January? You've got to be kidding. That's only six weeks away!"

"I know, but she's got the whole month of January off from her teaching duties."

Roxanne made a face. "What do you think? Can we do it that fast?"

"I know, it's pushing it. But, think about it. We don't need much prep. We don't need a script, but we do need that house up in Michigan. Doctor Hilton said she's confined to a wheelchair, but she could drive up there. She thought it was about six hundred miles north of her. She doesn't like to fly. So, you need to contact whoever sent you information about that house we talked about and make sure we can use it the first week in January. As soon as we secure the place, she'll start sending out invitations."

"I've got the woman's email right here and a phone number. How much do you want to offer?"

Brad thought for a moment. "I'm sure we can get it a lot cheaper than if we had to rent a place around here. Why don't you start out at five hundred a day?"

"How long do you want to use it?"

"We're only going to shoot a pilot, so...I don't know. Let's get it for ten days."

Roxanne turned back to her desk. "Okay. Let me give her a call."

Ruth heard someone knocking on the front door. Even before she looked out of the window, she knew who it was. She tip-toed over and peeked out. She was right. "Robert! It's that lunatic again!"

"You gotta be kidding! Put the leash on Fritz. I'm going to get my gun." He walked over to the front hall closet, pulled out a deer rifle, and grabbed the leash from Ruth. Fritz rushed out onto the porch as soon as Robert pushed the door open. "Damn-it, Joe, you need to turn around and get the hell off this property. I told you last time, Wilfred's not going to talk to you. I said I was going to call the sheriff the next time you came by and, by God, I'll do it."

Fritz was barking and snapping at the air. Long streams of saliva flew from his mouth.

Joe backed up several steps. He was weaving a little. "I ain't got no beef with you, Robert. I need to talk to the old man about Tony."

Even from a distance, Robert could smell alcohol. "Wilfred's not going to talk to you, and he's never going to take your calls, so you can stop calling here, too." Fritz jerked forward almost pulling Robert down the porch steps.

Joe stumbled backwards. "You don't need to sic that dog on me."

"Damn-it, Joe. We're all upset about your nephew and those other men, too. It's a damn shame, but you know as well as I do that fishing on the lakes is a dangerous game. You should know that. You did a little fishing when you were younger. You got to leave us alone. I don't want to call the sheriff, but this harassment's got to stop."

"It'll stop when I kick the shit out of that old bastard for killing them men," Joe said, slurring half the words.

"I'm giving you to a count of ten to get the hell off this property," Robert said. "When I get to eleven, we'll bring in the cops, and you know what that means." He stared down at Joe from the porch and began to count. "One...two...three...four...five...."

Joe turned around and staggered towards his truck. He grabbed onto the door handle for support, turned and yelled, "This ain't over yet. That old man's gonna get what's coming to him. You can bet your ass on that." He climbed into the truck, fumbled around for his keys for a moment, and then spun a doughnut in the driveway before heading back out to the county road.

Chapter 6

APRIL REFILLED HER coffee cup and sat down across from her mother at the kitchen table. "Where did you get your patience?" she asked.

Margaret gave her a puzzled look. "What do you mean?"

"Look at us. Here I am, thirty-two years old and living back home. And Eddy. He's twenty-eight and never left." She turned towards the window. "We're really making you proud, aren't we, Mom."

Her mother reached over and grabbed April's hand. "I wouldn't say you were back living at home. You're going through a very tragic time, and you need the support of your family. There's nothing wrong with that. That's what families are for. I'm very confident you'll be back on your feet soon."

April got up and gave her mother a hug. "Thanks, Mom. I think you're right. I'm starting to heal."

"What about Dennis? Don't you think it's time to see him again? You know, to talk things over."

"I try to tell myself it's time, but then I start thinking about what he did. How could he leave that gun..."

"But, you said he claims he didn't leave it out," her mother said.

"And that's the problem. He won't take responsibility for what happened. Even after his counseling. We'll never...." April dabbed her eyes with a napkin, "have Bobby back. But if you've done something horrible, you need to own up to it."

"You know he's suffering, too. I just think...."

April jumped up from the table. "Why can't he just...." She spun around towards the dining room door.

Margaret said quietly, "Come on. Don't leave. Let's talk about something else."

She walked over and sat back down. "I heard from work yesterday. They're holding my job."

"That's good."

April fiddled with her napkin. "Mom, I'm worried about Eddy. Ever since the accident, he seems more depressed than ever. I know this has been horrible for all of us, but I'm worried about him."

Margaret nodded her head. "I know. I've talked to his doctor about it. They've upped his medication, but he doesn't like to take it. It makes him tired and he says he can't think straight."

"Maybe he shouldn't take it," April said.

Margaret looked concerned. "Oh, no. He gets very depressed without it." She looked away. "And...he can be mean."

April leaned closer and grabbed her mother's hand. "Mean? Has he ever hurt you?"

Margaret shook her head. "Oh, no...no. Nothing like that."

"Maybe you should think about changing doctors," April said.

Her mother looked surprised. "Really? He's been seeing Doctor Craig on and off ever since what happened in Mayville."

"That's my point. That was twenty years ago. I put all that stuff behind me. Why didn't he?"

Margaret got up and refilled her coffee cup. "You're both so different. You were always outgoing. Strong, almost fearless. Your brother was always the quiet one. He holds things inside. He was younger when all that happened. The media attention scared him. I think you kind of enjoyed it."

April rolled her eyes. "I didn't enjoy it. Believe me. I just went with it. I didn't want them to think they were getting to me."

Her mother took a sip. "Then there was the teasing he got from his classmates. Calling him Ghost Boy and Haunted Eddy. That really bothered him even more than the incidents, I think."

"Yeah. I remember. Good thing we moved. I made new friends and tried to forget everything," April responded.

"And your brother didn't. He felt betrayed by those kids. I don't think he ever formed strong friendships again."

April looked surprised. "I don't know about that. I bumped into Joel Radke in Chicago just before...."

"Joel Radke? Oh my goodness. I haven't heard that name in quite a while. How's he doing?"

"He looked great. He's got a good job down in the Loop. He said he was going to stop by and see Eddy." She stopped and thought. "I don't know if that ever happened." April stood up, walked over to the window, and watched the snow fall into the back yard. "You know, you said you thought I was fearless a few minutes ago. That's really not true. But, I do face things and try and deal with them. That's where I think Eddy's problems come from. He hides them. He bottles them up. And by doing that, they never go away."

Margaret looked concerned. "But Doctor Craig thinks...."

"Doctor Craig's letting Eddy keep everything inside. I think Eddy needs to stand up and finally confront his demons."

"I know you mean well, April, but I think we should leave Eddy's treatment in the hands of a professional." She heard footsteps on the porch and then heard several pieces of mail drop onto the living room floor.

"I'll get it, Mother," April said. She walked down the hallway and picked up several envelopes and flyers that the mailman had shoved through the door slot. There was an electric bill, an advertisement for the local grocery store, and two letters that looked exactly the same. One was for Eddy and one was addressed to her. She walked back to the kitchen and handed Eddy's to her mother. "Looks like Eddy and I each got the same thing." She held up an envelope. "Who's Doctor Louise Hilton?"

Her mother looked at Eddy's envelope. "I don't know. Looks like it's from Western Michigan University in Kalamazoo."

April looked as the envelope. "I don't know anybody in Kalamazoo. Do you?"

"No."

April tore open her envelope and started reading. She quickly glanced over the paper and set it down. "Hmm, I can't believe it. Eddy's not going to be happy about this."

"What is it?" her mother asked.

"Some doctor who studies parapsychology wants us to go to a house up in Marquette, Michigan for some kind of study."

Her mother threw up her hands. "Oh! Not that business again!" She walked over to the sink. "Maybe I better toss his in the garbage. I don't want anything starting him off again."

Just then Eddy walked into the kitchen, poured himself a cup of coffee and asked, "Toss what in the garbage?"

Margaret shoved the letter into her apron pocket. "Nothing. Just another one of those people who what to bother us about what happened in Mayville."

Eddy looked over and saw a paper lying on the kitchen table in front of April. He grabbed it and started reading. After a minute, he looked up. "So, I got one of these, too?"

"I'm afraid so," she said with a smile. "I wonder how they knew I was living here?" April asked.

"They always come here," her mother replied. "I guess they forget you've both grown up. People find those old articles, send letters to the old Mayville address, and they forward them to me. I throw them away. Every year or so, I get another one."

Eddy tossed April's letter onto the table. "Now they want to study us. Examine us like lab rats."

"It didn't say that. It said there are going to be talks and seminars. Did you see the part where they want to pay us?" April asked.

"No. I didn't get that far."

"Take another look. I don't know about you, but I could use a few bucks. And I think it's about time we give Mother some money for groceries and stuff."

"Oh, you don't have to do that," Margret said.

Eddy looked defensive. "I'm...I'm going to get another job. It's just that...."

April picked up her letter again. "And, did you see where it is? It's not that far away. It's in the Upper Peninsula. Marquette. Probably only take us a couple of hours to drive up there."

"Are you serious?" Eddy asked. "You're actually thinking of going to this thing?" He stared at her in disbelief. "You don't want to dredge up all those terrible memories again, do you? I mean, I'm still seeing a shrink to try and forget all that crap."

"Eddy, this lady said they'd give us a hundred dollars a day for ten days! That's two thousand dollars for both of us. Think of Mother. Do you know how many groceries we can buy Mother for two grand?" April paused. "And, it might do us both good. We'd get out of the house for a while. God knows I could look forward to that. And, quite frankly, I think it might actually help you, too. Maybe it would do us both good to talk about what happened. You shouldn't keep everything bottled up inside like you do. And, did you notice, we're getting invited by a doctor. Maybe she can do something for you besides what Doctor Craig's not doing."

Eddy shook his head. "Not interested. Go by yourself if you want, but I don't think it's a good idea." He stormed out of the kitchen. April and her mother sat in silence as they listened to him stomp up the stairs to his room.

Margaret looked over at her daughter. "I can't believe you. He's spent the last twenty years in therapy trying to forget about what happened to us; but now all of a sudden, you want to take him up to some stranger's house in Michigan. To...to relive everything with some doctor you don't even know."

April looked over at her. "It's been twenty years and Eddy's still a basket case. His treatment's not working, Mother, but you won't admit it. Maybe it's time he did talk about what happened and finally get it out of his system."

Chapter 7

THE CIRCLES OF Hope facility was housed in an empty state mental institution four miles outside of Chattahoochee, Florida. It was an old, run-down, red brick building that at one time housed criminally insane inmates from all of the panhandle counties.

Closed down in the late fifties, it had stood abandoned until 1997 when part of it was refurbished and turned into a small private mental hospital.

Jeremy Taylor stared at his mother as she was led into the visiting room. A large man in green scrubs accompanied her. Jeremy thought he looked like Mike Tyson.

Mrs. Taylor turned to the guard. "I'll be all right, Mr. Johnson. You don't have to stay."

"I'm sorry, ma'am. I gotta follow the rules. Don't mind me. I'll just be sitting over in the corner."

Mrs. Taylor pulled out a chair across the table from her son and sat down. She looked nervous. "How are you feeling?"

Jeremy glanced over at the orderly. "I'm fine. There's no reason I should even be in here. I can't believe you *Baker Act*-ed me."

She looked surprised. "I had nothing to do with it. That was a decision the policeman made when your boss called 911."

"Overreaction. He hates me and he overreacted."

Mrs. Taylor let out a long sigh. "Jeremy, you pushed him to the floor and threw his computer out a four story window. I'd hardly call that an overreaction."

"How much longer do I have to be here?"

"They told me it's at least seventy-two hours for observation. You've only been here two days."

"Observation? That's a joke. I haven't talked to anyone yet. I'll be a complete lunatic if I have to stay here seventy-two hours. Have you seen the day room? Watching TV in there is like taking your life in your own hands. People are babbling and spinning around. I tried to stay in my room today, but they won't let you. I need to get out of here and get back to work. I can't imagine how many emails are piling up."

"You don't need to worry about that. You need to rest and tell the doctor what's bothering you."

Jeremy looked irritated. "Well, of course I need to worry about that. Do you have any idea of how many of those stupid emails I get every day? It's in the hundreds. I'll never catch up if I don't get out of here soon."

"Jeremy! I'm trying to tell you. They let you go. Those emails are not your concern anymore. Getting rest and feeling better is what you have to focus on."

He sat back in his chair. "They let me go! Are you kidding me? After twelve years? Call a lawyer. They can't do that."

His mother rummaged in her purse and pulled out a letter. "This came to your apartment. It looks important. Who is Doctor Hilton from Kalamazoo, Michigan?"

"From where?"

"It says Kalamazoo."

"Is that really a place? I thought it was just some made up name you heard on TV."

"Apparently not."

He tore open the envelope and pulled out the letter. After reading it he handed it to his mother. "Take a look at this."

She slowly read the paper and handed it back to him. "You haven't had any more episodes, have you?"

He unconsciously rubbed his left temple. "No, not for about a year."

"What about the police? Have you done anything for them?"

"Not since the Sinclair case."

"Good. Oh, by the way, Officer Patterson stopped by. Your boss wanted to press charges against you, but he talked him out of it."

"See, Mother. You hate it when I work with the police. Now they're doing something for me for a change."

His mother pulled out a tissue from her purse and dabbed her eyes. "I...I hate what it does to you. The nightmares. How you get so...tense."

"But I helped them solve those children's murders, didn't I."

Leon Johnson sat up and cocked his head towards the table.

"I don't understand what you do, I really don't. Going to those horrible crime scenes. Throwing yourself on the ground. And then the months of nightmares. And for what? Now you've gone and lost your job."

"Mother, you're talking about two different things. My boss had it in for me. He was new. He showed up and didn't know one thing about our clients. He couldn't stand it that I had to constantly correct him. He kept putting pressure on me. It's a miracle I didn't snap a few months ago. Really, that had nothing to do with my volunteer work with the homicide department."

"I don't care what you say. I think you need to stop it."

"If I wasn't doing something good, they'd stop calling me. It's only once or twice a year when they're completely at a dead end. Believe me; they'd rather not have to use me. That's why you never hear about what I do on TV."

Mrs. Taylor fanned herself with the envelope. "Thank goodness for that! Can you just imagine?" She looked down at the letter. "You're not thinking of doing this, are you?"

He smiled. "Why not? Apparently I don't have a job. They'll pay me every day and reimburse me for my transportation. I think it could be interesting. I've read about Doctor Hilton and her research. She was quite the deal back then."

His mother looked worried. "I...I don't think it's wise. You don't know these people or what their motives are. Michigan this time of year? You'll catch pneumonia. You've never even seen snow!"

"Just another reason I should go. And besides, it will give me something to think about when I'm stuck in this dump. Do me a favor and give the airlines a call. See what the flights are like. Looks like I would have to be there January 4th."

Chapter 8

DOCTOR HILTON SPENT the holidays with her sister in Grand Rapids. The first few days of January were spent thinking about what to take with her up to Marquette. She was excited to start her trip. If the weather cooperated, she thought she could drive there in about eight hours. She wasn't looking forward to crossing over the Mackinac Bridge, but she knew they had people that would drive your car for you, if needed.

Margaret knocked on April's door. "The phone, dear. Dennis is calling."

April put her book down. "I'm not taking it. Why does he insist on bothering me?"

"All right dear. I'll tell him." Her mother turned to go back down the stairs.

April jumped from the bed. "Wait! I'll take it." She followed her mother downstairs to the phone and picked up the receiver. "Hello."

"Oh, um…hi! Ah, I sure miss you, April. This…this was the worst Christmas of my life."

From the sound of his voice, April could tell Dennis was surprised she was speaking to him.

April stood there fighting back tears. "I know. I'm just glad it's over. I don't think Christmas will ever be the same."

Dennis tried to speak. He coughed. "Ah, I just wanted to tell you that I've been going to the V.A. every day for counseling. They're working on my PTSD, too. Look, I really miss you and um, I was wondering if…if I could come by and see you."

A wave of sadness washed over her. "I…I don't think that's going to be possible."

There was a long pause at the other end of the phone. "Why? We need to talk about this. I…."

Tears started streaming down her face. "Haven't we talked about it enough? Bobby's gone. He's not coming back. You…you…."

"I had the gun put away. Put away on the top shelf. I don't know how…geeze, April, what do I have to do?"

"Dennis, I can't do this right now. If you won't admit your part in this, there's no point in…."

"Look, we have to talk. I don't care what you say. I need to talk to you. I'm coming. How many times do I have to tell you…?" Dennis heard the phone click and the line went dead.

April hung up the receiver and slumped down into a chair. She wiped her eyes with her sleeve and tried to stop shaking. She could hear her mother moving around in the next room. She stood up, tried to compose herself, and walked into the kitchen. Her mother was washing the breakfast dishes. Eddy was sitting at the table, eating toast.

"I have to get out of here," April said. "I'm so tired of arguing with Dennis. He's made up his mind to come and see me. You know what? I'm going to go up to that place in Michigan. Don't tell Dennis where I am."

Her mother dried her hands and sat down at the kitchen table. "You're not going up there all by yourself, are you?"

April looked surprised. "I am unless you're coming with me." She looked over at her brother. "You heard Eddy. He's not interested."

Her mother frowned. "I don't know about this, April. On the one hand, I think it would do you good to get out of the house and meet some new people. But, I...I really don't think this is the answer! Who are these people? Why do they want to talk about what happened so long ago?"

"Who knows? Who cares? I need to get out of here. I don't want to see Dennis."

"But, they want you to remember all those terrible things that happened in Mayville. Those memories should be forgotten."

"That happened twenty years ago. I was twelve! I've forgotten most of it. Anyway, it doesn't matter. I'm going."

Eddy looked up from his plate. "I'll...I'll come with you."

April looked surprised. "I thought you weren't interested."

"I'm not. Not one bit. But, I don't want you going up there alone. And, I've been thinking about what you said. I probably need to take...take...um, stop sitting around and not doing anything. Like you said, that was so long ago. I looked up Marquette. It's right on the water. It looks like it could be an interesting place to see. When do you want to leave?"

Chapter 9

IT TOOK BRAD and his crew almost three hours to unload all of the cameras and video editing equipment from the van into the old Fredericks house. He had flown in from LAX. It had been a grueling trip. Four and a half hours to Detroit, a three hour layover, and then an hour and a half flight to Marquette. His crew had left three days earlier in a rented van. Everyone from Los Angeles was freezing. They knew it would be cold, but they weren't prepared for what greeted them. Brad had to take them all to a store so they could buy long underwear and warmer jackets.

From what he could see, the house looked perfect. It was dark, rambling, and the incessant wind from Lake Superior added a foreboding element.

As Brad was opening one of the boxes, Robert walked up behind him. "Ah, Mr. Feldman, do you have a moment?"

He stood up and turned around. "Yes." He saw an old man standing behind Robert.

"I'd like to introduce you to the owner of the house, Wilfred Fredericks."

Brad shook his hand. "Thank you for letting us use you magnificent house, Mr. Fredericks. I can imagine this will be a big change from your normal life. I promise I'll try and make our presence as unobtrusive as possible."

"Thank you. I'd appreciate that. Well, Mr. Feldman, I just want to say welcome to my house. But, just so you know, I want to be up front with you right from the start. You're more than welcome to use my place, but I want nothing to do with any of it. I'll probably spend most of my time upstairs in my room. Robert said he talked with you and the crew. He tells me everyone knows my room is off-limits. And, I really don't want to talk to any of the visitors you got coming over here, either. I'm gonna stay out of everybody's way and let them do whatever has to be done to get the job done."

Brad smiled. "Thank you for your frankness, Mr. Fredericks. Yes, Robert explained to us your thoughts, and we'll do everything in our power to make sure you're not disappointed. I understand where you're coming from. I'll do everything I can to make sure we don't bother you."

Wilfred nodded, turned around, and walked towards the staircase. As he disappeared upstairs, Robert said, "I hope you didn't think he was rude. He's fine with everyone here. At least, after a little convincing on my wife's part. But, he's a private man, and I'm sure this has to be pretty rough for him."

Brad smiled. "Don't worry. I appreciate his directness. Quite an uncommon trait where I come from. We'll try our best not to bother him." He looked around the hallway. "By the way, I need to thank your wife for thinking of us. This place looks wonderful. It has a lot of atmosphere. I'm hoping that, with the people Doctor Hilton's invited, we can walk out of here with an exciting pilot."

Robert grinned. "Hold on a minute, let me run and get her. She'd love to meet you."

A few minutes later Robert came back with Ruth trailing behind him. She was wiping her hands on a long apron. She reached out and accepted Brad's hand. "I...I wanted to go upstairs and freshen up a bit before I met you, but my husband insisted I come by now." She shot Robert a dirty look.

"Oh, I hope I didn't bother you. I just wanted to thank you for taking time and writing us about this house. It's amazing! The more I look around, the better it gets. I'm very excited about working on our pilot!"

Ruth blushed. "I'm so glad you think it will work. We're excited about having you here, too."

There was an uncomfortable silence. Brad smiled. "Well, I'll let you get back to whatever it was you were doing. I'm sure you have a lot of things to do, with all these people coming."

Robert winced when he heard Brad say that. Again, Ruth gave her husband a look. "Oh, we'll manage, somehow." She turned around and Robert followed her back to the kitchen.

Robert said, "Now, now, don't start. You know I tried to talk to Wilfred again about getting you some help, but he's so worried about money right now, he wouldn't hear of it."

"Does he understand he's going to get a big check for letting the production company use his house? And, it's only because of me! This is ridiculous. I'm the one who gets everything put together, and then I'm punished. I've got all this extra work to do because he's too damn cheap to hire someone to help me out."

"I know...I know. I'll help you the best I can."

"Once the crew leaves, there's going to be eight extra people I've got to feed and do laundry for. What's wrong with that man?"

Doctor Hilton was excited about meeting all the people she had invited. After reviewing her files, she had sent out twenty-three invitations. Five had accepted. She hoped they all actually showed up.

Her neighbor had helped her load her car the night before. As she was leaving, she checked to make sure that all the burners were turned off on the stove, the coffee pot was unplugged, and all the ashtrays were empty. It was only twenty degrees when she climbed behind the steering wheel at nine a.m. sharp. She had arranged to have Nicole meet her at a restaurant in downtown Marquette at six o'clock. That should give her plenty of time to get there, even with the snow. They would have dinner and then drive separately to the Fredericks house.

After driving north on I-75 for three and a half hours, Doctor Hilton saw dark gray snow clouds blowing in from the west. The wind picked up and Doctor Hilton worried about crossing the Mackinac Bridge. She remembered when a small car had blown off the bridge in the late eighties. It was a long way down to the water. She shuddered as she thought of what that drop must have been like.

An hour and twenty minutes later she approached the looming bridge. She wondered how strong the winds would be once she started to cross the straights.

She looked up at the giant girders and said to herself, "I can do it!" She gripped the steering wheel tightly and pulled onto the bridge. She kept her gaze on the roadway. She didn't allow herself to look down.

Ten nerve-wracking minutes later, she was entering St. Ignace in the Upper Peninsula. As she headed west on U.S. 2, she saw that the snowbanks were a lot higher than they were back home. After driving for another three hours, she pulled up in front of the restaurant in Marquette. Nicole stepped out of the doorway, helped her pull out her wheelchair, and they hurried into the building.

The restaurant sat on top of a big hill. Normally there was a beautiful view over Lake Superior. All Doctor Hilton and Nicole could see when they were seated at a table was a flurry of blowing snow.

After they finished ordering, Nicole looked out the window and said, "Looks like you got here just in time. I was beginning to get worried. It really started coming down about half an hour ago."

"I know. Once I got to Munising, the drifts off the lake started getting deeper. I'm glad I was driving an SUV."

Nicole looked up at Doctor Hilton. "I'm so excited. I can't believe I'm going to watch them film one of my favorite TV shows. I never thought that would happen. I can't wait to meet Brad Feldman."

Doctor Hilton smiled. "He seems to be a nice man. I've talked to him several times. He's been here a few days already. He came with a film crew. They wanted to put cameras around the house."

"That's so exciting!"

When their meals arrived, Doctor Hilton said, "I think we'd better eat quickly. I don't want to get this far and get snowed in. From what I understand, I think the Fredericks place is about fifteen miles from here. The map shows it's at the end of a point that sticks out into the lake. I can just imagine how hard the snow's blowing out there!"

The sky was a brilliant blue when April and Eddy carried their suitcases out to the car. "Is that it?" April asked.

"No, I've got one more upstairs, and I need to think about what books I want to take with me."

April turned. "You should have thought of that yesterday. Run up and get your bag. I want to get out of here."

"What's the rush? I figure it will only take five hours to get there. We've got plenty of time."

She glanced around. "Come on, Eddy. I want to get out of here before Dennis comes by again."

"You should have seen him when he was here yesterday."

"Like it's any of your business. Run up and get your bag. I'm leaving now with or without you!"

As Eddy dashed back into the house, April looked around to see if she could see Dennis's car anywhere.

After a few minutes, her brother ran back to the car and tossed his remaining bag into the trunk. He slid into the passenger seat. "Okay. Let's go!"

Margaret fought back tears as she watched April's car pull away from the house. Doctor Hilton's letter had brought back memories that she had tried to bury for such a long time. There were so many things April and Eddy didn't know about that had happened in the Mayville house.

They didn't know that the story about the desk bringing in the spirit had been concocted by a retired bishop who had been brought in to help get rid of the spirit. The bishop was summoned from the Archdiocese of Milwaukee when it became apparent to the local priest that what he was dealing with was way over his head.

Margaret witnessed the turning point when her husband, Frank, was taking the priest on a tour of the house. For several weeks, the children had been complaining about things that were making them scared. April had come into their room late one night crying because she had seen a witch that was wrapped in fire. Certain that this had been a nightmare, they comforted her and brought her back to bed. Two weeks later, Eddy started screaming in the middle of the night. When they went to investigate, he told them the same story.

Then Eddy's TV set started coming on by itself. It would rapidly change channels and then shut off. By this time, Margaret had started to become alarmed, but Frank dismissed it as bad dreams and electrical problems.

Things soon changed. He had been in the middle of painting the basement when things started to happen to him. One of the first occurrences had to do with his paint brush. It started on a Saturday morning when Margaret had taken the kids to the movies. Frank painted for several hours and then decided to take a break. He left his brush in the paint can and walked upstairs to the kitchen for a cup of coffee. When he returned ten or fifteen minutes later, the brush was on the floor ten feet away. The first time this happened, he thought that maybe he had set the brush down by mistake. After the third time it happened, he gave up painting the basement altogether. When Margaret got home, he told her about it, and she suggested that they talk to their priest after services the next day.

After hearing the story, the priest wanted to see the basement and determine if he could feel the presence of an entity. Frank escorted him downstairs with Margaret following close behind. Frank flipped on the basement light, and Margaret gasped in horror. The word *Satan* was painted on one of the concrete walls in red letters six feet high. Frank had been painting the basement white, and there was no red paint to be seen. When the priest walked over and felt one of the letters, it was still wet to the touch.

Being a devout Catholic, Frank was upset and somewhat embarrassed to see what had happened in front of his priest. He was sick of seeing his children being upset and scared in their own house. He walked over to the scrawled message and yelled, "Leave this house! Stop scaring my children! If you want to terrorize someone, pick a fight with me!"

Immediately the basement got about ten degrees colder and a gray mist started filling the room. The priest held up a large cross he was wearing around his neck and started shouting a prayer. When the ladder started shaking, everyone ran upstairs. Frank slammed the basement door shut and locked it.

From that point on, Frank's health started to deteriorate. Several large boils formed on his back and buttocks. It took several days for the local priest to convince the old bishop to come out of retirement and visit the house. From what their priest told them, he had had the most experience with things like this.

Margaret pleaded with the priest to get someone as soon as possible because it was becoming apparent that young Eddy was the focus of the entity. She and Frank started sleeping in his room to protect him, but his nightmares were getting worse. He pleaded with them to move away from the house. The morning the bishop arrived, Eddy woke up with several large welts on his stomach.

The bishop's first question to Margaret was "Do you have any idea why this is happening?"

When she showed him the Ouija board she had found under April's bed, he shook his head. He had seen several other instances where the board had been used to summon evil spirits. He cautioned them not to tell anyone about it because, in his view, the more teenagers heard about its use, the more they wanted to experiment.

After several exorcisms and the burning of the Ouija board, the spirit activity stopped. But by then, the family had had enough of the house, and they moved to Fond du Lac. Outwardly Frank's health gradually improved, but Margaret and the children watched as his mental condition slowly collapsed. Three years later, when the kids were away at camp, Frank sat in his car with the motor running and the garage door down. Margaret told them he had had a heart attack. They never knew he killed himself.

This haunted Margaret. She knew Eddy had suffered much more than April, and her worst fear was that Eddy might end his suffering the same way his father had. And now they were headed up to meet with some doctor and relive all the bad memories Margaret had worked so hard to put behind the family.

Doctor Hilton and Nicole ate quickly. "I'm very excited about meeting everyone," Doctor Hilton said. "Reading about them in the papers is one thing. Meeting them in person will be another thing, altogether."

"Did you contact anyone who you worked with at Duke?" Nicole asked.

Doctor Hilton shook her head and let out a soft laugh. "No. After what we put them through, I doubt if any of them would be interested and, that was so long ago, I bet most of them are dead by now."

Nicole wished she hadn't said anything.

When they returned to the parking lot, there was an inch of fluffy snow lying on top of their cars. The sun had gone down, and Nicole followed Doctor Hilton's taillights as she drove out of Marquette and headed north on Big Bay Road.

There were several places where she was glad Doctor Hilton's SUV was plowing through the drifts ahead of her. She doubted whether her small car would have been able to get through them if she were leading the way. Half an hour later they pulled into a long driveway. Several other cars were parked along the sides. Nicole pulled in behind Doctor Hilton's vehicle.

As she ran over and started helping the doctor with her wheelchair, Nicole noticed that a man had stepped out onto the front porch. He waved and yelled something to them. The strong wind blowing off of the lake made it impossible for Nicole to hear what he was saying. He jumped down the steps and ran over to them.

"Hello, I'm Robert," he yelled. He grabbed the wheelchair from Nicole. "I'll get this." He unfolded the chair and Doctor Hilton settled in.

He walked backwards up the porch steps, pulling the wheelchair up each step. Doctor Hilton was not a small woman, and it was all he could do to pull the chair up to the porch. He wheeled her into the foyer and returned to help Nicole with the suitcases. Once they were all inside, a thin woman with graying hair appeared. "Welcome! I'm Ruth. I see you've already met my husband, Robert."

Ruth took their coats and hung them in a closet off the front entry. Robert motioned to his left and said, "This way to the parlor. I'll introduce you to Mr. Feldman. Some of the others have already arrived. You can meet them, too."

Nicole grabbed the handles of Doctor Hilton's chair, and they followed Robert down a short hallway that led to a cozy room with several overstuffed couches and chairs lined against the walls. The front of the room was round with windows that looked out to the driveway. A long covered porch ran from the outside of the parlor all the way across the front of the house.

A man Nicole recognized immediately stood up and said, "Ah, this must be Doctor Hilton!" He walked over and shook her hand. "I'm Brad. Brad Feldman. So wonderful to meet you." He turned to Nicole. "And you must be Nicole! Thank you for taking time from your winter vacation to spend with us." Nicole thought he looked much more handsome in person than he did on TV.

She felt her face start to flush. "Um, nice to meet you, too."

Brad turned back to Doctor Hilton. "Come with me. I'd like to introduce you to some of the people you were kind enough to invite to our experiment." He guided her over to the couches. "This is Claudia Bishop. She's come all the way from San Diego,

California. I think she's probably a little in shock right now, as I am, because of the weather. But, thank goodness, it's nice and warm in here."

Doctor Hilton smiled and offered her hand. "Thank you so much for coming such a long way. I'm very interested in talking with you!"

"Thank you for inviting me, Doctor Hilton. I'm…I'm not sure what I've gotten myself into, but I hope it turns out to be a good thing."

Brad turned to a slender man with thinning long hair that was pulled back into a pony-tail. "And this is Reverend Peter Bowers."

The Reverend extended his hand. "It's an honor to meet you, Doctor Hilton."

As she shook his hand, Doctor Hilton noticed that his suit coat sleeve was frayed and discolored. "Thank you for coming, Reverend. Did you have any trouble getting here?"

"No trouble, but it took a while. I took a bus from Rapid City. It was a long ride."

Doctor Hilton was puzzled. She thought Brad's secretary had arranged an airplane ticket for the Reverend as she had done for the others who lived too far to drive. She was about to ask him why he took the bus, but then thought that maybe she hadn't heard correctly about what the preparations were going to be.

She smiled. "Well, I'm very happy that you made it safe and sound. I think it's very fortunate that we decided to start today. By the looks of the weather, I think tomorrow may have been a problem."

Jeremy stood up and walked over. "Hello, Doctor. I'm Jeremy Taylor."

Doctor Hilton's face lit up. "Oh, Mr. Taylor! So nice of you to come. I can't wait to talk to you about some of the things I've read about you. Your work with the police sounds fascinating. Just fascinating!"

He grinned. "Don't believe everything you read in the papers, Doctor!"

"We'll talk soon." She looked around the room and then asked Brad, "Have Mrs. Stoughton and her brother arrived yet?"

Brad shook his head. "No, we're still waiting for them." He glanced out the window. "I hope they're not stuck in a snow drift somewhere."

Robert walked over to a cabinet and pulled open two front doors. "In case anyone is interested, we have a fully stocked bar here. Mr. Feldman said that for the rest of the week he would like to have everyone come here to the parlor after dinner. The dining room is to the right of the front door. Behind us, through these French doors, is a library, in case anyone would like to spend some of their free time reading."

As if on cue, Ruth appeared in the doorway to the library. "Robert, please take Doctor Hilton and her assistant's bags up to their rooms." She turned to the two women. "I'm sure you'd both like to freshen up from your trip. Let me show you where you'll be staying."

Nicole grabbed the wheelchair and followed Ruth as she walked down a long, narrow, hallway which led to the back of the house. Ruth pushed open a door and stepped inside. "This is your room, Doctor. It's a little smaller than the bedrooms upstairs, but I thought you'd appreciate being on the first floor."

Her husband set down her bags. "Is there anything I can help you with?"

"No. I'll be just fine. Thank you." Doctor Hilton said.

Ruth turned to Nicole. "All the other guests are staying upstairs. Follow me."

They walked up the staircase and continued down a dimly lit hallway until they reached the third door on the left. "You're sharing a room with Mrs. Stoughton. She hasn't arrived yet. Unfortunately, we don't have enough rooms for everyone to have their own. I hope you don't mind."

Nicole looked around the dim surroundings. "Ah, no. That...that will be just fine."

April and her brother pulled into the driveway and parked behind several other vehicles. "Oh, Jesus! Take a look at that house!" Eddy said, peering out the windshield.

April sank back into the driver's seat and turned to Eddy. "We made it! I can't believe it!"

Eddy looked exhausted. "I don't know how you did it. I couldn't even see the road for the last thirty miles."

They grabbed their bags and quickly made their way up the steps to the front porch. Eddy knocked on the door. As they waited, Eddy said, "Listen to those waves! The lake must be right behind the house."

The front door opened and Brad stepped outside. "Eddy...and April! Welcome! We've been waiting for you. Come on in. You're the last ones to arrive. We were starting to get worried. Here, let me help you with your things."

Brad grabbed April's bag, and they followed him up the narrow staircase to the second floor. As they made their way down the hallway, Brad said, "Oh, Robert and Ruth are with Nicole now." He set April's suitcase down inside the room. "April, this is Nicole. You'll be sharing this room with her. She's Doctor Hilton's assistant."

April smiled. "Nice to meet you."

Brad introduced Robert and Ruth. Robert turned to Eddy. "Your room is on the other side of the house, all the way in the back. Your roommate, Jeremy Taylor, is downstairs. I'll introduce you to him later. Follow me." As they walked down the hallway, Eddy struggled to keep up. "Did you say roommate?" he asked Robert.

"Yes," he said, without slowing down. "Too many people for everyone to have their own room. You'll enjoy Jeremy. He seems to be a very interesting fellow." He walked to the end of the hallway and turned right. They passed by several other rooms before stopping at the last door on the left. "Here we are. It's a little hike. Why don't you put your things away, get your sister and Nicole, and come join us in the parlor. When you walked into the foyer that was the room to the left. The room where you saw all those people. We'll introduce you to everyone when you all finish up here."

Eddy had just finished hanging up his clothes when April and Nicole appeared at his door. "Ready?" April asked.

Eddy nodded and stepped out into the hall. He glanced around and said, "When do you suppose this house was built? It looks really old. Did you hear the floor creaking when that man took us to our rooms?" He laughed. "There'll be no sneaking around here at night! You could hear somebody coming from a mile away."

They followed the narrow hallway back to the stairs. As they entered the parlor, Brad waved. He pointed to a settee that was covered with a faded green flower print. When they had taken their seats, he stepped in front of the roaring fireplace. "Okay, looks like we're all here. Let me start things off by saying thank you all for coming. I'll briefly talk about what we have planned this week, and then I'll introduce you to a few other people." He paused and took in a deep breath. "My name's Brad Feldman. I'm the executive producer for *America's Most Haunted Locations* television show. As you know, nothing in television stays the same. We're working on a new pilot, and I'm so excited to have you all involved. Unlike *America's Most Haunted Locations*, the new show will pick one location and shoot the whole series there."

He looked around the room. "And, this happens to be the new location! Let me explain why we picked this particular house. As you can imagine, with our show being so popular, we get a lot of letters and emails. Seems like everyone wants us to use a creepy house in their hometown. When we were planning this pilot, we started reviewing all of the submissions we had received." Brad pointed to the back of the room. "One of the emails we received was from Ruth telling us about this house. Let me tell you some of the things Ruth wrote about that caught our attention. First, it's location. I'm sure all of you were thinking as you were traveling here, where in the world am I going?"

Eddy leaned over and whispered to April. "Did they plan on the blizzard, too?"

Brad continued, "Ruth told us about some of the strange things that have happened here. How the grandmother of the owner, Mr. Fredericks, wrapped a rope around her neck and threw herself off the second story landing. Sometimes, late at night, she can still be seen hanging from the staircase, twisting slowly in the moonlight."

Claudia Bishop felt a chill. She wrapped her arms around herself and looked over to see if anyone else felt anything.

Brad pointed to the ceiling. "How, upstairs they sometimes hear voices of the twins who fell through the ice and drowned over sixty years ago. They hear them up there talking to each other and singing songs."

Robert looked over at Ruth, but she kept her eyes focused on Brad.

He pointed to a shelf that was above a bookcase on the wall to his right. "See that violin? It belonged to Mr. Fredericks' great-grandfather. Legend has it that he would roam the moors of England late at night playing his violin. One night he came back to the house after a night of wandering, picked up an axe, and wiped out half his family. It was said that just before Mr. Fredericks' mother passed away, strange violin music could be heard moving from place to place throughout the house."

He was happy to see the startled looks on everyone's face. "So, you can see how excited we were when Mr. Fredericks told us we could use this place." He paused. "Now, let's talk about how you all were selected. Several months ago, I contacted Doctor Hilton and explained the premise of our new show. She graciously agreed to participate. She went through her extensive files and...." He stopped. "Why don't I just have her come up and explain the rest. Doctor Hilton?"

She wheeled herself to the front of the room. The warmth from the fire felt good on her back as she turned to face the group. "Hello, everyone. Thank you so very much for accepting my invitation. As you may or may not know, funding for parapsychology research dried up in the late seventies. In fact, it's not a subject that even gets any kind of recognition now, even though we were making real breakthroughs back when I was doing my research at Duke University, and later on my own. When Mr. Feldman contacted me, he made an offer that provided me an opportunity to reopen my studies once again."

Eddy shifted in his seat. He leaned over to April. "Jesus, this is one weird collection of people!"

April pretended not to hear him.

Doctor Hilton continued, "Even though I was out of the field, over the years, I've collected files of people who have had documented paranormal experiences. At the request of Mr. Feldman, I reviewed my files and sent invitations to those whose stories seemed the most interesting." She paused and gestured to everyone in the room. "And here we are! What better way to restart our research than to invite you all to this big old house and see what happens? I think our week here, isolated as it is from the cares and worries of day to day living, will prove to be quite exciting. We have an interesting series of meetings planned, and I hope you are as excited as I am to get started. Thank you again for coming." There was soft clapping as she turned and pushed herself back to the side of the room.

Brad returned to the fireplace. "Thank you, Doctor. Before I forget, I'd like to introduce you to Doctor Hilton's assistant, Nicole Peterson." Nicole stood up and gave a little wave. "Next, I'm going to call Robert Halstead up so he can tell you a little about the house we're staying in and some of the expectations we need to be aware of. Robert?"

Robert slowly shuffled to the front of the room and nervously glanced around. "Ah, as you all know by now, I'm Robert Halstead." He pointed to the back. "And, that's my wife, Ruth, standing over there next to the big dog. Don't worry about Fritz. He's about the gentlest German shepherd you'll ever find. He's very excited to have all this company. He belongs to Mr. Fredericks, the owner of this house."

Robert stopped and tried to organize his thoughts. He wasn't used to speaking in front of a crowd. "Anyway, um…this house was built in 1891 by Wilfred's grandfather. As you probably noticed, the house is filled with antiques. Most of them are things that the family brought with them from Europe when they immigrated to Canada."

He pointed to a large grandfather clock that was standing in the corner. "That piece came from Germany." He shuffled from one foot to another. "Anyway, Wilfred has agreed to let Mr. Feldman use his home, and he's very happy you all are here. Only thing is, he's a private man, and he really doesn't want to participate in what will be going on this week. So, if you see him around and he doesn't say much, don't feel bad. He'll be staying upstairs in his room most of the time."

Robert pointed to the doors that led to the foyer. "You've all been to your rooms by now. Upstairs, the first door down the hallway to the right is where his room's at. Please respect his privacy."

He stepped away from the fireplace for a moment and then came back. "Oh, if the weather ever breaks and you're walking around outside and you notice someone standing up on the widow's walk looking out over the lake, well that would be Wilfred. He likes to go up there and look out over the water." Robert looked around at the group as if he had something else to say, but then abruptly walked to the back of the room and stood next to his wife.

"The bar is now is officially open!" Brad said. "If you would like a drink, come over. I'll try and make you whatever you like. Then Doctor Hilton will introduce everyone."

The doctor wheeled herself over and requested a gin martini with three olives. The Reverend and Jeremy lined up behind her.

"Do you want me to get you a drink?" April asked her brother.

"Are you kidding? With all the medicine Dr. Craig has me taking, it would probably kill me."

"Oh, I didn't think about that."

"Go get one if you want. Don't stop because of me."

"I...um, no, I better not."

Doctor Hilton made her way back to the front of the room. She waited as Robert threw a few more logs on the fire. "Okay. Can I please have your attention? Brad and I have spent quite a bit of time talking about how we should structure our days here while we're all together. Every morning breakfast will start at nine o'clock sharp in the dining room. Then, depending on what we're doing, sometimes we'll move to the parlor or the library. Other times, you may have the morning to yourself. Read in the library or if the weather ever clears, you can walk outside. Robert tells me there's a set of steps that will take you down to the Lake Superior shoreline. But please be careful. He tells me they can be slippery, and for goodness sake, please don't walk out on the ice. At one o'clock lunch will be served, and after that we'll meet back right here in the parlor for a few hours. Then, depending on our activities, more free time until dinner which will be at seven o'clock. After dinner, we'll assemble right here again every night. Any questions?"

Claudia Bishop raised her hand.

"Yes?" Doctor Hilton asked.

"Ah, it seems like a long time between lunch and dinner. What if we get hungry before seven o'clock?"

Ruth stepped away from the back wall. "I'll have some snacks - nuts, fruit, cheese, sausage and crackers, things like that - set out on the sideboard between lunch and dinner."

"Oh, thank you," Claudia said.

"Any more questions?" Doctor Hilton asked. She waited. "Okay, well now, since we're all here, I'd like to take time and introduce you all and give a brief explanation of why you're here."

Nicole walked up and handed her a set of manila folders. The doctor adjusted a pair of glasses on the end of her nose, picked up the first folder, and opened it. "Let's start with Jeremy Taylor. When I mention your name, could you just stand up for a moment so everyone knows who you are."

Jeremy was wrapped in a thick sweater. He stood up and gave everyone a wave.

"Thank you, Mr. Taylor. Among other things, Mr. Taylor has the gift of retro-cognition. He has the ability to have perception of past events. Jeremy was brought to my attention when, at twelve years old, he helped solve a grisly series of child murders in Bainbridge, Georgia. He's been quietly working with police departments across the country ever since."

Eddy leaned over to April. "I didn't know the police really used people like that. Did you?"

She whispered, "I've seen it on TV shows, but I didn't know it really happened."

Jeremy stood up again. "Sometimes I'm able to see a little bit into the future, too. But, thankfully, not all the time."

Doctor Hilton pulled out another folder. "Next, we have the Reverend Peter Bowers. Mr. Bowers lives in Deadwood, South Dakota. Stand up Mr. Bowers."

He stood up and raised a glass that looked as if it contained ice and whiskey. He had a ruddy complexion and pale gray eyes. He looked like he had spent a lot of time outdoors. Eddy whispered, "Goodness, look at his hair! Looks like it hasn't been washed in weeks!"

"Shush," April whispered back. "What's wrong with you?"

"Did someone say something in the back?" Doctor Hilton asked.

"No, Doctor" April said. "Please continue." She felt her face flush as she elbowed Eddy in the side.

"All right then. The old Bowers Hotel in Deadwood has been in the Reverend's family for over a hundred years. The hotel is famous for its ghost sightings. According to an article in the *Deadwood Times*, dated August 5, 1964, when Peter was only three years old, his mother and his aunt both said they saw him surrounded by ghostly playmates when they entered his room. This went on for several months until they brought in a priest who sprinkled holy water around his bed. The hotel is still recognized as being one of the most haunted places in the country. People go there as a destination to see spirits." Doctor Hilton looked up. "I'm sure we'll be anxious to hear more of the story from the Reverend later."

As she pulled out another folder, the Reverend walked over to the bar and made himself another drink.

"Next we have Claudia Bishop."

Claudia stood up and smiled.

"My God, look how fat..." Eddy said under his breath.

"Stop!" April whispered, moving a few feet away from him.

"Claudia and her sister were living in Escondido, California, in 1981 when the face of the Virgin Mary appeared on their second-story bedroom window. At first, it only attracted a dozen or so people, but by the end of the week, there were several hundred folks coming to see the vision. As suddenly as it appeared, it vanished. One odd thing, the face seemed to weep blood. And, it appeared on the third anniversary of their little brother's death."

April gasped. Eddy moved next to her and took her hand. He said, "I guess we're next."

Again, the doctor pulled out a folder and flipped it open. "Oh, I almost forgot. Claudia is a registered pet psychologist." She turned to Robert. "So, if Fritz has any issues, make sure Claudia gets a chance to talk to him!" Everyone laughed. "Finally, last but not least, we have April Stoughton and her brother Eddy Russo." She pointed. "They're sitting over there."

"Oh, this is great!" Eddy whispered out of the corner of his mouth, as everyone turned to look. April smiled weakly as she stood up and pulled him with her. She squeezed his hand and prayed he didn't say anything.

"The Russo children were involved in a much publicized event in 1995 in Mayville, Wisconsin. This story made the national news, and I'm sure some of you will remember seeing it on television. Their parents had purchased a second-hand desk for April from a local Goodwill Store. Things started happening the same night they brought it home. At first, there were noises in the house. Strange lights. Things started moving by themselves."

Ruth turned to her husband and whispered, "See, these things do happen!"

The doctor continued. "At the beginning, for the first few days, it was amusing. A little scary, I'm sure, but nothing dangerous. Then, during the next few months things began to change. A knife sailed across the kitchen and almost hit their father. One night a misty fog appeared in April's bedroom where the desk was. Many more things happened, but when her father started hearing ominous voices, they moved out.

After putting a few coincidences together, they realized everything started happening the day they brought the desk home. Her father and a priest went back to the house, threw holy water on it, smashed the desk to pieces, and burned it in the back yard. Even after that, nobody in the family was anxious to return, so they put the house on the market. An older man, a widower, bought it, and moved in. Nothing has happened in the house since then."

Brad came bounding out of the shadows. "How about that for an interesting start! So now let me tell you what this is all about. As I briefly explained in the letter we sent out, we're shooting a pilot. I guess you could call it a new and improved version of *America's Most Haunted Locations*. The premise is that we find a group of people who have all experienced some form of supernatural or extrasensory event, or whatever you want to call them. We put you all in an old house, rig the house with cameras, and see what happens. Just so you know, there are no cameras on the second floor. We know everyone needs privacy, and that's where most of the bedrooms are; so we made the second floor off-limits. Not so for down here. Some of the cameras you will notice, but many more are hidden, and I doubt if you could ever find them.

Eddy twisted his head from side to side. "Hey, I see one of them over there!"

Brad continued, "Doctor Hilton and her assistant have a number of activities planned for you. Some testing protocols and things like that. Also, we'll be getting everyone together some afternoons or maybe after dinner just to see what happens. If we end up with some interesting video, and the pilot gets accepted, we'll bring everyone back; give you heaps of money, and shoot for another six weeks. We'll send you home every other weekend on our dime. Any questions?"

Jeremy raised his hand. "What...what if nothing happens?"

Brad laughed. "Then we'll have a pilot that's just as good as those other ghost hunter shows on TV." He paused. "No, if nothing happens, we wrap things up and call it a day."

Eddy leaned closer and whispered to April, "Like they're going to let that happen! They've already spent a pretty penny bringing all these freaks here from all over the country."

Brad looked around the room. "That's all I have. If nobody has anything else, let's spend the rest of the evening getting to know each other. Oh, Robert wanted me to tell you that there are several games set up in the library. Chess, checkers, cards, and puzzles."

Ruth walked back to the kitchen and came out carrying a tray filled with assorted snacks.

April walked over to the bar and made herself a whiskey and ginger. As she turned to head back to Eddy, Brad walked up, grabbed a vodka bottle, and made himself a drink. "That was an amazing story Doctor Hilton told us about what happened to you and your brother. It must have been terrifying."

While she was never a regular viewer, April had watched his show several times. She was surprised to find herself a little tongue-tied. "Ah, well, yes it was. Especially towards the end. Things started escalating quite a bit. Actually, things got a lot worse than what Doctor Hilton mentioned." She wondered what the name of the cologne was that he was wearing. It smelled wonderful.

"When something like that happens, does it live with you? Do you have nightmares?"

"I did for the first few years. My parents made sure we got counseling, but I only went for about a year. I felt okay." She paused. "It hit Eddy a bit harder. Actually, I'm quite surprised he agreed to come with me."

"Well, I'm certainly glad he did. I'm very excited to see what the week holds for us."

Claudia walked up. "Oh, excuse me. Mr. Feldman, can I ask you a question?"

Brad turned away from April. "Of course. What's on your mind?"

She stepped in closer and lowered her voice. "The dog. I'm getting a feeling that he has some issues. I was wondering if you think it would be okay if I set aside some time to meet with him."

Brad looked surprised. "Um, I don't know. I don't see why not, but I guess we'd have to run that by Robert or his wife first. It's Mr. Fredericks' dog, but as you heard, we don't want to bother him." Brad glanced around the room and then pointed. "There he is, talking to Jeremy. Why don't you go over there and ask him." He thought for a moment. "You're not thinking of charging him, are you?"

Claudia shook her head. "Heavens no! It would be a free consultation. It's just bothering me. I get the feeling that the dog needs to get something off his mind."

Brad smiled. "Well, you need to talk to Robert then."

He backed away and headed over to where Doctor Hilton was sitting. Claudia grabbed a plate, and started picking out some cheeses.

April walked over to Jeremy. "Very nice to meet you, Mr. Taylor. I hope we get to hear more about your amazing gift."

He smiled. "Not sure how amazing it is. Sometimes it can be quite frightful." He took her hand. "I remember seeing your story on the national news. It got a lot of press for a few months."

"I know. Our father was furious. He didn't want any part of all of that publicity."

"Believe me, I get it! When I work with the police, I request anonymity. Normally they don't have a problem with that because the public doesn't want to hear they've resorted to using somebody the likes of me!" He laughed. "But, every now and then one of those pesky reporters starts snooping around, and they make it difficult for all of us."

April glanced over and saw Eddy sitting by himself in an overstuffed chair in the corner. He looked miserable.

"So nice speaking with you," April said. "I hope we can chat again." She walked back to Eddy. "Brad said to circulate. You haven't moved from this spot."

"I see he made a bee-line to you! I'm not good at circulating. This is like being locked in a freak show with no way out. I can't believe I let you talk me into coming up here."

April stared at him in disbelief. "Talk you into it! You've got to be kidding. I was all prepared to go by myself; and then, out of nowhere, you said you wanted to come with me."

"I must have temporarily lost my mind. I can't imagine spending a week with this collection of loony-tunes. Good thing I brought a few books. I'm going to hole up in my room and read all day. Did you hear Brad say they have some sort of testing lined up for us? Are they out of their minds?"

April made a face. "Oh, come on. We've come all this way. Might as well jump in and enjoy yourself. And, don't forget, if the pilot gets picked up, we'll both probably take home some decent cash!"

"A lot of good that would do us," Eddy said. "Every nutcase in America who watches that show would recognize us. We'd have to move to Tibet and join a monastery."

April laughed. "Hey, it's not every day I get to hobnob with a celebrity. And a very handsome one, at that. And he smells so good! I'm going to have a great time, and you should make up your mind to have fun, too."

Jeremy slowly walked up to them carefully holding a very full martini glass. He took a big sip and then said to Eddy, "Evening. Looks like we'll be roommates for the week."

Eddy had forgotten that he was going to have to share a room. He grimaced for a second. "Oh, that's right...nice to meet you."

"Not drinking?" Jeremy asked.

Eddy smiled. "That was the plan, but I'm not so sure I'll be sticking to it."

Jeremy took another sip of his drink. "You know, I remember hearing about your story on the news. Incredible! Just incredible."

Eddy gave him a weak smile. "It was a long time ago."

Jeremy stood there thinking that Eddy may ask a question about what Doctor Hilton had said about him. Eddy yawned. After a long silence, Jeremy said, "Well, I just wanted to introduce myself."

"Okay," Eddy replied. "I hope you don't snore."

"Eddy!" his sister hissed. She turned to Jeremy. "Please ignore him. He's had a long day. Our ride up here was horrendous."

Jeremy smiled. "It's fine."

April asked, "I was wondering, do you work with the police often?"

"I try and keep it to only a few times a year," he replied. "I get calls from all over the country. It's...it's not easy, but...I feel I really can't say no. After all, these are children."

"I can only imagine, it must be very..." April said.

Eddy stepped in front of her, almost pushing Jeremy out of the way. "I just tried to call Mother on my cell, but I'm not getting any bars. Can you try? We promised her we'd let her know we made it up here okay."

"Oh, you're right. She's probably got herself tied up in knots. My phone's upstairs. Let me run up and see if I have any service."

Robert, who had been standing behind them, turned around. "It's not going to work. All cell phone are useless way out here. Closest place to get a signal is about ten miles down the road. If you need to call someone, you can use our land line." He stood in front of them somewhat awkwardly. "Uh, I just wanted to tell you how glad we are that you're here. My wife and I, we've worked here for fourteen years. We...we sure do hope this show takes off. We sure would hate it if we had to leave."

"Leave?" Eddy asked.

Robert looked confused. "Oh, nothing. I was...just...just rambling."

From the look on Eddy's face, April could tell he was going to say something inappropriate. She stepped in a little closer. "Well, thank you, Mr. Halstead. I hope it turns out well, too."

As he walked away, Eddy said, "Remind me to give Mother a call later."

"Okay, but I'd hate to run up a long distance charge for our hosts."

Eddy said, "I've got an idea. They said we'd have some free time tomorrow morning. Let's drive into Marquette and check out the place. We can call Mom from there."

"And make her wait all night?" April asked with a look of concern.

Eddy laughed. "It's not like we're ten years old. Tomorrow will be fine."

"Excuse me," Jeremy said. "I'm going to ask Robert if he can turn the heat up a little bit. Are you as cold as I am?"

"It's a little chilly," April said. "But it feels okay to me."

He shivered. "I don't know how you all can stand it. I've been freezing ever since I got here. There's Ruth. Maybe she can do something about it. I'll see you later."

Claudia, balancing a plate of hor d'oeuvres, walked up to Eddy. "Oh, Mr. Russo, I was so taken with your story."

He smiled. "That's nice." He turned and walked back to the chair he had been sitting in in the corner. Claudia stood there by herself, holding her plate.

The group had mingled for another hour when Doctor Hilton spoke up. "Everyone, if I can please have your attention. I want to thank you all again for coming. I've had a wonderful time chatting with everyone. But, it's been a very long day for me. Let's plan on meeting in the dining room tomorrow morning at nine o'clock for breakfast. Good night, everyone."

Nicole came over and walked next to her as they made their way to the back of the house where Doctor Hilton's room was located. When they got to the door, Nicole asked, "Is there anything I can do for you?"

"No. I have a little more unpacking to do, but I'm good. Thank you. Go back to the party and enjoy yourself."

"You know what," Nicole said. "I think I'm going to head upstairs, too. Driving in that blizzard really tired me out. And, did you notice? It's still coming down like crazy."

"I haven't looked outside, but the wind! It seems to have gotten even stronger since we got here. Have you heard the creaks? This old place makes a lot of noise."

"It sure does! Well, good night," Nicole said. As Doctor Hilton shut her door, Nicole took the stairs up to the second floor. She walked passed Robert and Ruth's room and stopped at the next door. She grabbed the doorknob and pulled. She let out a soft yelp and stepped back. This wasn't her room. It was a storage room filled with buckets, mops, old furniture, and piles of boxes. Ruth had mentioned the junk room in passing as she showed Nicole her room, but she had forgotten all about it. She shut the door and walked down to the next room. She pulled the door open and was happy to see that she was at the correct place. She yawned. Doctor Hilton had been right. It had been a very long day. She walked over to the closet and finished putting her things away. She glanced at her watch and wondered if she had enough time to grab a quick shower before April decided to come upstairs. She thought it would be okay if she was quick. She walked over and locked the door.

She pulled out her soap, shampoo and conditioner, and stepped into the bathroom. The hot water felt good as it cascaded down her skin. She rinsed off, twisted a towel around her head, dried off, and wrapped herself in a thick cotton bathrobe she had brought from home. She stepped into the bedroom and turned to comb her hair in the big mirror above the dresser. She froze. There was a message scrawled on the mirror. She let out a scream and ran to the door. She twisted and pulled the knob a few times and then remembered that she had locked herself in. She turned the key, pulled the door open, ran out into the hallway, and screamed again.

Brad and Jeremy were at the bar making themselves another drink. "What was that?" Brad asked.

"It sounded like a scream!" Jeremy said. "From upstairs!" They turned from the bar and ran out of the parlor, down the hall, and bounded up to the second floor. Nicole was standing in the hallway in front of her room. She had a sheepish look on her face. "I'm sorry. I get it now. Jokes on me, I guess!"

"What are you talking about?" Brad asked.

"I didn't know you guys were going to do things to scare us," Nicole said with a grin. "Well, congratulations. You really got me."

"What do you mean, scare you?" Brad asked.

"Like you don't know," Nicole said.

"Really. I don't know what you're talking about."

Jeremy stepped into her room and looked at the mirror. He called out, "The writing? Did your guys sneak in here and do this?"

Brad walked up next to Jeremy and read *"Bad things are coming! Leave now while you can!"* scrawled in big letters that showed up faintly in the mirror.

"We didn't do this!" He turned to Nicole. "When was the last time you were up here?"

"A couple of hours ago. Right when we arrived. I unpacked some of my things and then headed down to the parlor to meet everyone. I just came back now to take a quick shower. I know there was nothing on the mirror when I got here. I would have seen it."

"My guys all left yesterday. Everyone was still in the parlor when we left." He turned to Jeremy. "I didn't notice anyone leave, did you?"

Nicole turned to the door. "But, I locked the door before my shower. I know I did because I had to unlock it when I ran out."

Brad read the message again. "I don't know. I really don't know. But, we don't fake things. That's what's made the show so popular. What you see is what you get. No computer effects, no planting things. We don't mess around with any of that. I'm going to have to talk to Robert and Mr. Fredericks and get to the bottom of this."

Nicole grabbed him by the arm. "But...if you didn't do this, then who did?"

By this time, almost everyone else from downstairs had made their way up to the second floor. April, with Eddy right behind, walked over. "What's going on?" She looked at Nicole. "Are you all right?"

"Yes, I'm okay. I guess somebody thought they'd play a little joke on us." She pointed to their room. "Look at the mirror!"

April walked in and read the message. She stepped back into the hallway and looked at Brad. "What's this about?"

"Like I just explained to her, I don't know. It certainly wasn't something I did or asked someone to do."

Eddy walked in and read what was on the mirror. He marched over to Brad. "What the hell..."

April tried to calm him down. "Eddy, don't worry. It's only some kind of joke."

He glared at Brad. "Scaring young girls doesn't seem very funny to me."

Brad said, "I don't know who did this. Apparently, somebody thought this would be funny. I'm sure it's just a joke of some kind. A joke gone bad. Look, we're all tired. It's been a very long day for everyone. Tomorrow I'll see what I can find out about this. Like Nicole said, I'm sure it was just somebody's idea of misguided humor."

"I'll get a rag and wash it off," Ruth said.

Eddy leaned over and whispered to April. "I don't like this. Maybe we should leave. This reminds me too much of what we went through. We can't risk starting those things all over again."

She could see he was sweating. "Don't be ridiculous. This is some stupid prank. We aren't leaving."

"I sure hope nothing's been done to my room," Claudia said with a touch of uneasiness.

Jeremy put his arm around her. "I'll come with you, and we can check it out."

As Robert turned to walk back to the stairs, Eddy asked, "Where's Bowers?"

"Passed out in a chair. I think the bourbon and the heat of the fire got to him."

"Well, I guess it wasn't him who wrote this crap," Eddy said. He turned to April. "You going to be all right? You want to stay with me tonight?"

"With you? I doubt your roommate would be happy about that!"

A pained look crossed his face. "Oh, yeah. I keep forgetting about that. Hey, maybe you can stay in Bowers' room. He'll probably spend the night passed out downstairs in the chair." He thought for a moment. "Wonder how he got a room to himself?"

"Go to bed, Eddy. I'll be fine. See you in the morning."

Eddy slowly walked down to the end of the hallway and stopped in front of Claudia's door. "Everything okay?"

Jeremy stepped out and pulled the door shut behind him. "Looks fine. I wonder if we got any cryptic messages."

At the end of the hallway they turned to the right and walked past another room. The door was open and Eddy peeked inside. "I guess this is where Bowers is staying. Lucky for him. He's got a room to himself."

Jeremy laughed. "With a message writing ghost running around this place, maybe it's better to have a roommate!"

Eddy didn't respond. He slowly pushed their door open and glanced around the room. "Everything looks okay in here."

Brad and Robert returned to the parlor. Brad shook Reverend Bowers a few times. "Hey, time to wake up. Everybody's gone to bed."

The Reverend shook his head a few times and looked around. He struggled to his feet. "Oh, sorry about that." He smiled. "My God, what was in those drinks?" He blinked a few times and then turned towards the door.

"Are you going to be all right?" Robert asked.

"Don't worry about me," the Reverend replied. "See you guys in the morning."

Brad looked over at Robert and tried not to laugh.

"I don't know about you," Robert said, "But, I have a feeling it's going to be a very interesting week!"

Robert said good night and Brad made his way over to his room. Finally the house was quiet. He sat on his bed, kicked off his shoes, and looked around. He had set up a tiny command center where he could monitor all of the different cameras that his crew had located throughout the first floor. He thought about taking a look at some of the footage and seeing if he could see if someone had sneaked upstairs to write the message in Nicole and April's room. He yawned and decided to wait until morning when he felt more alert. He glanced down and saw a picture of his wife that he had set on the nightstand. He slipped his shoes back on and walked out to the kitchen. He picked up the phone that was mounted to the wall and dialed his home number. After four rings his wife answered.

"Hello, honey. I just thought I'd give you a ring. I was hoping you'd still be up."

He waited for her to respond.

"I just put the kids to bed. It's only ten o'clock here." She paused. "How's the project going?"

Brad's heart started beating a little faster. It actually sounded as if she were happy to talk to him. "It's...it's going good, I guess. Actually, we just got started. What a place! It's colder than hell here and snowing like crazy. I haven't seen snow since we went to Colorado on our honeymoon. Believe me, this snow is nothing like what we had there. I've never missed California more than I do right now. How are the kids?"

"They're fine. I ran into Quentin from the network. He tells me if they pick up this pilot, you wouldn't have to do so much traveling. Is that right?"

"Yeah. We'd pick one spot and shoot everything from there. I'd probably go a few times, but the crew could handle most of it without me. I'd stay back at the studio and work on the rushes." He waited for a moment. "I miss you."

He heard a child's voice in the background. "Yes, it's Daddy. No you can't talk to him. Get back to bed!" There was a pause. "Well, okay. Thanks for calling. Don't work too hard and…stay warm. Bye." She hung up.

He put the receiver down. *What was that all about?* At first she had sounded like her old self, but then, after he told her he missed her, she just ended the conversation. He wondered if she had a boyfriend. He had asked her that before and she claimed she didn't, but now he wondered even more.

He knew the reason she had left was because of his constant traveling. He was hardly ever home. He knew raising the kids like that wasn't easy. But, he also knew she liked the money he was bringing home. They had bought a new house in Laguna Pines, and it had cost a fortune for the decorators. He thought about calling her back but then decided it would probably be better if he didn't.

Upstairs Nicole looked over at April and said, "Oh my God! Can you believe how handsome Brad is? He looks even better in person than he does on TV. And he's not even stuck-up one bit! I never met anyone from TV before. Have you?"

"No. Well, I saw John Candy once at the Milwaukee airport, but I didn't talk to him."

"I've never seen anybody famous before. Just Brad."

They talked for another half hour, then April yawned and said, "I'm sorry, but I can't seem to keep my eyes open. We had a nerve-racking drive up here. I think it wore me out."

"Oh, okay. I'm sorry. I guess I'm a little wound up." Nicole turned off the lamp that was on the night stand next to her. "Good night."

"Night." April settled into her bed and pulled the covers up to her chin. She enjoyed listening to someone who was so young and full of excitement. Excitement about the project, excitement about life and the future."

April had almost drifted off to sleep when Nicole sat up in bed. "What was that?"

"What?" April asked.

"I heard a noise."

April listened. "Was it the house creaking?"

"I...I don't know. Maybe?"

"I noticed this place makes a lot of noises. With this wind, I think we're in for a lot of different sounds tonight."

"Oh. That's probably what it was. Boy, I'm sure glad you're here with me. If I was alone, I don't think I'd get a wink of sleep!"

April laughed. "I'm glad we're roommates, too."

Nicole lay back down and quickly fell asleep. April lay in bed and listened to all the sounds around her. The wind was blowing even harder, which seemed impossible. It felt as if she could feel the house sway when a strong gust hit. She heard the old timbers in the walls creaking and groaning against the onslaught. *How many storms had this old house weathered?*

She thought about Dennis and wondered what he was doing. He wouldn't have been too happy about this trip. Whenever she tried to talk about what had happened to her and her brother back in Mayville, he never wanted to hear about it. Her thoughts moved on to Bobby and she started to sob. Tears ran down her cheeks and fell onto the pillow.

She reached for a tissue. *What was that?* She held her breath. It sounded like footsteps coming down the hallway. *Yes! Those were footsteps.* She propped herself up on her elbows and stared at the door. As they got closer, she heard the steps slow down and stop in front of their door. She saw two dark shadows at the bottom of the door illuminated from the hallway lights. She heard the doorknob start to turn. She pulled the covers up to her chin. She wanted to shake Nicole and wake her up. Someone was pulling on the doorknob, but, thankfully, she had remembered to lock the door. After a few moments, the shadows disappeared and she heard the footsteps continue down the hallway.

April gasped for air. She had been holding her breath the whole time and had not even noticed it. She took several deep breaths and tried to get her heartbeat back to normal. She wondered how Nicole could have slept through all of that. It sounded to April as if her heart was pounding loud enough to be heard in the next room. She glanced over at the mirror to see if any new messages had shown up. Thankfully, there were none. She pulled the covers over her head and tried to go to sleep. Even being under a thick quilt, she could hear waves pounding out on the lake. It felt like the house was responding to every one of them.

Chapter 10

MARGARET MADE COFFEE and looked at the clock. It was nine a.m. *I wonder why nobody's called me. I hope everything's all right.*

As she walked out to get the morning paper, she noticed a car idling across the street. It looked as if the man sitting behind the wheel was watching her house. She grabbed her glasses that were hanging from a chain around her neck and looked again. It was Dennis. She wondered if she should ask him to come in, but then thought better of it.

She returned to the kitchen, spread open the newspaper on the table, and started reading. Every fifteen or twenty minutes, she would glance at the clock. *I wonder why they aren't calling.*

From across the street, Dennis sat in the car and stared at the house for another hour. He was sure April's mother had seen him. He was hoping she would tell April that he was out there and have her come out. He waited another ten minutes, put the car in gear, and drove a few miles until he came to a small strip mall. He pulled in front of a restaurant and decided to have breakfast.

Robert walked into the kitchen and immediately saw that Ruth was not having a good morning. "How's it going?" he asked. "Anything I can do?"

She glared at him. "Is there anything you can do? Are you kidding me? You could walk around and pick up all the plates and glasses these people have left sitting everywhere."

"Okay. Sure, not a problem."

"I swear, I've never seen people eat like this group. I've done catering before, but this is something else. And that Claudia! I can't keep up with her. How much baking does a person have to do?"

Robert walked around the parlor and library collecting cups, saucers, plates, and glasses. Ruth was right. There were dirty dishes sitting around everywhere. He brought them back to the kitchen and set them in the sink. "I'll wash them. I can see you have your hands full with breakfast."

People started showing up at five to nine. Ruth set out platters of scrambled eggs and ham. Everyone seemed to enjoy their breakfast. After they had all eaten, Doctor Hilton asked everyone to move into the parlor. Claudia hurried over and took a seat next to Eddy. The doctor wheeled herself in front of the fireplace next to where Fritz was sleeping. "This morning Nicole and I would like to start testing everyone for some basic ESP traits." She held up a deck of cards. "We're going to use the same cards I used during my work with Doctor Rhone. They're called Zener cards. Each pack contains twenty-five cards with five different symbols. I'll pass them around so you know what's on each card." She handed a pack to Brad to distribute. "Then, I'm going to have Nicole take you one by one into the library while I turn over twenty-five cards. Each time I turn over a card, I'll ring a bell and you will try and predict what the card is. We'll do this three times for each of you. Nicole will keep track of what your answers are and we'll come up with your score. Anything over twenty percent would prove to be very interesting. Who would like to go first?"

Claudia raised her hand. "Oh, pick me! Pick me!" She turned to Eddy. "Isn't this exciting?"

As Nicole headed to the library, she made a detour to where April was sitting. "Can I ask you a question?"

"Sure, what is it?"

"Did you see my emerald ring this morning?"

April looked surprised. "I saw a pile of your jewelry sitting on your nightstand, but I didn't pay any attention to what was there. Why?"

"After you left this morning, I was getting ready, and I was going to put my ring back on. It was a birthday present from my mom. It's my birthstone. I always wear it. Last night I set it with my other jewelry, but this morning it wasn't there."

"No. I'm sorry, but I don't remember seeing it. Maybe it rolled off the stand. Did you look under the bed?"

"Yes. I pulled out the bed sheets. I looked behind the bed. I looked everywhere. Were you missing anything this morning?"

"No. But, I don't wear much jewelry. I have a small box in my suitcase."

"You might want to double-check and make sure it's all there."

"I will. Why don't we both go upstairs when this is done and look over the room? Sometimes two sets of eyes are better than one."

Nicole saw that Claudia was waiting in the library doorway. "That would be good. Thank you." She escorted Claudia into the library and partially closed the door.

Doctor Hilton wheeled herself back to a corner of the parlor far away from the others where a small table had been set up. She shuffled the deck of cards and started turning them over. After each card was turned over, she rang a small bell and wrote down what it was on a pad of paper next to her.

Eddy sat on the couch and said to April, "This is stupid. I'm not going to do this."

She turned and gave him a little push. "Don't be such a downer. Did you forget that they're paying us to be here? We have to participate. Just play along. Who cares if you can tell which card is going to turn up or not."

"Just my luck everyone will be able to do it but me."

She smiled. "I seriously doubt that. Just because we've all had some kind of experience, doesn't mean we all have ESP. I don't remember us having any kind of premonition that came true or anything like that, so I doubt either of us is going to do very well."

"I've never predicted anything that came true. So, why would I waste my time with this crap?"

"Who cares?" Let's just have fun with it."

As they were talking, Brad walked over and pulled up a chair. "Good morning."

"Good morning," April said.

"Morning," Eddy mumbled. He stood up. "I think I'll walk around a bit."

"I didn't mean to scare you off," Brad said with a laugh.

"You didn't. I'm going to practice for my ESP test."

"Good luck with that!" As Eddy walked away, Brad pulled his chair a little closer to April. "How did you sleep last night? Any issues?"

"I slept very well, thank you. No more tricks." She thought about the footsteps but decided not to mention it.

"I'm afraid I haven't come up with any ideas about who wrote that message in your room. It certainly wasn't any of my people. Like I said, they all left a few days ago. And, after talking with Robert and his wife, I still don't have a clue as to who would do that."

"I'm sure whoever it was thought it was just a funny prank, but it did bother my brother. And, I think it upset Nicole, too."

"Let's hope whoever it was got it out of their system and won't do anything stupid again." He reached over and put his hand on her arm. "By the way, I want to tell you how sorry I am for the loss of your son. I can't even imagine...."

April looked surprised. "How did you know?"

"My secretary did research on everyone before we sent out our invitations. We wanted to make sure everyone would be compatible." He smiled. "I'm not sure how effective we're going to be with that."

"Well, thank you for your kind words."

"My niece was killed in L.A. a few years ago. A drive-by. Mistaken identity. It was so sad."

"Oh, how awful. How old was she?"

"Fifteen."

"How are her parents doing?"

"My sister. She's...you know... doing the best she can. She's divorced now. Their marriage couldn't take it."

"That's a shame," April said. She didn't mention what she was going through with Dennis. "Do you have children?"

"Yes, I have a boy and a girl. He's seven and the girl's five." He paused. "But, I'm separated. My wife...it's...it's a long story."

"I'm sorry to hear that."

Eddy, who had been talked into playing a game of chess with Reverend Bowers, watched as Brad sat down next to his sister.

The library door swung open and Nicole and Claudia stepped into the parlor. Nicole handed Doctor Hilton Claudia's results.

"April, would you like to go next?" Doctor Hilton asked.

She turned to Brad. "Looks like I'm the next lab rat."

He stood up. "Good luck!"

As April neared the library, Claudia walked by carrying a small plate with several powdered doughnuts piled on it. "Look, they have treats!" she said. She walked over to Fritz, bent down and whispered. "We need to talk. I know you want to tell me something."

Fritz stood up, grabbed a doughnut from her plate, and wandered out into the foyer. Jeremy, who was sitting nearby, looked up from his book and said, "Apparently, Fritz doesn't want to share his secrets."

Claudia stood back up and turned towards him. "They usually don't when they're very troubled."

"How did you do with the cards?" he asked.

She shrugged her shoulders. "Don't know. I felt I was picking up on some of them, but you never know."

After an hour and a half, Eddy was the last one to participate in the library. The door opened and Nicole led him out.

"That was the most ridiculous thing I've ever experienced," he said to Nicole.

"I bet you did very well," she replied. She waved his answer sheet. "I've got a good feeling about it."

"Hmm. I bet I didn't get a single one of those right. I couldn't see any shapes no matter how hard I tried."

He walked back to the chess table where the Reverend was waiting. Eddy sat down, glanced at the board, and looked up at the Reverend in surprise. "You've moved my knight."

"What?"

"My knight. It wasn't there when I left." He pointed to a square on the board. "It was right here!"

"My good man, are you accusing me of cheating?" the Reverend asked, raising his voice.

"I'm not accusing you of anything. All I'm saying is, my knight is in a different place now than it was when I left."

The Reverend pushed himself away from the table. As he attempted to stand up, his knee caught the corner of the chess board, and all of the pieces tumbled to the floor.

"Now look what you've done!" Eddy cried. "You...you did that on purpose to cover up your cheating!"

Everyone in the parlor stopped what they were doing and turned towards the commotion. The Reverend took a step towards Eddy. "Hey, man! I never moved your damn knight and my knee hit the board as I was standing up. It was an accident."

Eddy's face was getting red. "You did that on purpose!"

The Reverend stared at him in disbelief. "For your information, I don't appreciate being called a cheat in front of these fine people. You owe me an apology!"

"An apology!" Eddy yelled. "I don't owe you jack shit!"

April ran up and grabbed him. "Eddy! Please!"

He struggled out of her grasp and stared at the Reverend. "I catch you moving pieces to your advantage when I was in the library, and...and you want me to apologize!" He laughed. "It'll be a cold day in hell before you get an apology out of me!"

Brad walked over as April bent down and started picking up the chess pieces from the floor. "Gentlemen, I'm sure this is just some sort of misunderstanding. I suggest we all just forget it and move on." He stepped in-between them.

Eddy turned and headed for the stairs as Reverend Bowers bent down and helped April pick up the remaining pieces.

"I'm sorry, Reverend," April said. "My brother's been quite isolated from other people for a few years and if he doesn't take his medicine, it makes him...ah, edgy. I'm afraid he doesn't know how...."

He put his hand on her shoulder. "Don't trouble yourself. It's fine. No hard feelings. Chess can be very competitive at times. May I suggest that we switch to a less combative game in the future?" He picked up a queen. "I'm thinking checkers might make a better choice."

April placed two pawns and a rook back onto the board. "That may be a good idea." She let out a long sigh. "I better go find Eddy and talk to him."

As she was walking out to the foyer, Nicole came up to her. "Can you help me look for my ring?"

"I'm on my way to...." She paused. "Sure, let's go." As they walked to the stairs, Nicole said, "I hate to say this, but that man is starting to give me the creeps."

"Who?"

"The Reverend. The way he looks at me. Maybe it's my imagination, but it seems like he's always staring at me."

"Really! He does seem to be a little odd. And he looks a little rough. Not the look I was expecting for a minister."

Once in the room, Nicole pointed to the pile of jewelry on her nightstand. She held up a green necklace. "I had this on, too. With these earrings." She picked up a bracelet. "This, too. But my ring is gone."

"What about the bathroom? Did you take it off to wash your hands?"

"I don't think so. But, I'll look."

After half an hour of searching every conceivable place, April said, "I don't know where to look next. It seems to have vanished."

"What about your things?" Nicole asked. "Have you checked your box?"

"Not yet." She walked to the small closet, pulled out her suitcase, and unsnapped the two brass latches. She picked up a small satin bag and dumped everything out onto the bedspread. She separated the few pieces with her fingers and then stopped. "My wedding ring! It's not here!"

"Are you kidding?" Nicole asked.

"No. I know I brought it. Wait a minute. A pair of my earrings are gone, too! Eddy got them for me this Christmas."

"Somebody's been in here!"

April slowly put the remaining pieces of jewelry back into the pouch. "We're going to have to have a talk with Doctor Hilton."

Nicole jumped up from the bed. "Let's go."

"Hold on a minute. I need to talk to my brother. Give me a few minutes. I'll stop by and get you."

April stepped out into the hallway, still shaken from what had just happened. She knocked softly on Eddy's door and waited. She pushed it open. He was sitting in a chair staring out the window.

"Eddy, what in the world happened down there?"

He spun around facing her. "Don't lecture me! That bastard moved some pieces to make sure I'd lose. He must be some kind of idiot if he thought I wouldn't notice."

"Have you stopped taking your medicine? Mom told me that you...."

"That shit makes me feel like a Zombie. If I'm going to be cooped up in this creepy old place, I sure as hell need all my wits about me!"

April frowned. "Having your wits about you doesn't mean you had to make such a scene!"

"Me make a scene? What are you talking about? He's the one who made the scene. He's the one who knocked over the board. Not me."

"Maybe so, but you shouldn't have...."

Eddy stood up and grabbed her by her shoulders. "I have to tell you something."

From the look on his face, April got concerned. "What?"

"Last night. When Jeremy came up to go to bed. We sat here talking for a few minutes and... he said something." He paused.

"What? What did he say?"

"About the desk. He knew it wasn't the desk."

"What desk?" April asked.

"You know. The desk we told everyone had brought the spirit into the house. He knows."

April gave a start. "How could he know? We've never told anyone. At least, I haven't."

"And neither have I," Eddy said quietly. "But he knows. He told me it was the Ouija board."

"Impossible. You must have slipped and told him something."

Eddy let her go and took a step back. "No! No! We were talking about something else altogether, and he just turned to me and said he knew it wasn't a desk. You and your sister were fooling around with a Ouija board, and that's what brought the spirit into your house."

"What did you say?"

"I just looked at him with my mouth open. I wanted to run out into the hallway. Then I just nodded. He just smiled and then went to bed. I didn't get much sleep. Believe me; I've been trying to figure out what happened all morning. That's the reason I snapped at the Reverend. I've been on edge all day."

April walked over and gave him a hug. "Doctor Hilton's brought all these people together because they either have some gifts or they've experienced some very unusual things. Don't talk to him again about what happened. If he brings it up, just say you don't want to talk about it. We've done a good job of never mentioning it to anyone, and I'd hate to have that come out now." She stopped. "Not that anyone's even interested. But how would we explain lying about that for so many years. Just change the subject if he brings it up again."

Eddy nodded and wrapped his arms around her. She could feel him trembling. "I wish I had never come up here. It was a mistake."

April thought for a moment. She didn't want to tell him about the missing jewelry.

Eddy asked, "And those words on your mirror. What about that?"

"It was just some dumb prank."

"But, who would do something like that and think it was funny?" he asked.

"I...I don't know. I just don't know."

Sitting at the bar in the Whitefish Tavern, Joe Casperson had just finished his second boilermaker, when Tom Sunquist walked in and took a seat next to him. Tom ordered a beer and turned to Joe. "How you been? Last time I seen you was at your nephew's funeral. Damn shame what happened to him."

"Sure was. And those other guys, too." Joe took a drink. "You know, I'm almost glad my sister passed before we lost Tony. That would have killed her sure as hell."

"That was rough, all right. All them funerals. Did you ever tell old man Fredericks what you thought of him? You told me you were going to go over there."

"Naw. The chicken-shit bastard won't take my calls, and I got runned off the place twice. That handy man of his told me next time I show up, they're gonna call the cops."

Tom took a long drink. "Aw, hell. It's better for you if you stay away. You don't want them jerking your parole." He waved the bartender over. "Two

126

more. One for me and get another one for Joe." He turned back. "How long were you downstate anyway?"

"I did twenty-eight months in that hell-hole."

"Yep. Like I said. Better stay away." He threw a ten dollar bill on the bar. "Oh, did you hear what's going on over there?"

"Where?" Joe asked.

"Fredericks' old place."

"No."

Tom smiled. "This don't sound right, but from what I heard, he's got some movie people over there making some kind of TV show."

Joe gave him a look of disbelief. "A TV show? About what?"

"I don't know. My cousin is friends with Robert's wife. She said Ruth's been bitching about all the work she has to do because they moved in a bunch of people for a week or so."

"Really! Joe said.

"It just don't seem like something old Wilfred would put up with."

Joe picked up his glass. "Wait a minute. I bet I know what's going on."

"What?"

"The old bastard needs money. Talk is, the county was going to foreclose on his place because he hadn't paid his taxes. He's broke."

Tom scratched his chin. "Must be some kinda reality show. I wonder what they pay you for something like that."

Joe thought for a moment. "Must be a bunch. No way Wilfred would put up with all that bullshit if the money wasn't good."

Tom glanced out the bar window. "Looks like I'd better be heading home. I got a four wheel drive, and I still had a hell of a time getting over here." He scooped up his change. "I hope those folks over at Fredericks' place plan on being there awhile. Out on that point like he is, with all that wind, they may get snowed in for a week."

Joe put on his cap. "Yep. They could all get trapped out there. Stuck there for days."

Chapter 11

WILFRED SET HIS book down and looked at the clock. It was 2:00 a.m. He got up from his desk and walked over to the window. The wind was still blowing strong. He wondered how big the snow drifts were in the driveway. He quietly pulled open his bedroom door and slowly walked to the stairs. He stopped and looked down the long corridor. All the doors were closed. He could hear snoring coming from one of the rooms. It sounded like a radio was playing softly from somewhere at the end of the hallway. He walked down the stairs stepping as lightly as possible, trying to be careful on the steps he knew squeaked the loudest. He headed towards the kitchen.

Once all of the guests had arrived, Ruth had been bringing dinner to his room after everyone had finished eating in the dining room. Tonight she had forgotten to bring him desert, and he was getting hungry.

He pulled the refrigerator door open and found a piece of apple pie. He sat down at the kitchen table and started eating. After the second bite, he heard footsteps coming down the hallway. Whoever it was wasn't doing much to quiet their steps. The kitchen was dark except for a small amount of light streaming in from an outside porch light.

Wilfred put his fork down and listened in the darkness. The footsteps were getting closer. Suddenly, the kitchen door swung open and a large woman stepped towards the refrigerator.

Out of the corner of her eye, Claudia spotted a dim figure sitting at the table in the dark. She threw her hands in the air, let out a high pitched shriek, and stumbled backwards. She fell over a kitchen chair and rolled onto the kitchen floor.

Wilfred rushed over and stared down at her. "Who the hell are you?"

She rubbed her head. "Um, Claudia. One...one of your guests."

"Oh. Are you okay?"

"Ah, I think so," Claudia stammered. "You...you scared me!"

"I didn't mean to startle you. I was just sitting here having a piece of pie." He reached down and held out his hand.

She grabbed it and pulled herself to her feet. "I was just coming down for a little snack. Oh, my...." She fanned her face. "My heart...it's pounding. You gave me quite a fright!"

He righted the overturned chair and guided her into it. "Sit down. Calm down. How about I get you a piece of this pie?"

She nodded.

He sliced her a piece and set it down on the table. "Let me get you a fork." He walked over to the sink, poured her a glass of water, and rummaged through the utensil drawer. He handed her the glass and fork and sat back down across from her.

Between bites of pie, she tried to think of something to say. "I...I think your dog has some anxieties."

Wilfred looked up from his plate. "What?"

"Your dog. He has some issues I'm trying to deal with. I'm a certified animal psychologist."

Wilfred shook his head. He stood up, grabbed his plate, walked over and set it down in the sink. As he passed by Claudia on the way out the door, he muttered, "That's very interesting." He took a few steps into the hallway and then turned back. "Ah, you might want to keep your eyes peeled when you get to the staircase. Granny's restless tonight. Too many people here. When I came down, she was mumbling to herself and walking back and forth at the top of the stairs. She didn't look very happy." He winked and disappeared into the darkness.

Claudia sat motionless in her chair. *Granny? Is he putting me on? Is that his idea of some kind of joke?* She felt a chill run down her back. She sat immobile in the chair. After several minutes she forgot about her half eaten piece of pie and made herself get up. She tiptoed back out to the hallway. Her eyes were wide as she approached the stairway. She glanced up at the top of the railing. She was pretty sure she'd faint if she saw the old woman's ghost.

She pressed herself against the wall and inched herself up the staircase one step at a time. When she got to the landing, she ran down the hallway as fast as she could, glancing behind several times. She threw open her door, jumped into bed, and pulled the thick quilt over her. It was cold in her room. It seemed colder than when she left. She pushed herself further down in the bed and squeezed her eyes shut.

Back up in his room, Wilfred sat down at his desk and picked up the calendar. He had a feeling it was going to be a very long week. He reached down and scratched Fritz behind the ear. *I think that lady's got it all wrong. There's nothing wrong with my dog. I'm the one that's going to have some issues!*

Claudia poked her head out from underneath the covers and stared at the door. She had heard something. In the darkness, she strained to hear what the noise was. There it was again. It sounded like...children. It was very faint and it sounded like it was coming from under her bed. She tilted her head and listened. *Yes, there it is.* Two soft voices were singing a song.

She spun around and stared at the window. Now the sounds were coming from that direction. She noticed the curtains were moving ever so slightly. She buried her head under the covers again and started to pray.

Eddy sat next to April at the breakfast table. Claudia walked in and sat down in the chair next to him. He glanced over at her, turned to April and whispered, "Looks like she's had a rough night. Check out the bags under her eyes."

April sneaked a quick peek. "Looks like she didn't get much sleep. How about you? Did you sleep okay?"

"Not at first. My roommate sure likes to talk about himself. Did you know he just got out of a mental institution! How great is that? I tried to sleep with one eye open all night hoping he didn't snap and try and smother me with a pillow or something!"

April looked alarmed. "Maybe you can move!"

"Where to? Bunk with Reverend Bower? I don't think so!" He glanced around the table to see who had come in. "This whole place is full of nutcases. If you ask me, I think Doctor Hilton dropped the ball on the vetting process."

As Robert walked by, Eddy jumped up and grabbed him by the shoulder. "Can I ask you a question?"

Robert stopped. "What?"

"How do people live up here?"

April gasped. "Eddy!"

He looked over at her. "I'm not trying to be a jerk. It's a good question. I mean, what do they do for work? We didn't see any factories or big businesses. I'm wondering how most people make a living up here."

Robert laughed. "That's a very good question." He thought for a moment. "Some people fish the Great

133

Lakes, like Wilfred did. And, we've got the timber industry."

Eddy nodded. "Yeah. With all these trees, I can see that."

"And then we've got the mines."

"Mines?" Eddy asked.

"Yes. Iron ore. They've been pulling ore out from the Marquette iron range for over a hundred years."

"Mines! I had no idea."

Robert glanced over and saw Ruth motioning for him in the kitchen. He gave her a wave. "I've got to go. Hope that answered your question."

"It did. Thanks!"

Robert turned and headed back to the kitchen. After another few minutes, more people came in and took their places at the table. Doctor Hilton took her place and asked if everyone had a good night. Claudia raised her hand.

"Yes, Claudia?" Doctor Hilton asked.

"Um, I had come downstairs for a little snack, and I ran into Mr. Fredericks in the kitchen. It was all dark, and he about scared me to death. But, he seems to be a nice man. He got me a piece of pie." She paused.

"That's nice dear. Does anyone else have …."

"No! I'm not finished. I…I have a question. When he was leaving to go back to his room, he told me to be careful because he had seen his granny. He said she was at the top of the stairs, and she was mad because there were too many people in the house. Um, do you think he was telling the truth or…maybe just trying to scare me?"

Ruth stopped what she was doing and looked over at Robert who was standing with a huge grin on his face.

Robert let out a little cough. "Um, I can answer that. I think he was just making a joke."

Claudia frowned. "I don't think it was very funny!" She paused. "And then, when I got back to my room I ...." She glanced around the table. "Oh, nothing."

"What? What were you going to say?" Brad asked.

She lifted up a fork full of home fries. "Nothing. It's nothing."

Doctor Hilton surveyed the table. "Okay, then. Does anyone else have anything to report?"

No one did. After breakfast, Doctor Hilton announced that she wanted everyone to meet in the parlor. As they were taking their seats, Claudia ran over and plumped herself down on the other side of Eddy. She turned to him and let out a little giggle. Eddy looked at his sister and rolled his eyes. Jeremy sat at the chess table across from the Reverend. Jeremy pointed to one of the paintings and said to Reverend Bowers, "Aren't those pictures switched?"

He looked to where Jeremy was pointing. "What do you mean switched?"

"I swear the picture of Mr. Fredericks' grandfather was over on that wall and the picture of his mother was where his grandfather's portrait is now."

The Reverend looked back and forth from one wall to another. He studied the picture of the old lady that was hanging over an antique china hutch. "I really never noticed. Why would someone move them?"

"I don't know. But I'm sure they were the other way around when we went to bed last night."

Doctor Hilton wheeled herself to the front of the room. "Nicole spent quite some time tabulating the results of yesterday's Zener tests, and I'd like to let you know the results. Just a reminder, the way the cards work, someone guessing randomly would be expected to get around twenty percent of them correct. Anything above that number would be very interesting."

She picked up a piece of paper and pulled out her glasses. "Here are the results." She glanced back up from the paper. "Oh, before I continue, please don't be upset if your score wasn't over twenty. For many of you, the experiences you've exhibited, had nothing to do with having ESP." She glanced back down at the paper. "Reverend Bowers, you scored eighteen percent."

Eddy stifled a laugh and whispered to April, "Guess his pickled brain couldn't even get him to the random guessing stage."

She gave him a poke. "Shh. What's wrong with you?"

Doctor Hilton looked up. "Did someone have a question?"

This time Eddy answered. "Ah, no, Doctor. Sorry." He gave her a big smile.

Claudia stood up. "Ah, did anyone hear anything strange last night?"

Doctor Hilton looked around the room. "Anybody?" Nobody answered. "I guess not. Why do you ask, Claudia?"

Claudia looked embarrassed. "Oh, nothing. I guess I had a weird dream. Oh, if anyone finds a tennis bracelet, can you let me know? I think mine must have slipped off me yesterday."

Nicole gave a start and looked over at April. Eddy noticed and whispered, "What's that all about?"

"Nicole said she misplaced a ring. We looked for it in our room yesterday just before I came over to talk to you."

"Wait a minute. She lost a ring and Claudia misplaced a bracelet all on the same day?"

She couldn't bear to tell him about her wedding ring and the earrings he had given her for Christmas. "I know. Sounds strange, doesn't it."

"All right. Next, we have…." The doctor paused and looked directly at Eddy, "Mr. Russo. He scored a twenty-three." She waited to see if anyone had anything to say. "April scored a twenty-five, Claudia's score was nineteen, and…." She stopped and put down the paper. "Here's where things get very interesting. Jeremy got forty-one percent of them correct!"

Reverend Bowers jumped from his chair, ran over, and shook his hand. "Great job, Jeremy. But I'm not surprised after hearing about all you do for the cops and everything."

"That's amazing!" Claudia said from the other side of the room. She looked at Eddy. "Isn't that amazing?" April looked over and saw that Eddy had a panicked look on his face.

"What's wrong?"

"I bet that's...that's how he knew about the Ouija board!" Eddy said.

April saw beads of perspiration starting to form on his forehead. "Are you okay? It looks like you're sweating. You look a little pale."

Eddy pulled out a handkerchief and wiped his face. "I'm okay. It's just that the guy's starting to give me the creeps."

April shook her head and whispered, "Why? He seems like a nice man to me. You don't seem to like anyone. You've made nasty comments about..." She nodded her head towards Claudia. "I know you don't care for Reverend Bowers and...."

Eddy leaned closer and whispered, "Reverend! Right! What kind of church do you think he's a reverend at? The church of Bowery bums? Oh, wait! Maybe it's the church for problem drinkers."

Just as April was going to respond, across the room she saw Jeremy walk over and stop Robert as he was headed towards the library. Jeremy pointed to the pictures and said something to him. Robert stopped, studied one of the portraits for a few moments and then took a step back and scratched his head.

April noticed that the wallpaper around the frame of Wilfred's mother's picture was slightly browner than the rest of the wallpaper. She watched as Robert removed Wilfred's grandfather's picture and leaned it up against the wall. April put her hands to her mouth and let out a little yelp.

Eddy spun around. "What?"

She pointed at the wall. Under the paining someone had scrawled a message in red, drippy paint. She read, *Roses are red, like the color of bleeding. To the person who gets them, it's help they'll be needing.*"

Hearing April's gasp, everyone turned towards where she was pointing. Robert stared at the writing.

Claudia grabbed Eddy's hand. "Wha...what is that?" Her voice sounded weak and shaky.

Brad walked over and stood next to Robert. He reached out and touched one of the letters with his finger. It felt cold and sticky. He turned to the group. "Apparently we have another example of someone trying to be funny." He picked up the painting that was supposed to be there and handed it to Robert whispering, "Here, cover this up."

Sensing tension in the room, Doctor Hilton said, "Okay folks, we've given everyone their Zener scores. That's all I had this morning. Why don't we all take some time off? Read, relax, and take a nap if you want to. Let's plan on meeting again after lunch around three o'clock."

As everyone got up, Reverend Bowers asked, "Who's interested in a game of chess?"

Nobody responded. "I think I'm going to take a walk outside," Eddy said.

April stared at him. "Outside? Are you kidding? Have you looked out a window this morning? The wind's blowing like crazy, and it hasn't stopped snowing since we got here."

"That's okay. It's stuffy in here. Everybody's breathing in everybody else's air. I need some fresh air." Eddy turned towards the stairs. "I'm getting my coat. Do you want to come with me?"

April looked at him. "Are you serious?" She waited until he had left the room and then she walked over to Jeremy. "Um, I was wondering if I could have a word with you."

He smiled. "Sure. What do you want to talk about?"

She pointed to the far corner of the room. "Let's talk over there." He followed and sat down next to her. "Is this good?"

"Yes. I'm sorry. I wanted to ask you about something that my brother said, and I didn't want the others to overhear us."

Jeremy looked puzzled. "Okay, what did he say?"

"Eddy told me you mentioned that you thought the spirit that bothered us when we were kids came from a Ouija board and not the desk."

Jeremy frowned. "Oh, my. I was hoping that didn't cause a problem. I could see that bothered him." He drummed his fingers on the arm of the chair. "But, it did come from a Ouija board, didn't it?"

April looked around and whispered. "Yes, but we never told anyone that. We found one in the basement, but our mother hated it and wouldn't let us play with it. One day she grabbed it and threw it in the garbage. I snuck it back out and hid it in my room. How...how did you know?"

140

He let out a sigh. "It's almost impossible to describe. I...I get these feelings. Maybe intuition is a better word. And then I see...I don't know, call them visions. When Doctor Hilton was telling your story, I saw you and your brother playing with a Ouija board. I could feel darkness coming from the board. I knew immediately that your experience had nothing to do with a desk."

April looked disturbed. "It was awful. We had locked ourselves in my room, and we were fooling around with the board. I can't remember what we had asked it, but all of a sudden we felt all of the warmth just slip out of the room. A gray mist started coming up from the floor, and our hands were trembling. The mist smelled like old...old musty dirt and death. I'd never felt anything so terrifying before. I tossed the board under my bed, and we both ran out of my room. That's when everything started happening."

"And you don't think your mother found the board?"

"I don't know. Later that night I was going to take it and bury it or something, but when I went to get it, it was gone."

"I'm sure your mother found it. Maybe she just didn't want to...."

"I don't think so. She would have said something. As much as she hated it and told us never to play with it. I'm pretty sure she would've killed me if she had seen it. I mean, we didn't grow up in a house that didn't believe in punishment." She laughed. "If you don't believe me, just ask Eddy!"

"How was it that the desk got the blame for starting this?" Jeremy asked.

"My father had just bought me a second-hand desk from Good Will. That was the only thing different in the house that he knew of, so he came to the conclusion that the spirit was in the desk when he brought it home. Eddy and I agreed because we knew we'd get punished if they ever found out about the board. I've never told a soul, and I know Eddy hasn't either."

Jeremy took her hand. "I'm sorry I spilled the beans. I promise to keep it a secret!"

She smiled. "It really doesn't matter anymore. But, it did freak Eddy out when you told him."

He shook his head. "I'm so sorry. I just never know when something like this turns around and bites me a good one."

"Don't beat yourself up. You have an amazing power."

As Eddy approached the staircase he noticed Claudia was ahead of him halfway up the stairs. He thought that the sweat pants she was wearing looked two sizes too small. Not a pretty sight. He slowed his pace to make sure she made it to her room before he walked by. He had noticed that she was taking every opportunity to sit next to him, and he didn't want any part of that.

He continued down the hallway and was almost to his door when he heard her scream.

He spun around and ran back down the corridor to her room. She stepped into the hallway and pointed inside the room. Her face was pale and her whole body was shaking.

"What? What is it?" he asked.

"Look...look!"

He poked his head into the room and saw a large vase of red roses sitting on her dresser.

Downstairs, Jeremy jumped up and asked April, "What was that?"

"It sounded like a scream! From upstairs!"

Jeremy ran out of the parlor. He met Brad at the foot of the stairs, and they both ran up together. Brad got to Eddy first.

"What is it?" Brad asked.

"The poem," Eddy said. "It came true!"

Chapter 12

MARGARET HEARD SOMEONE knocking on the front door. She jumped up, and for one quick moment thought that it might be April and Eddy. As she hurried to the door, she saw that it was April's husband standing on the porch. "Oh, Dennis. I'm glad to see you. Come in. Please come in."

He stepped into the living room slightly puzzled, but happily surprised by her welcome. It wasn't the greeting he was expecting. He followed her back to the kitchen.

"How about a cup of coffee? You take it black, don't you?"

"Yes."

She poured him a cup. He took a seat across from where her cup and a newspaper were sitting. As he sat down, she said, "I'm glad you stopped by. I'm a little worried about April and Eddy."

Dennis looked up from his coffee. "Worried? Why? What's going on?"

"I knew this wasn't a good idea. I told April not to go."

"Go where?"

"They drove up to the Upper Peninsula."

"Are they going skiing?"

Margaret let out a nervous laugh. "No. They both got letters from some doctor asking them to go up to Marquette. They're shooting some kind of TV show."

Dennis put down his coffee. "TV show? You're kidding, right?"

"No. It's got something to do with the things that happened to them when they were kids." She looked at Dennis for his reaction. "Um, I'm sure April told you about that, didn't she?"

He nodded. "Yes. You mean that haunting stuff, don't you?"

"Yes. I told her not to do it. Eddy's never gotten over that. At first, she was the only one that was going; but then, at the last minute, Eddy decided to go, too."

"Okay," Dennis said, with a quizzical look. "So, what's the problem?"

"They were supposed to call me the minute they got there, but I haven't heard a word from them. I've tried both of their cells phones, but it goes straight to their voice mail. Nobody's called me back."

Dennis straightened up in his chair. "Did you say this was a couple of days ago? And you haven't heard from them?"

Margaret looked down at the table. "Yes."

Dennis took a sip of coffee. "From what I've seen on TV, the weather's been pretty bad up there. But if they'd been in some kind of an accident, I'm sure you would've been notified by now." He thought for a moment. "They probably got all involved with the TV show and just forgot to call. Do you have a number for this doctor?"

"No. I'm afraid I don't"

Margaret looked as though she was about to burst into tears. "The thing is, they're both so dependable. And they know how I worry. I can't imagine why I haven't heard from them."

"Do you know where they're staying?" Dennis asked. "I could drive up there and check the place out."

She got up and grabbed a piece of paper that was hanging from the refrigerator. "They're staying somewhere called the Fredericks place. And…." She read more from the paper. "It says it's about fifteen miles outside of Marquette." She handed him the paper. "There's a little map."

"Why don't I drive up there and see what's going on?"

"Oh, gracious. No, I couldn't ask you to do that!"

"It wouldn't be a problem. I took a week off to come down here and see if I could patch things up. I don't have anything else to do. Let me drive up there and check out the place."

Margaret thought for a moment, then shook her head no. "Oh, she'd be so mad. She didn't want me to tell you where she was going." She glanced down at the table. "I…I just think she needs a little more time, Dennis."

He finished his coffee and stood up. "How about this. I'll stop by again tomorrow. If you still haven't heard from them, we'll talk about me heading up there. Does that sound okay with you?"

She nodded. "Yes. That sounds good. Thank you. Thank you so much."

Just as everyone was finishing their lunch, Reverend Bowers stood up from the table and said, "Doctor Hilton, some of us have been talking, and we'd like to have everyone, including Brad, meet with us in the parlor right now."

She looked surprised. "I don't see a problem with that. Let's take our coffees and go right now."

As Eddy and April headed towards the parlor, Robert walked up and handed something to Eddy.

He looked at the hard, round, shiny ball in his hand. "What's this?"

"It's an iron ore pellet," Robert replied.

Eddy rolled it around in his fingers. "Where did you get it?"

Robert laughed. "There's millions of them alongside the railroad tracks. They fall off the cars as they're taking them to the docks."

"Really!" Eddy said as he handed it back.

"Keep it. I've got a whole coffee can of them down in the basement."

Eddy smiled. "Thanks!"

Brad and Doctor Hilton made their way to the front of the fireplace while the others got settled in their favorite chairs and sofas. The Reverend stepped out in front of the group and turned to face Brad.

"Like I said, we've been talking, and we think that you're behind some of the nasty little things that have been going on. We understand the need for drama while making a television show, but we feel your antics are upsetting some of the women, and we'd like you to admit it and to tell us all this is going to stop."

Eddy whispered to April, "Some of the women? Scared the hell out of me, too! And I bet he's about crapped in his pants a few times himself!"

Brad cleared his throat and stepped forward. "I appreciate everyone's concern, but please believe me; I'm not doing any of this. My crew left a few days after they set up everything, so I'm the only one here. Personally, I think it's one of you who thinks these little pranks are funny, but believe me, they aren't. And, if whoever is doing this thinks it will help the pilot get sold, it won't. I suggest we just go along with what Doctor Hilton has planned for us. I know she has several activities lined up. We're lucky to have someone with her expertise in the field. Everyone, please give her your full support, and whoever it is that thinks these little pranks are funny, please stop the foolishness. You're putting this whole pilot in jeopardy." Brad looked over to where Doctor Hilton was waiting.

"Thank you, Brad. This afternoon I thought we'd talk about any new paranormal experiences you've had since the first ones that brought you all to the media's attention. Who would like to go first?"

Everyone turned and looked at each other, and after a few seconds, Jeremy stood up and said, "I'll start."

Doctor Hilton looked relieved.

"Well, the last case I worked on was the disappearance of a little four-year-old girl in Palatka, Florida. The girl lived in a trailer park and was being watched by a sixteen-year-old baby sitter. According to the babysitter, she had put the girl down for a nap around three o'clock, and when she went to check on her at around four-thirty, the girl was gone. Well, when I got called into the case...."

As Jeremy continued, April jumped up and quickly walked into the library. Brad watched as Eddy got up and followed her. From the look on April's face, Brad knew something was wrong. He excused himself to Doctor Hilton and joined them. April was sitting at a wooden table and Eddy was standing over her. Eddy asked, "Are you okay?"

She looked up and saw Brad. She waited until he walked over and then said, "I...I just couldn't hear about the death of another child. I'm sorry, but...."

"No need to be sorry," Brad said. "We understand completely."

"What was Jeremy thinking?" Eddy complained. "He should have known better than to start rattling on about some kid...."

Brad turned to him. "I doubt very much that he knows anything about the loss your family's experienced."

Eddy stopped and thought for a second. "Well, maybe not, but I don't think talking about some kid being murdered is really appropriate. You know, I even wonder if those stories of his are true. I find it hard to believe the cops are beating his door down to listen to a bunch of his mumbo jumbo."

"Eddy!" April said. "From what we've all heard, he clearly has a gift. Look at his Zener scores. How could he guess forty-one percent of them correctly if he doesn't have some kind of ability?"

"Who knows?" Eddy looked at Brad. "It's...it's probably a setup for the show. That guy gives me the creeps. Try rooming with him for a while." He stepped back and crossed his arms. "Look, I'm not in the mood to argue with you about him. Why don't I go back in there and subject myself to another dose of his bullshit." He spun around and walked back into the parlor.

"I'm sorry," April said. "I don't know why he's so bitter. Ever since he got here, he's had some kind of nasty attitude. I...I wish I hadn't brought him."

Brad pulled over a chair and sat down. "I'm sure Jeremy would never have started talking about those things if he had been aware of what you've been through. And don't worry about Eddy. This house seems to bring that out in people. Even my team started crabbing at each other. They've worked together for three years, and I never heard them barking at each other like they were doing here." He looked around. "You have to admit, this place is a little gloomy."

"Let's talk about something else," April said.

"Okay, good idea. What do you want to talk about?"

April thought for a moment. "I know. Last night I was talking with Nicole. It was so refreshing to hear how excited she is about graduating and starting her life. She told me about all her travel plans. That got me thinking. You know, I've never left the Midwest. I was born in Wisconsin and moved to Chicago. That's only a hundred and fifty miles away! Then I started thinking about what you told me. About California. I wish I would have taken some time after school to go places and see things. I can't even imagine what California must be like."

Brad smiled. "Some parts of it are great and some, not so much. You know what you should do?"

She gave him a quizzical look.

"You should come to California. I can show you around."

She looked thrilled for a second and then frowned.

"What's wrong?" Brad asked.

"I've been living with my mom since Bobby died. I've taken a leave of absence from my job. I'm afraid I don't have any going-to-California money just sitting around."

"Don't worry about that. You're part of the show. I can have the studio pay for it, and I can write it off. You're a consultant."

She laughed. "Well, I don't know about that. Before I do anything, I really have to get myself together and start working on my future." She stopped and looked at him. "But, thank you for allowing me to dream. I haven't done that for a long time."

He stood up and offered her his hand. "Shall we go back?"

She reached out to him. "Yes. Let's see what other gruesome tales are being told out there."

As they walked back into the parlor, they heard Claudia from the back of the room. It sounded like she was almost hysterical. "What's going on?" April whispered to Brad.

Claudia continued, "We...we didn't know what to do. My sister drew that face on our window because she had seen a story on TV. It was just a joke. Then, before we knew it, there were people coming to see it. I tried to get her to take it off. But by then, there were TV crews outside and everyone wanted to interview us. We were both afraid. What if they found out this was just a joke. There were all kinds of people coming from far away to see it. We knew we were going to be in big trouble if we said what we had done." She looked over at Doctor Hilton. "I'm sorry. I'm so sorry."

Reverend Bowers chuckled to himself. The whole story about ghosts in the family hotel had been dreamed up by his father. The hotel was about to go under, and his dad was desperate to come up with something to save it. He made up a story about the hotel being haunted and talked his friend, who worked on the local paper, to print it. The *Associated Press* picked it up, and in a few weeks, there were so many gullible people trying to book a room that they had to turn some of them away. And then, just like magic, people started seeing ghosts in the hotel. *People are assholes. So easily manipulated. You won't be seeing me bubbling away to the Doc telling her my whole story is a bunch of shit, too.* That letter from Doctor Hilton had come at a perfect time. He needed to get out of town for a while.

Claudia walked over to the sideboard, picked up a napkin, and wiped her face. "Now, there's a message written in blood about me and then it comes true and flowers show up in my room. I'm scared. I...I shouldn't be here. I just want to go home!"

Doctor Hilton wheeled herself over to her. "Now, now. Everything's going to be okay. There was no blood involved in that message. It was red paint. If you want to go home, we'll see what we can do. I'm sure Brad understands."

Robert, who must have been standing just outside in the foyer, suddenly appeared. "Ah, that may be a problem, Doctor. We're officially snowed in. There's about three feet of snow in front of the front door and six-foot drifts in the driveway. We're just about the last road to be plowed by the county since we're the only house down here. I'd say we'll all be stuck here for at least a few days." He paused to let them comprehend what he had told them. "Oh, by the way, the phone lines are down, too.

A look of panic swept over Claudia's face. "But...I want to go now!"

Robert shrugged his shoulders. "We got a pair of snowshoes out in the garage if you want. But they're not very easy to walk in, and it's sixteen miles into town. I guess you could make it, but...I wouldn't bet my life on it. Not in this weather."

She turned to Brad. "Mr. Feldman, I really have to get out of here!"

He looked over at Robert. "I'm sorry. There's nothing I can do. Why don't you go up to your room and rest for a while. Maybe you'll feel better after a nap. Mother Nature has a way of taking things out of our hands."

"I'm...I'm afraid to go up there. I don't want to find more roses or something like that."

Jeremy motioned to her. "I'll go with you. I'm sure your room's just fine. Come on, let's go check it out."

Doctor Hilton noticed that everyone had a slightly shocked look after hearing Robert's statement. "Well, with that said, I think it would be a good idea for us all to relax a little and contemplate our predicament. I'll see you all later for dinner."

As April headed for the stairs, Eddy walked up behind her. "How did your little talk with Brad go? You seemed to be in there a long time."

She turned. "Ah, do I detect a little jealousy, my little brother? We had a very nice talk, if you must know. In fact, he invited me to come out to California. How about that?"

"A trip to California! Well, imagine that. Did he offer to show you his casting couch as part of the deal?"

"Eddy! He's not like that!"

He laughed. "Right! Too bad you're still married. I'm not sure Dennis would think that was such a good idea."

"I'm separated, as if you don't know, and guess what? So is Brad. In fact, we have a lot in common.

And you know what? The more I'm around all these people from all over the country, the more it dawns on me that I need to expand my horizons a little." She stepped closer and lowered her voice. "And I think that's something you should be thinking of, too. Look at us. It's shameful both of us are living with Mother like two little kids. You know, I'm really glad I decided to take this trip. It's made me see things in a whole different light. We only have one life, and I think we're both wasting ours horribly."

Eddy took a step back. "Well! I wasn't expecting that!" He grinned. "Talk about being on different pages! I can't wait to get out of this house of freaks, and you're making plans to take a trip to California." He shook his head. "What a difference a day makes!"

She put her hand on his shoulder. "I...I guess I came on a little strong. Sorry. No, I'm not running off to California. Not yet, anyway. But this trip did get me thinking."

They walked up the staircase in silence. When they got to her room, she asked, "What are your plans this afternoon? Do you want to come with me and read in the library?"

"And interrupt another beautiful moment with Brad. No, I don't think so. Actually, I'm going to take that walk I've been talking about."

"How are you going to do that? Robert said there's a three foot drift by the front door."

"The back door's okay. I already checked it with Robert. The porch roof kept most of the snow off."

"Well, be careful. It sounds like it's still blowing like crazy out there."

"I don't care. I've got to get out of here. Get away from these lunatics and clear my head."

April gave him a hug. "If you change your mind, I'll be in the library. And...sorry about the little lecture."

Claudia and Jeremy walked down the hallway. She pointed to one of the lamp fixtures. "Look! It's covered in cobwebs. This place needs a good cleaning." She stopped in the middle of the hallway. "I feel so claustrophobic here. And now we can't even leave if we wanted to. I shouldn't even be here in the first place. I'm...I'm being punished for coming. It was wrong for me to...."

"Please, Claudia!" Jeremy said. "Calm down. You're only making things worse. You're here now. You can't go anywhere because of the storm. You can't change that. Try and turn this negative into something positive. Talk to some of the others. Get to know Doctor Hilton a little more. She's a fascinating woman."

"I've tried to talk to Eddy, but he doesn't seem very interested."

"Then pick someone else. Talk to Nicole about her studies or Robert about his past or Reverend Bowers about his congregation."

"Oh, I don't know about the Reverend. He kind of scares me." She moved closer and whispered, "I think he needs to wash his hair!"

As they approached her door, she slowed down and turned to him. "Um, would you mind checking my room? I...I don't like surprises."

"Not at all. That's why I came with you." She pulled out her key and unlocked the door. He pushed it open, stepped in, and looked around. "Looks okay to me."

Claudia stepped in and glanced at the big antique dresser. "Yes. Nothing seems out of the ordinary."

As Jeremy turned to leave, she grabbed him by his shirt sleeve and pointed to a chair. "Would you like to sit and chat for a minute?"

"Sure!" He smiled and took a seat.

"I...I was wondering. How did you get such a high score on your Zener cards?"

He laughed. "Everybody asks me that, and I really don't know. All of this started when I was seven years old. I got scarlet fever real bad and almost died. When I got better, I had the...gift." He stopped. "If you can call it a gift."

Claudia sat in amazement. "How did you know you had it?"

"My grandmother passed away. My mother's mother. And I knew it was going to happen. I didn't tell anyone, but I knew she was going to go."

"That's what I'm so fascinated by," Claudia said. "Do you see something? What tells you?"

Jeremy thought for a few moments. "Like I told April, it's...it's like a combination of a feeling and a vision, but it's not really either one. I can't describe it because it's something so different. Like the cards. I can't actually see them, but I get a feeling and then I seem to know which one is going to turn up next."

"That's got to be terrifying, knowing when someone is going to die!"

"Thank goodness it doesn't happen all the time. Like when my father passed. It was a complete surprise to me. I didn't see or feel anything before he died."

"Well, it surely is a gift!" Claudia said.

Jeremy smiled and patted her hand. "Well, thank you, but I think everyone has it. It's just a question of how can we all bring it out. It took scarlet fever for me." He stood up and gave a little shiver. "I think I'll head back to my room and put on another layer. I'm freezing."

Claudia stood up. "Thank you for walking with me."

Back in his room, Eddy put on his thick winter jacket, gloves, and boots. He pulled on a Green Bay Packers knitted cap, stepped out into the hallway, and saw Jeremy headed his way.

"What's this?" Jeremy asked, looking him over. "You're not going outside, are you?"

"I guess your paranormal powers are firing on all cylinders!" Eddy said. "How did you know?"

"Very funny," Jeremy replied. "Be careful out there. You'd never get me outside in this weather. I can't seem to get warm in the house! Be careful the wind doesn't sweep you right over the cliff. It looks like there's a hundred foot drop down to the lake."

"I'll be fine," Eddy said. He walked down the stairs and made his way to the back of the house. He was thankful he didn't run into anyone else. He was in no mood to rationalize his walk to anyone else. As he pushed the back door open, he felt the wind hit him like the wash from a propeller driven plane. He stumbled to stay upright. He had to turn his back to the lake just to catch his breath. He tightened the scarf around his neck and pulled it over his nose. He slowly turned, and holding on to the railing, he took the porch steps down to a giant snow bank.

He plowed through three feet of snow and slowly made his way over to the old iron fence that meandered along the edge of the cliff. In some places, the sharp spikes on the iron posts were buried beneath the snow drifts. Eddy wished he had a camera. He stared out over the lake. Ice and snow extended out from the shore about a hundred feet. Huge waves of dark gray and black water were breaking on the ice sheet. The wind was blowing the sound of the waves back towards the shore, making them even louder than they were.

April was right. The temperature was probably around ten degrees, but with the blizzard conditions, it felt like it was twenty below zero. His forehead was tingling and started to feel numb. As he turned to walk back to the porch, he glanced up at the widow's walk and noticed a thin figure bundled up in a long black Mackinaw coat staring out over the lake. He wondered how Mr. Fredericks could possibly stand up there. At that height, the wind had to be much worse than what he was experiencing.

Heading back to the house, Eddy tried to retrace the path he had made in the deep snow, but the wind had already covered it over in places. Finally, he stumbled up the porch steps, stomped his feet, and pushed the door open. He peeled off his jacket and hung it on a hook. He walked down the hallway, turned into the parlor and walked over to the fireplace.

Jeremy was standing with his hands outstretched towards the fire. He looked over at Eddy. "My God, man! Your face is as red as a beet! You really went outside in that gale?"

Eddy leaned closer to the fire. "I was getting tired of being cooped up in here." He rubbed his hands together and then felt his forehead. "Probably not a good idea. It's brutal out there!"

Jeremy glanced out the window. "I've got to hand it to you. Very brave of you. I would've never given that a thought."

Eddy smiled. "And I even got to see the elusive Mr. Fredericks."

Jeremy looked surprised. "He was outside, too!"

"Well, kind of. He was standing out on that widow's walk, looking out over the lake. I can't imagine how cold and windy it must be up there."

"I guess he's a tough old bird. But, he seems to be something of an odd one. Not very social. I wonder how they ever talked him into letting us all come and stay in his house."

"Beats me. I sure wouldn't be throwing open my house to all these nut...um, people."

Chapter 13

AFTER DINNER EVERYONE sat in the parlor waiting for Doctor Hilton. After a few minutes, she wheeled herself in. Nicole followed behind, pushing a tea cart filled with boxes.

Eddy walked over to the window. "If this wind gets any stronger, I'd swear we were in some kind of winter hurricane. I sure hope this old house can stand up to it."

April had been hearing the house bending and creaking all day as the storm continued to pound them. She called to him, "Eddy, come over here and sit down. I think Doctor Hilton has something to say."

Eddy sauntered over and took a seat. "Big deal!" He was rolling the iron ore pellet around in his fingers.

Doctor Hilton clapped her hands together and said, "Okay, everybody. I think we have an activity that everyone will enjoy. God knows we need something to keep our minds occupied. Nicole has several Ouija boards that she will pass out to you."

Jeremy glanced over at Eddy and smiled.

Doctor Hilton continued, "I'd like you to pick a partner, take a board, and sit with each other for half an hour and see what happens. You can ask the board anything you like, but after thirty minutes, I'd like you to change partners. If anything interesting or unexpected happens, please let Nicole or me know right way. Any questions?"

April whispered to Eddy, "I don't think we should do this together." He turned to her with a panicked look. "I don't think we should do this, period!"

From the other side of the room Claudia yelled, "Ouija boards! Oh, I love those!"

Jeremy picked up a board and walked over to April. "Would you like to be my partner?" She put on a weak smile and looked back at Eddy. "I...I guess so."

Eddy stared at her, shaking his head no.

As Nicole handed a board to Reverend Bowers, he put his hand on her arm and pulled her closer. "Hmm. That's some sweet smelling perfume you're wearing!"

She stepped back and pulled away. "Ah, um, thanks."

The Reverend motioned for Eddy. "Come on, Eddy, let's see what kind of damage we can do with this thing."

"Ah, no thanks. Not my cup of tea."

Reverend Bowers looked around the room. "Hey, Brad. Come over and be my partner." Brad smiled.

"I'm just an observer here. I can't put myself into the show."

"Oh, come on. Look, everybody else has someone."

Brad walked over to him. "Okay, if you insist."

The Reverend smiled, "Good! Sit down. I know it's a bunch of hokum, but what the heck, we gotta keep the Doc happy." He set the board down on the table where the chess pieces normally were and picked up the planchette. "Do you want to drive or should I?"

"I thought we both put our fingers on it," Brad said.

The Reverend let out a laugh. "We do, we do. Come on. Maybe we can summon up some of them ghosts we have back at the hotel."

Jeremy pulled out a chair for April.

She stared at the board. "I...I'm not sure I want to do this."

Jeremy smiled. "I know. I'm going to bring it back to Nicole. I just wanted you to sit with me."

She sighed. "Oh, thank goodness!"

Claudia ran up to Eddy. "Come on, let's do it together!"

He turned. "What?"

"You know," she winked. "The board."

"No. Not for me. Sorry."

She laughed and pushed him down in a chair. "Don't tell me you're afraid of it?"

"To tell you the truth, I had a bad experience once, and I...."

"That's ridiculous," Claudia laughed. She moved her chair so their knees were touching and she slid the board onto both of their laps. "Here, put your hands on the thingy." She reached over and placed both of his hands on the heart shaped piece of wood. She plopped her fingers down on the other side and said, "Okay, let's think of a question we can ask."

As she was thinking, Eddy felt the planchette start to move.

"Oh, it's moving!" Claudia squealed.

It started moving slowly at first and then picked up speed. She called out the letters it stopped on. "T...E...L...L." There was a pause. "I think it said 'tell!" Claudia blurted out. The planchette continued to move. "Y...O...U...R...S...I...S...T...E...R."

Claudia struggled to put the letters together. "Yoursis...tell...? Oh, it said 'tell your sister!'"

At this point, the planchette started twirling around. Both Claudia and Eddy pulled their hands away from the board. It spun faster and faster and then flew off the board and hit Eddy in the forehead. The planchette clattered to the floor, and a thin trickle of blood bubbled from his head.

Claudia let out a scream. "It kept moving!" She glanced up at Eddy. "Oh, my God! Help! He's bleeding! It...it was moving by itself!"

Eddy pulled out a handkerchief, pressed it over his wound, and ran towards the foyer. As he left the room, the lights suddenly went out, and everyone was left sitting in the dark.

"What happened?" Claudia screamed. "Who turned off the lights?"

"I don't know," Doctor Hilton called out from the corner. "Everything just went black."

The door from the foyer squeaked open, and Ruth said, "The power went out. Robert's going down to the basement now. We got a generator down there. Lights should be back on in a few minutes."

Brad sat in the dark across from Reverend Bowers. "What do you think that was all about?" he asked.

"Probably Eddy just wanting some attention. He seems to thrive on it," the Reverend replied with a hint of disgust in his voice.

April reached out and grabbed Jeremy. "Eddy's hurt. I've got to find him!"

"It's pitch dark in here. Wait until the generator kicks in. I'll come with you."

After a few minutes, Doctor Hilton whispered to Nicole, "Go try and find Ruth. See if she can give us some candles or flashlights so everyone can get back to their rooms."

"Okay," she said, feeling her way to the door. As Nicole entered the foyer, she could see a yellow glow down the hallway coming from the kitchen. She followed the light and saw that Ruth had lit a kerosene lantern and had it sitting on the kitchen counter. Ruth had her back to the door and she gave a start when Nicole walked up to her.

"Sorry to scare you, Ruth. Doctor Hilton was wondering if you had a few flashlights or candles we could use. She wants everyone to go back and stay in their rooms until the lights come back on."

"I do. But everything should be back to normal any second now. Never usually takes this long. All he's got to do is get the generator going. Only takes about a minute or so."

Nicole stood there not knowing what to say. Finally, she said, "I think it's been like at least fifteen minutes. Maybe he's having trouble getting it going. Do you think we could have...?"

"Yeah. Hold on. I've got to find them." Ruth pulled out a stool and pushed it over to a tall cabinet. She stepped on it, reached up, and pulled open a door. "We keep 'em in here. Don't ask me why. They should be someplace where you can lay your hands on them when you need them. I know they're in here someplace." She reached her hand further into the cabinet and felt around. "Can you pick up that lantern and hold it up here?"

Nicole grabbed the handle and held it up as high as she could. Ruth got on her tip toes and peered into the opening. "Here they are."

She pulled out several long, white candles and handed them to Nicole. "Let me get you a little saucer for each one. Don't want hot wax dripping all over the place."

Nicole lit one of the candles from the lantern, held it over a plate, and turned towards the darkened hallway. "Thank you."

"I bet you the lights come back on before you even make it to the parlor," Ruth said.

"I hope you're right!" She slowly walked back down the hallway making sure her one glimmer of illumination didn't blow out. As she got halfway to the parlor, she heard something at the far end of the darkened hallway. She stopped and turned her head. It sounded like music. She listened as faint sounds from a violin came drifting down the hallway. *Violin music! Didn't Brad talk about a violin? What was it he said?*

The music was getting closer. She peered into the darkness to see if she could see anything. As the sounds got nearer to the kitchen, the glow from the lantern suddenly disappeared, plunging the hallway into total darkness except for the faint glow from her candle. Nicole turned and started walking towards the foyer. She tried to walk faster, but as she did, the feeble light from her candle flickered and almost went out.

The music now seemed to be coming from somewhere past the kitchen, and it was getting closer. She glanced back but still couldn't see anything. The music seemed to be gaining on her. She turned and started running towards the parlor. The candle flame fluttered out and Nicole ran blindly down the corridor. She held her arms out in front of her and ran faster. The music was right behind her. Her right hand slammed into the front door. She stumbled and fell against the door with a bang. She slid down to her knees. Her forehead was throbbing as she reached up to feel her face. Broken pieces of candles rolled in all directions on the foyer floor.

Hearing the commotion, Reverend Bowers ran out to the hallway and almost tripped over her. "What happened?" he asked.

"I was coming from the kitchen. Ruth gave me some candles. I heard someone playing the violin down at the end of the hallway. It was dark and I couldn't see who it was. The music was getting closer, and then Ruth's lantern went out and the hall got dark. I started running because the music was right behind, me and I didn't know who was there!"

"Are you all right?" the Reverend asked.

"I...I hit my head pretty hard." She felt her hand. "And my wrist. It's really sore."

She heard Jeremy ask, "Did you say you have candles?"

"They went flying when I slammed into the door, but they should be around here someplace."

Jeremy and the Reverend knelt down and started feeling around the floor. "I've got one," Jeremy called out. "Does anyone have a match?"

"Yep, hold on a minute." Reverend Bowers fumbled in his pocket, pulled out a book of matches, and struck one. Jeremy reached over with the candle and got it lit. He held it over Nicole. "Let me look at you." He pulled her hair away from her forehead. "Well, let's see here...you've got quite a lump starting to form on your head, but I don't see any blood." He reached down and helped her up. "Come on. Let's get you into the parlor where you can sit down."

As they entered the room, Doctor Hilton wheeled herself over. "My goodness! What happened? I heard an awful racket out there."

As Jeremy started to explain, Reverend Bowers lit a candle and walked over to the shelf above the bookcase. "It's gone!"

April walked up behind him. "What's gone?"

"The violin that was sitting here." He held up his candle. "The shelf's empty."

Jeremy walked over and handed April a piece of candle. "Here. Doctor Hilton wants everyone back to their rooms for the night. It's probably a good idea to lock your door, too. Even if the generator gets the lights going, the activities down here are cancelled for the night."

April and Jeremy each held their candle stub in front of them as they walked upstairs and slowly walked down the hallway to Eddy's room. Jeremy pushed the door open and April saw Eddy sitting on the bed holding a wash cloth against his forehead.

"How are you?"

"I guess I'm going to make it," Eddy said.

"So, what exactly happened down there?"

Eddy glanced at April and then looked over at Jeremy. "I think that Crazy Claudia threw the planchette at me."

"Come on, Eddy. Why would she do that?"

"How the hell would I know? She's some kind of kook from California. She keeps sitting next to me, and she's probably pissed because I don't give her any attention."

April held her candle up close to his head. "How bad is it? Can I see?"

Eddy slowly pulled the wash cloth away.

"It's stopped bleeding. It's not too big, thank goodness."

"You know how head wounds bleed," Jeremy said. "Looks like you're going to live to see another day."

Eddy frowned. "Just what I need. Another day in this madhouse."

"Tell me again what happened. I…I find it hard to believe Claudia would through it at you."

Eddy glanced over at Jeremy and lowered his voice. "That damn planchette had a mind of its own. It started spinning around like it was possessed." He brought his voice down to a whisper. "And then it flew off the board and slammed against my head." He patted his forehead with the wash cloth. In a louder voice, he asked, "What's with the lights?"

"I guess the storm knocked out our power," Jeremy said. "Ruth said an emergency generator should get them back on any time now."

"I about killed myself on the stairs. The lights went out just as I got to the staircase. I crashed into the stairs and about knocked myself out. I had to crawl on my hands and knees back to the damn room."

Upstairs, Wilfred heard people walking past his doorway. He wondered what was taking Robert so long getting the lights back on. Robert had started the generator many times in the past. There wasn't much too it. Push a button and the battery kicked it in. He knew it had plenty of fuel. Wilfred had used a flashlight to find a candle and it was burning in an ash tray on his desk.

He started for the door and then stopped. He wondered how many more of those people would still be hanging around downstairs. *To hell with it. Let Robert take care of it.* He grabbed a book, lay back in bed, and tried to read. After struggling in the dim light for two paragraphs, he blew out the candle. In less than fifteen minutes he was snoring.

Four hours later, Wilfred woke up. He had to pee. He reached over and switched on the lamp sitting on his nightstand. It clicked but no light came on. He fumbled for the flashlight that he had left on his nightstand. He switched it on and peered at the clock. It was 3:22 a.m. *What the hell. Why wasn't the generator working?*

He grabbed his robe, walked over to the door, and pushed it open. He played the light up and down the hallway. All the doors appeared to be closed. He walked over to Ruth and Robert's room and knocked softly on their door. He had to knock several times before he heard movement in the room. The door opened slightly and Ruth peeked out. Her hair was disheveled; and she was wearing a heavy quilted robe. "Wilfred! It's you!" she whispered through the door. "I thought it was one of those damn guests. What's going on?"

"The generator? Why didn't Robert turn it on?"

"He tried. He spent about an hour down in the basement. Something happened, and he couldn't get it working. He was going to come and get you, but he thought he'd look at it one more time in the morning."

Wilfred yawned. "I'll head down there now and see what the problem is."

"Do you want me to wake Robert up and have him go with you?"

Wilfred shook his head. "No. Let him sleep. I'm sure all these people are running him ragged. I'll go take a look."

"Okay. Well, goodnight."

She closed her door, and he made his way down to the first floor, hoping all the while that he didn't meet any of the guests. As he walked by the door to the kitchen, he noticed a red stain on the hallway floor. Wilfred stopped and looked down. The marks continued down the hall, all the way to the parlor, but it looked like they came from the kitchen.

Wilfred leaned into the doorway and shined his light onto the kitchen floor. The beam reflected off a large pool of brownish-red liquid. He stepped into the kitchen, careful to avoid the stain. He bent down and played his light over the area. It looked like blood.

He stood up and walked back into the hallway. He followed the markings down the hallway and into the parlor. As he stepped through the parlor door, he noticed one of the chairs was turned over. As he bent over to pick it up, he noticed the red streaks continued across the floor on into the library. He played the light around in ever-widening circles. He noticed that the markings were getting longer and darker the closer they got to the library. He squatted down and dabbed his finger into a small red puddle. It was dry but still a little tacky.

He made his way into the library, being careful to walk next to the streaks and not disturb them. He shined his light over to the left and stopped. A man was sprawled out on the floor. He was lying on his back with a huge butcher knife sticking out from the middle of his chest. Wilfred ran over to the body and bent down. He grabbed the man's wrist. It felt cold. There was no pulse. He stood up and played the light around the room. Nothing else looked out of the ordinary.

Wilfred slowly backed out of the room, staring at the body the whole time. When he got back to the parlor, he shined the light in a big circle. He noticed that a lamp, a small table, and a potted plant were all knocked over.

He made his way back up the steps as fast as he could and knocked again on Robert and Ruth's door. This time the knock was louder and more urgent. After a minute or so Robert pulled the door open. "Hey. Did you get it going?"

For a moment, Wilfred didn't know what Robert was talking about. "Oh, that...no. I never made it to the basement. We've got a big problem downstairs."

From the look on his face, Robert knew this was serious. "What?"

Wilfred grabbed him by the arm, pulled him out into the hallway, and shut the door. "There's a dead man lying in the middle of the library floor."

"A dead man! Who is it? Did somebody have a heart attack?"

"It's a heart problem all right. There's a big knife sticking out of the guy's chest."

"What! A knife? Who is it?" Robert asked, pulling his bathrobe tighter.

"I don't know. One of the guests. I never met most of 'em. Come on. I'm sure you'll know who the guy is."

From inside the room, Robert heard his wife ask, "What is it?"

He pushed the door slightly open. "I don't know yet. Something's happened downstairs, and I want you to stay here. Lock the door and don't let anyone in but Wilfred or me."

Ruth appeared in the doorway looking concerned. "What? Don't let anyone in? What's going on?"

"I'll tell you later. Shut the door and lock it." Robert pulled the door shut and waited until he heard the lock click shut. He turned to Wilfred. "Let's go."

Chapter 14

DENNIS SAW THE red flashing lights as he approached the *Welcome To Trenary* sign at the intersection of US 41 and highway 280. A state trooper waved him over.

"What's going on?" Dennis asked.

"You're going to have to turn around and go back. Road's closed."

"But I need to get to Marquette!"

"Not today. Eight-foot drifts. County plows have been out all night."

"When will the road be cleared?"

The trooper shrugged his shoulders. "I don't know. Listen to the radio. We'll make an announcement when it's good to go."

Dennis couldn't believe it. "Okay." He turned the car around and headed back south. He tried to remember where he had seen the most recent motel. He thought about the call he had received that morning from April's mother. She sounded frantic. He was glad she asked him to drive up and see what was going on. It would give him a good excuse to see his wife again. And besides, he was a little worried about her, too.

He stopped in Rapid River, but every motel was full. He finally found a place fourteen miles down the road in the town of Escanaba. He checked in, turned on the clock radio, and stretched out on the bed. He listened as the announcer read a long string of announcements updating all of the most recent weather closures.

Joe Casperson walked into the kitchen as his wife put down the phone. "That was Dee. Marquette's shut down. They've closed US 41 from both directions. Got cops at Munising and Trenary both."

"I ain't surprised. This is the worst I've seen for about the last ten years."

Madge thought for a moment. "Yep. That was the year my cousins were trying to get here for Ma's funeral. They never made it. Had to turn around at the bridge and go back to Lansing."

Joe nodded. "Yeah. That was the second year I had my plow. Remember? Made a killing with that damn plow. Paid for the truck and everything that year."

Madge poured herself a cup of coffee. "Speaking of making a killing. Dee said old man Fredericks is in for a big windfall."

He straightened up in his chair. "Why's that?"

"She talks to Ruth sometimes, and she said they're using his old house for some TV show. Paid him a lot of money for it, too."

Joe scratched his head. "His house? Why in the hell would they want to use that old falling down piece of shit? The place ain't been painted for twenty years."

"I guess because it looks so old."

He looked around. "Hell, we got an old double wide. Why didn't they call us?"

"Who'd want to make a movie in a trailer?" Madge asked.

Joe pushed himself away from the table and stood up. "That damn Fredericks. He kills them guys and look what happens. Before you know it, he's got a ton of money coming his way. It just ain't fair. Poor Tony. Cut down before he had a chance to live. And that old bastard's got more money rolling in. Probably got a stack of dough from those Hollywood guys just sitting there waiting to get to the bank."

Robert and Wilfred waited until 5:30 a.m. before waking Doctor Hilton. She threw her robe on and wheeled herself out to the hallway where they were waiting. "What is it?"

"It's bad. Real bad," Robert said, staring down at the floor.

"What? From the looks of you two, it looks like someone died!"

Robert looked up. "I'm afraid that's exactly what happened."

Doctor Hilton gasped. "What! Someone's died?""

Both Robert and Wilfred nodded their heads. "Jeremy Taylor," Robert softly said.

Doctor Hilton jerked in her chair. "Jeremy's dead? What happened? When? Where? Are...are you certain?"

"Wilfred found him early this morning. He was going down to the basement to check the generator when he saw blood on the floor. He followed it into the library and found poor Jeremy lying on his back, dead."

Doctor Hilton fanned herself. "Oh, my God! Goodness!" She took a deep breath. "So what happened? Did he slip and hit his head?" She looked up at them. "Did he have a stroke?"

"It wasn't no stroke that killed him," Wilfred said.

"What was it?" she asked.

"Um," Robert looked at the floor again. "Wilfred found a butcher knife...stuck in his chest."

The doctor gasped and looked up at them in horror. "He was...murdered?"

"Ah, I don't think he could have fallen on it like that," Wilfred said.

Doctor Hilton grabbed the wheels of her chair and slowly pushed herself back and forth. "What are we going to do?"

"Not much we can do right now," Robert said. "We can't call the police. The phone's out. We don't have a snowmobile. I figure it would take about a day to snowshoe back to Marquette; and in this weather, like I told Claudia, I'm not sure you could even make it."

"But...what do we tell...them?" Doctor Hilton asked.

"I think we keep the library closed and tell them the man died," Wilfred said.

"Wait a minute!" Doctor Hilton said. "The man was murdered. You want to have some kind of lunatic murderer roaming about without anyone else knowing about it?" She rubbed her forehead. "No, that's impossible."

"I think you're right," Robert said. "People have to know what happened."

"You're going to have a house full of panicked people," Wilfred said.

"As you should have!" Doctor Hilton exclaimed.

"I can lock the library door to the hallway," Robert said. "That lock still works. But we're going to have to shove one of the sofas in front of the door that opens up from the parlor. That locks been busted for years."

"You're sure it's Jeremy, and you're sure he's...dead?" Doctor Hilton asked.

"Quite sure," Robert said quietly. "Do you want to see?"

She thought for a moment. "No...no. Goodness, this is terrible. It's all my fault. I invited all of these lovely people here."

"I don't think it's your fault," Robert said.

Wilfred stared down the hallway. "And one of them people isn't so lovely," Wilfred said. He looked back down at Doctor Hilton. "But the question is, which one?"

An hour later there was complete silence in the dining room. Everyone was staring down at their breakfast plates unable to eat. April and Claudia were sobbing quietly, their faces buried in their napkins.

Eddy reached over and put his arm around his sister. Doctor Hilton glanced over at Nicole. She was completely pale, and it looked like she may be sick at any moment. Doctor Hilton let out a little cough and said, "Under the circumstances, we'll be canceling all of our activities. I...I don't know what to say. Some of us will be in the parlor if you don't want to be alone, but if you would rather stay in your room, please keep your door locked. We're hoping the weather clears in a day or two so we can notify the authorities. I'm sure they will want to talk to each of us and see what they can figure out. I'm...I'm so sorry. I feel that I must...."

Brad stood up. "Excuse me, Doctor. I know you must feel awful. We're all in shock. But, please don't blame yourself." He looked around the table. "I hate to contradict you, but personally, I don't think we should sit around here and twiddle our thumbs and wait for the authorities to try and figure out what happened. I think it behooves us all to get to the bottom of this. We're stuck here together. Somebody killed a man. Will there be more? I think we all need to go into the parlor and start asking questions. Did anyone hear anything?"

He looked at Eddy. "What about you? You're Jeremy's roommate!"

Eddy looked surprised at being called out. "Me? What are you trying to say? That I killed him?"

"I'm not accusing anybody of anything. I'm just asking you a basic question." He motioned towards the door. "Come on everyone. The parlor."

Everyone stood up and quietly filed into the room except Claudia. She remained motionless in her chair. Brad waited for her to get up. She just sat there.

He walked over. "Are you all right?"

She buried her face in her hands and started sobbing. "He...he...was so nice. He always was looking out for me." She looked up at him. "How could this happen?"

Brad patted her on the shoulder. "That's what we're trying to find out, dear. Come on, let's go into the parlor."

Brad helped her up and walked with her down the hallway. He guided her into a chair and stepped over to the fireplace. Just as he was about to say something, Eddy blurted out, "What about Mr. Fredericks? Shouldn't he be here? Robert said he's the one who found him."

"Yes, you're right," Brad said. He turned to Robert. "Look, I know he likes his privacy, but we need to hear what happened last night."

Robert nodded. "I know. I'll go see if I can get him to come down."

A few minutes later Robert returned with Wilfred trailing behind him. He stood next to Robert and looked around the room. "In case you're wondering, last night Robert and I checked all the windows and doors and everything looked okay. Nobody broke in here and done this." He took a deep breath and was about to start talking again when

Ruth walked up to him and handed him a cup of black coffee.

"Thanks." He took a sip and continued, "Last night I woke up around three-thirty. I switched on my light, and it didn't go on. I figured Robert would have gotten that damn generator going by then. He done it a bunch of times before, so I thought I'd go down to the basement and take a look at it. When I got to the hallway by the parlor, I saw a chair was turned over. When I went in to pick it up, I noticed some marks on the floor." As he said this, everyone glanced down and started looking at the floor.

"They're gone," Robert said. "I cleaned them up."

"That wasn't very smart," Reverend Bowers said. "You destroyed evidence."

"I probably did, but I didn't think everyone would want to be sitting around big streaks of blood. Believe me," he pointed to the door to the library which was now blocked by a heavy loveseat. "There's plenty more in the library."

Claudia let out a gasp. Nicole leaned over and buried her head in her hands.

"Anyway," Wilfred continued, "when I followed the marks, I found a man lying on his back. He was dead. I went upstairs and got Robert. He looked at him and told me it was that Taylor fellow."

Eddy stuck up his hand like he was in school. "What about the generator? Considering what happened, I think we'd all feel better if we had some lights."

"After Robert and I barricaded the library, I went down to the basement. Somebody's cut off the terminals and made off with the battery. You need a battery to start the damn thing. Until I get to town and buy a new one, or find the old one, the generator's not going to start. It's got plenty of fuel so it's ready to go once we get it going."

"Sounds like it's a setup to keep on killing," Brad said.

"Or, maybe somebody had a fight with their roommate?" the Reverend said, looking over at Eddy.

Eddy bolted to his feet. "Hey, wait a minute! Just because I'm rooming with the guy doesn't mean I had anything to do with this!" He glared at him. "You're the guy nobody can get along with. You can't even play a simple game without having some kind of hissy fit!"

Brad stepped into the center of the room. "Now, now, now! Please gentlemen. This isn't going to do us any good. I understand all of our nerves are shot, but I didn't bring everyone in here to throw accusations at each other. We need to calmly talk about what we know happened before Mr. Taylor's...um, demise." He turned to Wilfred. "Thank you, Mr. Fredericks. You've given us what we wanted to know."

As Wilfred turned and walked out into the foyer, Brad said, "Okay. Now Eddy, what do you remember about last night?"

"I got beaned by that Ouija board, and I was headed up to my room when the lights went out. I about killed myself trying to find my way back in the dark. My sister and Jeremy came in, and she checked out my head. She left and Jeremy wanted to talk about the Ouija board. He was always wanting to talk about things. I had a hell of a headache, and I told him so. Then, I went to bed." He stopped and looked around the room. "This is a bunch of bullshit! I don't see anybody else getting the third degree!"

April said, "Eddy, please! Jeremy was your roommate. You've probably got the most information. This is important! We need to know what we're dealing with here."

He glared at her. "I haven't got jack shit! He wanted to talk about what happened to us when we were kids. I...I'd rather forget about all that, and I told him so. I crawled into bed and fell asleep. The last thing I remember was him trying to read a magazine by the flickering light of the candle.

"This morning I got up, looked around, and didn't see him. I thought he must be downstairs having breakfast. When I came down, I didn't see him at the table. Then, when we were all in the room, Robert came in and told us what happened." He glanced around the room again. Everyone was staring at him. "That's it. There's nothing more." He turned to Brad. "What about all those cameras you got planted all over the place? Have you checked those?"

"We don't have any power, remember? I need electricity to make everything work."

Eddy turned to Robert. "What about heat? How are we going to stay warm with the power off? It's getting cold in here."

"Don't worry about heat. We use oil for our furnace. We went to that because the electricity goes out here all the time. We're pretty sure we've got enough oil, but since we don't know how long it will be until the truck can get here, we've turned the heat down a little to try and conserve. We'll keep the fireplace going in the parlor. That will help heat the downstairs but it may get a little nippy up on the second floor. If you need more blankets, just ask Ruth."

Brad looked over at Reverend Bowers and then at Claudia. "Think about last night. Does anyone remember anything else?"

Claudia stood up. "I...I think I may have some information."

"You do?" Brad asked.

"Well, I had come downstairs for a snack, and when I got near the kitchen, I heard voices. They were arguing. Two men. I couldn't hear exactly what they were saying, but I could hear that they were mad."

"Whose voices were they?" Doctor Hilton asked.

"I...I couldn't tell. They were muffled. The door was closed. But, then they got louder, I got scared and ran back upstairs to my room."

"What time was that?" Brad asked.

"Um, I don't really know. I didn't look at the clock. But, if I had to guess, I'd say about one or one-thirty."

"So, looks like we've narrowed it down to a man," April said.

Reverend Bowers grinned. "Whew! Good news! Now I don't have to watch my back whenever Nicole's around."

"Oh, that's funny," Eddy sneered. "Got to watch those comedians. They're always a little twisted inside."

The Reverend stood up and lunged towards him. "Comedian? Are you calling me a comedian?"

Brad jumped in front of the Reverend. "All right now. Calm down. Gentlemen, this isn't going to help! Damn-it! We have to be civil to each other and work together. People, we have a serious situation here."

April reached over, grabbed Eddy, and pulled him back to his seat.

Doctor Hilton pushed herself over to Brad. "It sounds like we know as much as we're going to. If nobody has anything more to add, I suggest we all retreat to our rooms. Maybe say a prayer for poor Jeremy. Claudia, why don't you come to my room or maybe sit with April and Nicole."

"Thank you, Doctor," Claudia said. She looked at April. "Could I come to your room for a while?"

"Sure!" April said.

"Thanks." She turned to Doctor Hilton. "After that, maybe I'll try and take a nap in my room." She glanced over at Eddy. "Can I say something?"

"Certainly," Brad said. "Did you think of something else?"

"Ah, I know what Mr. Fredericks said, but...um, what if someone broke in? I mean, everyone here seems so nice. I...I just think that maybe someone from the woods broke in, and poor Jeremy ran into him when he was going to the kitchen for a sandwich or something."

Eddy pointed to Robert. "I don't think you people even lock your doors at night. Do you?"

Robert coughed and looked over at his wife. "Um, we've never had any problems here. We're so far from anybody. We don't have any neighbors or anything."

Eddy looked exasperated. "So the answer is no. The doors were unlocked last night, right?"

"It's not like we live in the big city or anything," Robert said. "I really don't think this has anything to do with...."

Eddy jumped up. "So any hermit or hunter or crazy person out in the woods could have marched right in here and killed us all in the middle of the night!" He winced in pain and rubbed his forehead. "This is great! Just great!"

"We'll be locking the doors from now on," Robert said. He turned and walked out to the hallway.

Eddy stared in disbelief. He turned to April. "Can you believe that guy? It's a little late for that!"

"I know, Eddy. But, I guess they do things a little different up here." She paused. "You want me to move my stuff into your room?"

Eddy looked surprised. "What?"

"I don't want you to be alone," April said, taking him by the arm.

"Oh. No. That's okay." He looked around and saw everyone was leaving. He whispered, "I probably shouldn't say this, but I'm looking forward to some quiet time. That guy never shut up. He kept asking me questions."

"What kind of questions?"

"All kinds of stuff. He wouldn't stop about that damn Ouija board."

As they approached the stairway, Brad caught up with them. "April, got a minute?"

April looked surprised. "Oh, hi, Brad." She turned back to Eddy, "I'll come up and see you in a bit."

Eddy glared at Brad. "Yeah. I'll be there."

She followed Brad back to the empty parlor, and they sat down on a loveseat. "I just wanted to see how you were doing."

She sat quietly for a moment, let out a sigh, and then tears started to flow. "I...I can't believe what's happened. He...he seemed like such a nice man. How could this be?"

He moved closer. "Let it out. Don't keep it in."

She leaned into him. He felt solid and warm. Suddenly, she felt very fragile and alone. She started sobbing. "I'm...I'm sorry. I don't know what's wrong with me." Her shoulders were shaking.

"That's okay. It's good to let it go."

She wiped her eyes with her sleeve and tried to control her crying. After a few minutes she took a deep breath. "Thank you. I'm sorry I broke down. I don't know what happened. It just came out. I mean, he was...was murdered!"

"I know. It's terrible."

She stayed in his arms, listening to his breathing. After another few minutes she asked, "What should we do? Who do you think would do something like this?"

He thought for a moment. "I don't know. I was hoping we'd hear something more when we were all together."

"Should we be afraid?"

"I...I really don't know. It sounded like he had an altercation with someone for some reason, and it got out of control." He took a deep breath. "I sure hope that's what happened. The other alternative is that some madman is roaming the halls...in the dark."

April jerked forward. "Like that violin music and what happened to Nicole!"

Brad nodded. "Yes. What was that all about?"

April shook her head. "It's all too much. I can' take it. Let's change the subject."

"Okay, what do you want to talk about?"

"Have you heard from your wife?" April asked.

Brad jerked. "Oh, I wasn't expecting that! No, I haven't. But then how could I? We're completely isolated here. We couldn't even get a letter delivered."

"Oh, that's right. I forgot about that. My poor mother. I was supposed to call her to let her know we got here safe and sound. We were supposed to take a drive back to Marquette the day after we got here and call her from there, but then the weather got crazy."

"What about your husband?" Brad asked. "Do you think you'll get back together?"

April sat up and looked at him. "How did you know about that? I never said anything about...."

"Your brother told me," Brad said. "I was a little surprised because we had talked about our past, and you never mentioned him."

"The past few months have been a nightmare. There were things I just couldn't bring myself to talk about."

"I'm sorry. I should never have mentioned it."

"No. It's okay. I should have told you." She leaned into him again. "It's so sad. When I got here, I was so excited. It felt so wonderful to be out of my mother's house. I felt like I was about to take back my life. I started thinking about new things. New places. And...and now this. Poor Jeremy." Her eyes welled with tears again. "Why did this have to happen?"

"Don't let something that you had nothing to do with put a stop to your plans. I still want you to come to California. I think it would do you good. Why don't we try and focus on that. Something positive."

She turned her head and looked into his eyes. "Thank you. I will. It sounds wonderful."

Just then they heard a noise from the foyer. Robert was struggling with a huge armful of firewood. Brad moved to get up. "Looks like he could use some help."

As Robert stumbled over to the fireplace, several pieces of oak fell out of his arms and crashed onto the floor.

"Hold on!" Brad called out. He ran over and picked them up.

"Just stack them there on the rack," Robert said, bending down with the remaining logs. "We're going through wood like crazy with that damn generator out." He stood up and brushed pieces of bark off his flannel shirt. "But, don't worry. We've got a lot more."

"So, what do you think happened to the generator's battery?" Brad asked.

"Sabotage, I guess. I don't think anyone broke in to steal it. Won't take long to replace once we get to town. But who the hell knows when that's going to be."

"Well, it better be soon. We've got a dead body in the library and a house full of terrified people."

Robert spun around and pointed his finger at him. "Hey, I don't need a lecture. If you've got any brilliant ideas, please share them with me, because right now, I'm plum out of them."

Brad took a step back. "I'm sorry! I didn't mean to offend you. It's just...I guess it's just nerves. Sorry."

Without replying, Robert turned and walked back out to the foyer.

Brad walked back to April who was now standing next to the loveseat. "What was that all about?" she asked.

"I really don't know. I guess I said something that made him mad. I certainly didn't intend to."

"Everyone's on edge and I don't blame them." She glanced over at the door to the library. "Just to think what's in there. It's...it's all too much." She looked back at Brad. "I better run up and see how Eddy's doing."

"Good idea. It must be hard for him. He spent the most time with Jeremy. I'm going to check on Doctor Hilton. Let's talk again, soon."

She reached up and took his arm. "Yes. And thank you for listening. I'm sorry I came apart like that."

He put his hand over hers. "I enjoyed our time together."

As she walked up the staircase, the sound of Brad's voice echoed in her head. She could still smell his cologne. She walked up to Eddy's' door and knocked softly. She waited a few seconds and knocked again. The door opened, and he motioned for her to come in. She saw an unfamiliar suitcase on the bed. It was half filled with assorted items.

"What's this?" she asked.

"His stuff. I'm packing it up."

"Packing it up? Should you be doing that?"

He looked at her. "Why not? It's more than a little creepy sitting here surrounded by a dead man's things. Why wouldn't I pack them up?"

"Well, I know it must feel funny. But, the police. Don't you think they would want to go through everything just as they were?"

"Be my guest! I'll hand them the suitcase, and they can do whatever they want."

"I don't know," she said. "I don't think they're going to be very happy about this."

Eddy slammed the lid shut. "You worry about the wrong things."

"What is that supposed to mean?"

"Instead of worrying about this guy's possessions, you should be worrying about what happened to him."

"You don't think I'm worried about that? Of course I am."

"It doesn't look like it to me."

"How can you say that?" April asked with a hurt look on her face.

"You and Brad. Every time I turn around, you two are cozying up together."

"First of all, that's not true. And, secondly, what does that have to do with not worrying about what happened to poor Jeremy?"

"Think about it. I hate to break this to you, but who's the only person set to gain anything from someone getting knocked off in this damn house?"

She looked at him incredulously. "You're not suggesting Brad had anything to do with it?"

"I'm not? Let's just say, up until that time, everything around here was dullsville. All of Doctor Hilton's little experiments were duds. Nothing was happening. Brad's chances of turning this into a TV show were less than zero. Then...bam...the action starts. Who wouldn't tune in now?"

April sat on the edge of the bed, stunned. "I...I can't believe you just said that. No. I know you don't believe that."

Eddy smiled. "Think about what I said. Who else would want something like this to happen?"

April stared at him. "You're...you're too much! So, you think Brad would actually kill someone to make his TV show more interesting?"

"Hell, I wouldn't put anything past those Hollywood people. They're ruthless."

She shook her head. "I knew it was a mistake to bring you up here. You only came to be nice to me. From the minute we got here, you've only had mean and nasty things to say about everyone. But, this...this is beyond anything I could even imagine you saying."

Eddy stood up and grabbed her by the shoulders. "Be careful. I'm telling you to be careful. You're cozying up to a rattlesnake. Who knows? Maybe two murders make for better TV than one? I'm probably next on his list. I know he doesn't like me. He probably thinks it would be a lot easier to sweet talk you without your annoying little brother around."

April stood up and walked to the door. "I can't listen to any more of this."

Chapter 15

DENNIS BOLTED UPRIGHT from the bed and looked around. He had fallen asleep on top of the covers in the Delta Motel. He was bored and disappointed that he couldn't get to Marquette. The only thing he could find in the room to read was a two-year old, large print-edition of *The Reader's Digest.* After glancing through two or three pages, he had drifted off to sleep.

He got up and splashed water from the bathroom sink on his face. The dream. What in the dream had awakened him? It was the question he had reviewed in his head so many times in the last few months. He couldn't stop dreaming about Bobby.

How had Bobby climbed up to the top shelf of his closet and taken his gun? Why? It was no secret that the gun was up there. Bobby knew it. He had had many talks with him about the danger it posed. Bobby had never expressed an interest in seeing or playing with it before. In the recurring dream, Bobby had taken a chair from the kitchen and reached up to the shelf where the gun was kept. Then, in the dream, Dennis was running towards him in slow motion, not making any progress. He watched in horror as Bobby loaded the gun and tried to spin it around his finger like they did in the old western movies. He helplessly watched as Bobby's finger hit the trigger and the gun went off in mid-spin. That was when Dennis jumped up from the bed, damp with sweat, and fully awake. He had had so many dreams just like it. Something was wrong. It seemed that there had to be a reason he kept having the same dream over and over. He had even moved one of the kitchen chairs over to the closet and measured the distance to the shelf. It looked to him that Bobby still could not have reached the gun. Was there something in the dream that he was missing? Was Bobby trying to tell him something?

He walked over to the window and looked outside. It had stopped snowing, but the wind was still blowing hard from the north. Across the street he saw a bowling alley. It looked open. He decided to run over and see if he could get something to eat.

The smell of onions frying greeted him as he pushed the door open to the Super Rama Bowling Alley. He sat down at the bar and ordered a beer. The place was just about empty. He could only see three people bowling down at the lanes. When the bartender brought him his beer, Dennis ordered the deluxe hamburger plate special.

"You from around here?" the bartender asked. "I don't remember you coming in before."

"No. I'm from Chicago."

"Up here on business?"

"No. Actually, I was on my way to Marquette. I almost made it, but the cops turned me away. Road was impassable."

"I bet that was near Trenary," the bartender said. "It's always snowing there. Must be some kind of lake-effect thing. I swear, I've driven to Marquette in May, and it's been snowing there."

"It's so frustrating to get so close but have to turn back. I really need to get up there. I'm worried about my wife."

"Give her a call." He pulled out his cell phone. "Need a phone?"

"Tried that. It never connects."

"How bad do you want to get there?" the bartender asked.

"Pretty bad. Why?"

"I belong to a snowmobile club. I know a bunch of guys that would be able to get you there if you wanted to ride on a snowmobile. Probably cost you a hundred bucks, but they'd get you there."

"From what I understand, the place I'm looking for is about fifteen miles outside of town. Would that be a problem?"

"Fifteen miles? Are you kidding? That would be nothing." A waitress walked up and set down his lunch. "Just let me know what you want to do. You want to go, I'll give my friend a call and see what we can put together."

Dennis didn't hesitate. "Call him! Here's my number. I'm staying across the street at the Delta Motel."

Madge poured Joe a cup of coffee. "You got up early this morning."

He pulled out a cigarette from a pack on the table. "Couldn't sleep. Kept thinking about old man Fredericks."

She sat down across from him and grinned. "You're thinking about that money, aren't you? It's driving you nuts, ain't it."

Joe blew out a cloud of smoke. "Them Hollywood people don't fool around. I bet they gave that old bastard plenty to use his place."

"So what? It ain't any of your concern."

Joe gave her a wink. "Now don't you be worrying about what's my concern and what ain't."

Doctor Hilton heard a soft knock on her door. When she opened it, she saw Claudia standing in the hallway with Reverend Bowers. A cloud of stale smoke poured out of her room into the hallway. "Can we come in and speak to you for a moment?" Claudia asked. She coughed and waved her hand.

"Of course. Come in."

They squeezed into the small bedroom and sat down on the edge of the bed. Claudia coughed again.

"Sorry," Doctor Hilton said. "Bad habit. What's on your mind?"

Reverend Bowers spoke up. "Well, Doc, Claudia and I've been talking. We feel like we're sitting ducks in this house. A man's been killed, and we don't know who did it or why. We'd like to know what you think is going on."

She took a deep breath. "I feel awful that I've put you all in this position. I...I've been talking with Brad about the same thing and we...."

"Brad!" Claudia exclaimed. "Be careful. We think he could be the one behind all this stuff."

Doctor Hilton shook her head. "I know what you're thinking. You think he's been behind all the little scares we've had to make the show more interesting. And who knows, maybe he has. Personally, I don't think so, but we don't know. But a murder! Do you really think the man is desperate enough to kill somebody? Do you think he's willing to risk everything? His reputation, his standing in Hollywood, for an unsold pilot?"

"But, who else has anything to gain?" Reverend Bowers interjected.

"I don't know. But I don't think Brad killed anyone."

The Reverend turned to Claudia. "We don't know much about that Eddy guy. Personally, I think he's got a few loose screws. And that temper! Did you see him go after me when the chess board fell over? I thought he was going to start punching me."

Claudia didn't respond right away. Finally, she said, "I don't know about that, but what about the old man who owns this house? We never see him. Robert just about came out and told us he didn't want us here. Maybe he went nuts for some reason and stabbed poor Mr. Taylor."

"Speaking of that, what do we know about Robert...or his wife?" the Reverend asked. "Nothing. For all we know, he could be on some kind of parole or something. I get the feeling he's hanging around us a little too much. Remember how sometimes he'd just happen to be behind a door and step out and say something. And his wife. She's given me a few surly looks now and then. Even yelled at me to pick up my cup of coffee."

Claudia jumped up from the bed. "Oh, me too! Once I asked her when she was going to be putting out the snacks, and I thought she was going to take my head off. She looked at me like she was going to kill me."

Doctor Hilton smiled. "What about me? Maybe I've been creeping around late at night arranging everything so my research would show some positive results."

They both turned and looked at her. She smiled again. "I only said that so you could hear what you're saying. It's a lot of speculation. Believe me, I've been doing a lot of thinking, too. But it all boils down to one thing. We don't know. That's why we all have to be very careful. Try not to put yourself into a vulnerable position. Make sure your door is locked at night. During the day, spend time with several people. Being in a crowd is much safer than being alone."

The Reverend stood up. "Thank you, Doc. We've taken up too much of your time."

"Not at all. And please, if you see something that you feel is important, please let me know."

They thanked her again and stepped out into the hallway. Halfway down the corridor, Claudia said, "Well, that was a waste of time!"

"She doesn't have a clue," Reverend Bowers responded. "You know, I'm a little disappointed. I mean...she's the one who's put us in this position. She should have done a little more research before putting this together. I wonder how much she actually looked into the backgrounds of Mr. Fredericks and Robert and his wife. You'd have to be a little crazy to like living way out here in the middle of nowhere. For all we know, one of them could be a serial killer."

Claudia shuddered. "Please. Don't say things like that. Things are bad enough."

It was eerily quiet the rest of the morning and afternoon. Almost everyone had made the decision to remain cloistered in their rooms. Only Reverend Bowers and Brad had made it to the dining room for lunch. After they had eaten, Brad went back upstairs and knocked on the ladies' doors, trying to get them to join them, but they told him they would rather stay in their rooms. He gave up and retreated to his room like the others.

Just before dinner, one by one, everyone started showing up in the dining room. Absent was the normal excitement and chatter of conversation. It seemed that somehow, everyone had spent a day of contemplation, and now nobody trusted each other. The quietness was interspersed with furtive looks around the table. Even Ruth served the cold meal in silence.

Claudia ate quickly. She finished first and excused herself to return to her room. She seemed to be the first one upstairs. Eddy sat next to April, but even they had little to say during the meal. Nicole, normally full of smiles and enthusiasm, stared down at her plate, her brow furrowed with tension.

Brad put down his napkin and looked around the table. He stopped his gaze at April. "I don't know about anybody else, but I'm going nutty sitting in my room listening to the clock tick. I'm going to have a drink in the parlor, and I sure would like some company."

April turned to Brad. "That's a good idea. I can only read and sleep so much."

Eddy gave his sister a disgusted look and pushed himself away from the table. He threw his napkin down and stomped off down the hallway.

"I'll drink to that!" Reverend Bowers replied. They pulled their candle stubs out and lit them from the lantern.

Doctor Hilton said she had something to go over with Nicole, so they would not be joining them.

As Robert and Ruth started to clean up the kitchen, Brad held up his candle and led April and the Reverend into the parlor. "I'll be the bartender tonight. What are you having?"

April glanced around the room. "It...it doesn't seem right, us having drinks in here."

"We're not celebrating," Brad said. "We're just trying to cope."

"In that case, I guess I'll have a martini, please. Dry and no olives," April said. She looked around and gave a shudder. "I don't know. Maybe we shouldn't be here."

"Whiskey for me," the Reverend called out. Brad handed them their drinks and the Reverend raised his glass. "Here's to poor Jeremy. He seemed like a nice guy." They clinked glasses and everyone took a sip.

There was an uncomfortable silence. Then Brad raised his glass. "And here's to looking out for each other." He walked over and sat down on the loveseat next to April. Reverend Bowers took a seat in an overstuffed chair next to them.

April took another sip and asked, "Reverend, tell me about your church. How large is your congregation?"

The Reverend was in the middle of taking a drink. He coughed and wiped his mouth with a cocktail napkin. "Well, I'm…I'm not preaching at the moment. Decided to take some time off." He smiled.

"Really!" she said, looking over at Brad.

"So, what are you doing now?" Brad asked.

"I'm…ah, actually I'm working on a ranch." He took another drink. "You know. Going back to my roots. Getting back to some hard labor." He looked at his hands. "Took some time to get those calluses back."

"Do you miss it?" April asked.

"Miss what?"

"Preaching."

"Oh, sure I do. But, you know there's a whole lot of politics that goes with running a church." He laughed. "And I sure as hell don't miss that!" He noticed that April had moved over and was pressed against Brad. The room got quiet. The Reverend stood up and tossed another log onto the fire. He stood at the fireplace warming his hands for a few minutes and then turned and said, "So, Brad. Can I ask you a question?"

"Sure, go ahead."

"Well, with everything that's happened. I imagine the pilot's a dead deal." He stopped. "Oh, bad choice of words. The pilot. It's probably not going to make it, don't you think?"

Brad thought for a moment. "Well, probably not. We can't profit from the death of poor Mr. Taylor. But, maybe we can edit some of the footage from before the...before he died. We'll see. I'll have to see what we can salvage when I'm back in L.A." He put his arm around April. "Maybe April can help me with some of the editing."

She felt her face start to get warm.

The Reverend arched his eyebrows. "Oh! Really!"

April smiled. "I've never been to California, and Brad was kind enough to invite me." She laughed. "Editing? I don't think so!"

Reverend Bowers took a step towards the door. "Ah, that's very interesting. Well, if you don't mind, I think I'll just take my drink and mosey back up to my room. Goodnight."

When he was out of hearing range, April asked, "Is it my imagination or did he seem to choke when I asked him about his preaching?"

"I know! I was thinking the same thing. He definitely wasn't expecting that question."

"I was just trying to make conversation. That wasn't the reaction I was expecting."

"Pretty interesting. Too bad we had to cut the pilot short." Brad shook his head. "Damn, it's a shame. I think that with this group, we could have gotten into some very exciting interactions."

She sighed. "I know. You're right. Such a shame."

Brad pulled her closer. "Let's focus on something more positive."

"What could that be?"

"You. I'm so glad we were able to meet. I wish it had been under better circumstances, but just the same, I'm so happy I got to meet you."

She snuggled into him. "Me too."

"When do you think you can come out and see me?" Brad asked.

"Are you serious about this?"

"Of course I am! I think it would be good for you, and it will give me something to look forward to." She felt him move his face closer to hers. "And I sure need that."

She turned her head. He leaned over and kissed her. She twisted around and wrapped her arms around him. As he kissed her again, she could feel her heart pounding. He pulled her closer.

Reverend Bowers slowly walked up the staircase, holding his candle out in front of him. He was mad at himself for letting April's question throw him off like that. Even though his credentials had been bought from some university he had found on the internet, he actually had worked in a church for a couple of months as an associate pastor. He missed working with the youth group. If it hadn't been for that one overly developed girl, he'd probably still be there. But, it wasn't a total loss. It was amazing how having a *Reverend* in front of your name caused people to relax their guard. It gave you an edge. And there was nothing wrong with having an edge.

Nicole ran her fingers through her hair. It needed washing. She got out of her clothes and quickly threw on her robe. She walked into the bathroom and turned on the shower. She held her hand under the water and waited for it to get warm. After a few minutes she remembered. There was no electricity.

Reverend Bowers walked down the narrow hallway and paused at Nicole and April's door. He reached out, turned the door-knob, and was surprised to feel the door open slightly. He put one foot into the room and stopped. He heard water running in the bathroom.

He quickly made his way over to the closet and pulled out April's suitcase. He remembered that she had had several other pieces of jewelry that looked promising. When nobody had brought up the subject of the missing jewelry, he thought he'd take another look at what was there. He snapped the two locks open, pulled out the silk pouch, and stared down at the jewelry. He dug out two pieces and slipped them into his pocket. He put the pouch back and slid the suitcase back where it had been. He stepped closer to the bathroom. The door was open. He stood in the shadows and watched as Nicole bent over the tub.

April heard a cough from the parlor entrance. She pulled away from Brad and saw her brother's face illumined in a small yellow glow. She sat up and straightened her hair.

Eddy sneered, "Don't mind me. I was only getting a drink, but I'm not really in the mood for one now." He turned and stomped off towards the staircase.

April stood up. "I'm...I'm sorry. This was wrong. I... I need to talk to Eddy." She grabbed her candle and walked towards the door. She could see the light from Eddy's candle bob up and down as he walked along the hallway. She caught up to him at the bottom of the stairs. As she approached, he held up his hand. "Stop! I don't want to hear it. You disgust me! Did you forget you're a married woman with a grieving husband who you won't even talk to?" He spun around and stomped up the stairs.

She stood there alone. The harsh reality of Eddy's words echoed in her head. This whole trip, including her stupid infatuation, was nothing but a failed attempt at escape. Escape from the death of her son, escape from a crumbling marriage, and an escape from the fact that she, just like her brother, was living back home with her mother. Tears streamed down her cheeks. Sobbing, she tried to hold her candle still as she slowly made her way up the stairs.

She stopped in front of her door and tried to compose herself. She didn't want Nicole to see her like this. She wiped her eyes, took several deep breaths, and then reached for the doorknob. April was surprised to see that the door was slightly ajar. She pushed the door open and held her candle out in front of her. "Nicole?"

She noticed a faint light coming from the bathroom. As she turned to set the candle down on the dresser, she noticed a quick movement from in front of the bathroom door. There was a noise, and she felt something hit her alongside her head. She fell to the floor. Someone was on top of her. More blows rained down on her. She screamed and tried to cover her head. She heard someone mutter, "Shut the hell up!" and then felt strong fingers wrap around her neck.

Nicole thought she heard something from the other room. She called out "April?" and waited for an answer. She called out her roommate's name again. She listened for a response and then heard a loud thud. She turned off the water, grabbed her robe, and peeked out of the room. From the glow of April's candle, she saw two figures grappling around on the floor.

She screamed "April!" and frantically looked around for something to use as a weapon. She saw one of her high heels lying next to the bed. She reached down, grabbed it by the strap, and ran over. She could see April struggling on the floor with someone on top of her. She swung her shoe and smashed the heel down onto the dark figures back.

April felt the grip loosen around her throat. She wildly punched the air trying to connect with whoever was on top of her. When she felt her right hand connect with the person's face, she dug her nails deep into flesh and raked her hand down.

There was a loud yell. The man stood up and pushed Nicole over onto the bed. April heard footsteps as the intruder scrambled for the door. She heard the door slam shut and then heard Nicole mutter, "Oh...oh, my God!"″

Nicole pulled herself up from the bed and bent over April, "Are...are you okay?"

April took a deep breath and crawled to her knees. She lay on the bed and tried to catch her breath. "I...I think so. My face...he punched me."

Nicole helped her to her feet. "Come into the bathroom. Let's see...."

April held on to Nicole and they stumbled into the bathroom. April grabbed the candle and looked into the mirror.

Nicole stared in horror. "Your left cheek is really red and swollen."

April moved her jaw back and forth. "I...I don't think anything's broken." She unbuttoned the top two buttons of her blouse and looked at her neck.

Nicole saw that it was scrapped and bleeding. "Did he try to choke you?"

"Yes. I screamed when he knocked me down. He kept hitting me. He told me to shut-up, and then he grabbed me by the throat. I...I think I scratched him and then he let go."

"I hit him! I hit him real hard with my shoe."

April tried to smile. "Good! Thanks."

"I was in the bathroom when I heard something and I called to you. When you didn't answer, I peeked out, and saw you both on the floor. I...I looked around for something to hit him with, but the only thing I could find was one of my high heels. I grabbed it and started beating him as hard as I could."

April held a washcloth under the cold water and patted the side of her face. "You probably saved my life!"

April held the cold washcloth tight against her cheek, and they both stepped back into the bedroom and sat on the edge of the bed.

"Who would do something like that?" Nicole asked.

"It could only be one person."

"Who?"

April paused. "Reverend Bowers!"

Nicole turned to her in shock. "Reverend Bowers! No! Are...are you sure?"

"He was sitting with Brad and me in the parlor. He had just left. I think I made him mad when I asked him questions about his church. It was late. Nobody else was up. Who else could it be?"

"What about that Robert guy?" Nicole asked.

"I...I don't know. I never thought about him. He's hardly ever around." She glanced over at the door. "Oh, my God!"

"What is it?"

"The door! It's still unlocked!" She jumped up, ran over, and twisted the key in the lock. She leaned against it and took a deep breath. "We have to be more careful!"

Nicole stood up from the bed. "We need to tell someone about this!"

"Not tonight! I'm not setting foot in that dark hallway tonight!"

"But...they should know what just happened!"

"Be my guest. Go out there if you want. Not me!"

Chapter 16

THE NEXT MORNING, Nicole and April stayed in their room longer than usual before going downstairs for breakfast. They wanted to make sure everyone was there before they arrived. As they entered the dining room, April took a seat next to Eddy. He took one look at her and yelled, "What the hell happened to you?"

Everyone turned to look. She surveyed the room to see if anyone's face had scratch marks. She noticed that Nicole was giving everyone a close look, too.

"The Reverend!" she whispered.

"What?"

"Where is he?" she whispered.

Eddy glanced up and looked around the table. "Not here. Why?"

She whispered, "You're not going to believe this!" She stood up and addressed everyone sitting at the table. "Ah, can I have your attention! I have something to tell everyone."

Doctor Hilton turned away from Claudia and looked over at April. "My goodness! What happened to your face?"

"That's what I want to tell you. When I went upstairs last night, someone was in our room. They knocked me down, punched me in the face, and tried to choke me."

Brad looked at her in disbelief. "What!"

Robert stood in the kitchen doorway, holding a large platter of hash browns.

"Thank God Nicole heard me struggling. She ran over and started beating him with her shoe. I was able to reach up and scratch his face." She looked around the room. "I see that everyone's here except Reverend Bowers. And…nobody here seems to have any scratches on them."

"I knew it!" Eddy said, jumping up. "I knew that guy was a creep! I'll show him a thing or two!"

Brad also stood up. "Hold on for a moment. Before we start accusing him of anything, I'll go get him and see what he has to say for himself." He looked over at Eddy. "You stay here and try and calm down." Several minutes later, he returned alone.

"Where is he?" Eddy asked.

"Claims he's not feeling well. He wants to skip breakfast and rest in bed."

"Isn't that convenient?" Eddy said. "He's afraid to come down here and face the music." He pushed himself away from the table. "He attacked my sister. I think it's time he told us what's going on."

Brad held up his hand. "Wait a minute. Let's not rush to judgment. I say we let the man rest until

212

lunch. He's going to have to eat sometime. If he has scratches on his face, they aren't going to disappear by noon. Let's let him rest as he requested and see what happens at lunch."

During the rest of breakfast, Doctor Hilton asked Nicole more questions about what happened the night before. Brad came over and talked with April. Eddy looked like he was getting more furious by the minute.

Once everyone was finished eating, Robert walked over to Brad. "Um, can I talk to you in private for a minute?"

Brad looked up from April. "Sure." He stood up and followed Robert into the foyer. "What's on your mind?"

"Ah, I been going into the library every once in a while to make sure everything's the same in there."

"Yes?"

"Well, there's a vent from the fireplace in the parlor and you know, that room doesn't get that cold. Last time I went in there, I could, um...smell something. I...I think we need to move him."

"Oh, shit!" Brad said. "Where do you suggest?"

"We could put him out on the porch, but then there's snow, and who knows what kind of animals could get a whiff of him and...."

"That won't work!"

"Yeah, I know. But, I'm thinking the basement is a better idea. It's cold down there now with the electricity off, and it's protected."

Brad rubbed his chin. "Okay, but we can't do this when anyone's around. Maybe we can talk to Doctor

213

Hilton and make sure everyone just stays up in their rooms until lunch time."

"Good idea. Why don't you go talk to her? Get everyone out of here and then meet me in the library. Both of us should be able to get him down the stairs."

Brad shook his head. "I...I can't believe I'm doing this."

"Hell. It ain't no picnic for me, either."

Brad went to talk to Doctor Hilton, and Robert walked back to the parlor. He pushed the worn leather sofa away from the library door and walked in. Jeremy was lying exactly where they had found him. Robert wondered if they should remove the butcher knife before they tried to move him. He cautiously sniffed the air and stepped back, coughing. *It probably would have been a better idea to move him a little sooner.* He walked back into the parlor and waited for Brad.

A few minutes later, Brad walked in. "Doctor Hilton said she'd send Nicole around and talk to everyone." They walked into the library and immediately Brad started coughing. He waved his hand in front of his face. "Oh, Jesus!" Brad said. "I thought you said it wasn't that bad in here? I'm going to throw up."

"I know. It's worse than I thought. I'm going to have to take off the storm window and air this room out a little."

Brad pulled out his handkerchief and covered his nose and mouth. "I...I don't know if I can do this!"

Robert stared at him. "What? Who's going to help me? The Reverend? I don't see Eddy being much help."

"Okay, okay. Let's get this over with."

Robert bent down and grabbed Jeremy by the shoulders. Brad kneeled and tried to pick him up by his feet. "Shit! This guy's heavy!" Brad sputtered.

"Wait, you got to pick him up closer, by his ass."

Brad rearranged his grip. "Okay, let's go."

They struggled with the body as they slowly made their way through the parlor and out to the foyer. "Here...careful now," Robert said, panting. "Okay, set him down. I'll get the door to the basement."

They heard footsteps in the hallway and then a piercing scream. Brad turned and saw Claudia running back towards the stairs, her hands flailing in the air. He turned back to Robert. "Can't everybody just listen for once and do as they're told?"

"I bet she'll be seeing that in her dreams for the next couple of nights!" Robert said. "I know I will."

Brad stared down the steep wooden steps that led to the basement. "How are we going to do this?"

Robert tried to catch his breath. "I don't know. If I miss a step, I sure as hell don't want this guy landing on top of me." He looked around and said, "Wait a minute!" He walked back to the hallway and grabbed a long rug that was in front of the front door. "Here. We'll put this on the stairs. We'll set him on it and drag him down with the rug."

Brad stared at the rug. "You think that will work?"

"Better than have him roll down and land on top of you!"

"Yeah. Okay." He grabbed the rug and tossed it onto the first several steps. They lifted Jeremy and set him on the carpet, headfirst. Robert got in front, grabbed the rug, and started pulling. Brad grabbed the back of the carpet and they slowly eased the body down to the basement. The butcher knife wobbled back and forth as the corpse bounced down the staircase.

When they finally got to the bottom, Robert said. "Let's put him over here away from the landing. I don't want Wilfred stumbling over him if he comes down here. He's got a workshop over there."

Brad rubbed his hands together. "It's freezing down here. I don't think he'll be doing any woodworking projects in this cold."

Robert laughed. "He's a Yooper. The cold don't bother him."

They dragged Jeremy's body over to the side and left him lying on the rug.

When they returned upstairs, Robert went back to the foyer and shut the door to the library. He pushed back the heavy sofa.

"I need to wash up," Brad said. "Sure wish we had some hot water."

"I know. If the wind stays down, I'm hoping they'll be able to plow the road sometime tomorrow."

"That would be wonderful. I'm not looking forward to another night in this house without any lights."

"What about that Reverend?" Robert asked. "What do you want to do with him?"

Brad looked at his watch. "It's three hours until lunch. Let's see what happens then. Oh, don't forget about the library window. You said you wanted to get some fresh air in that room."

"Oh, yeah. Let me do that right now."

The phone rang in Dennis's motel room, waking him from a nap. He fumbled for the receiver.

"Dennis, this is Sam from the snowmobile club. Look, I've got a change of plans for you."

"Oh, no!" Dennis replied, his heart sinking.

"Don't worry. It's a good thing. I just checked and the road from Trenary to Marquette's open. It wouldn't make sense for you to pay me to take you all that way now. I've called a friend of mine who's in the Marquette club. His name's Hank. I'll give you his number. Call him when you get up there, and he can run you over to that house you're looking for. I told him a little bit about it, and he thinks he knows where it is. Hank's a good guy. I told him you'd be calling him."

"That's great!" Dennis said. "If the road's open, I'll head up there right now."

As everyone gathered around the table for lunch, April nervously watched the door to see if Reverend Bowers would show up. Again, he was a no-show. Ruth came in with a platter of sliced ham and beef. She had several types of bread already on the table along with assorted mustards, mayonnaise, tomato slices, and cheeses.

Eddy made a sandwich and glared at the door. "Well, it looks like our favorite minister isn't going to show up again."

Brad glanced over at the doorway. "No. It sure doesn't."

"Just how long are we going to put up with this shit?" Eddy asked. "Frankly, I'm getting a little sick of it. Clearly he's the one who attacked my sister, and I'm pretty sure we all know who killed Jeremy, too."

Brad glanced at his watch. "It's still a little early. Let's just eat our lunch. If he hasn't shown up by the time we're finished, we'll go upstairs and make him come out and talk to us."

Eddy grabbed a piece of cheese. "For all we know, he's slipped out the window up there, and he's halfway back to North Dakota by now."

Doctor Hilton looked up. "He's from South Dakota."

Eddy tossed down his sandwich. "I don't care if he's from the damn moon; this guy's dangerous and needs to be dealt with!"

"He attacked April!" Nicole said. "And...and he was watching me in the bathroom when she came into the room. I can only imagine what he was going to do to me!"

Brad pushed his chair back. "Okay, let's go talk to him right now."

Eddy stood up. "I think we need to get Robert, too."

Brad looked at him. "You don't think we can handle it?"

"Who knows what he's got up there? He may have a whole set of butcher knives. He's from cowboy country. For all we know, he's packing a bunch of guns, too."

Doctor Hilton let out a gasp. "I thought it was strange that he took a bus here, not an airplane! Do they check for weapons on the bus? Is that why he did it?"

Just then Ruth walked in with an apple pie. Brad pulled her aside and whispered, "Ruth, could you send Robert over to Reverend Bower's room? Eddy and I are headed up there now."

Ruth set the pie down on the table. "Certainly, Mr. Feldman. I'll send him right up there."

As they walked up the stairs, Eddy asked, "How do you want to do this?"

"Since I already asked him if he was coming to breakfast, let me ask him about lunch. You and Robert should stand on each side of the door in case something happens."

Eddy looked concerned. "Oh, okay."

They walked to the Reverend's door and waited until Robert showed up. Everyone took their places, and Brad knocked forcefully on the door. "Lunch time, Reverend. Time to eat."

There was a muffled response from inside the room but they couldn't make out what he said.

"Speak up, please!" Brad yelled. "It's time for lunch."

This time the response was louder. "Like I told you, I'm not feeling well. Thank you, but no lunch today."

Brad looked over at Eddy and Robert. He took a step closer to the door. "Mr. Bowers, I have something I need to discuss with you. Please open the door."

Eddy noticed Brad didn't call him Reverend.

"I'm sick. I'm in bed. Maybe tomorrow."

"Please Mr. Bowers. I must insist."

"No. I'm in...."

Robert motioned for Brad to step aside. He stepped across the hall, ran a few steps, and planted his size eleven shoe next to the doorknob. The door flew open and the three men burst into the room.

Reverend Bowers was sitting at a small desk near the window. He jumped up with a startled look. Eddy saw long scratch marks running down the left side of his face. He ran up and grabbed him by the front of the shirt. "You ass-hole! You tried to strangle my sister!"

Brad jumped between them and pushed Eddy aside. He turned to Robert. "We need a rope."

"No problem. I'll be right back." Robert turned and ran down the hallway.

"Rope?" the Reverend repeated, with a look of fear. "What are you going to do, string me up?"

"That's a damn good idea," Eddy said. "You killed Jeremy and almost killed my sister. What do you think we should do with you? Come listen to one of your sermons?"

"I...I didn't kill anyone!" Reverend Bowers exclaimed.

"Right! And you got these scratches from shaving with a dull blade, I suppose," Eddy sneered.

The Reverend pushed Brad away and lunged at Eddy, knocking him onto the bed. He jumped on top of him and started punching him in the face.

Brad grabbed him by the neck and pulled him off of Eddy. Eddy scrambled to his feet, ran up, and drove his fist into his stomach. The Reverend doubled over.

"Eddy!" Brad yelled, "Just help me hold him!"

Robert came running back down the hallway with two long pieces of rope dangling from his hand. "Turn him around. Get his arm's behind his back." He wrapped one rope tightly around the Reverend's wrists.

Brad looked over at Eddy. His face was bleeding in a few places. "Go wash off in the bathroom." He turned to Robert. "What should we do with him?"

"I say we tie him to a chair in the library. I'll tie the door going into the parlor shut. The other door's still locked from when..." He stopped. "From before."

"Will it be warm enough in there?" Brad asked.

"We'll throw a blanket on him. He should be fine," Robert replied.

They marched him downstairs, through the parlor, and into the library. Brad grabbed a wooden chair from one of the library tables, and Robert started tying him to the chair.

Eddy walked in holding a wet towel against his face.

Brad stepped back from the chair and looked at Eddy. "Looks like you might end up with a black eye. He got you pretty good."

"That dirty bastard. He's no minister. Killing Jeremy, probably getting ready to rape poor Nicole, and then attacking my sister." He looked over at him tied in the chair. You're...you're a damn monster!"

The Reverend ignored him and then turned to Robert. "It's...it's freezing in here." He turned his head and sniffed. "What...what's that smell?"

Robert walked over to the window and slammed it shut. "I'll find a blanket for you. It won't take long for the room to warm up."

Eddy sniffed and backed up towards the door. "Whew. That's nasty!""

Brad pointed down to the round rag rug that the Reverend's chair was sitting on. "It's the rug. He...he must have...leaked out or something. You know...onto the rug."

"Serves you right!" Eddy said. "You killed the man, and now you should have something to remind you of it."

Reverend Bowers struggled in his chair. "I...told you. I didn't kill anyone!"

Robert looked down to the rug. "I'll come by tomorrow and get it out of here."

"What about eating? How am I going to eat? I'm hungry."

"Hungry?" Brad repeated with a touch of sarcasm. "I've been begging you to come downstairs for both breakfast and lunch. You weren't very hungry then."

"We'll bring you something tonight after dinner," Robert said. "You can go to the bathroom then, too. All three of us will walk with you."

"Oh, great!" Eddy said. "Just what I wanted to do."

Robert checked the rope and knots once more, and they walked out of the library. He wrapped the other rope around the two French door handles and finished it off with a square knot.

Brad said, "I think we should take a look at his room. I'm curious as to what's up there."

"Good idea," Eddy said. "Let's go."

"If you guys don't mind, I need to let Wilfred know what's going on." He stared down at the floor and let out a long sigh. "I know he thought this was a crazy idea."

"Go ahead," Brad said. "We'll handle it."

When they got to the Reverend's room, Eddy walked into the small closet and pulled out the Reverend's suitcase. Brad decided to start with the dresser drawers. He was rummaging through the second drawer when he heard Eddy yell something from the closet.

"What is it?" Brad asked.

Eddy stepped out holding a magazine with young naked girls on the cover. "Don't think this is appropriate reading material for any preacher I know!" Eddy said. "And this isn't the only one."

"Now we know why he was sneaking around peeking at Nicole."

"Yeah. Maybe it was a good thing my sister barged in there when she did. Who knows what was about to happen."

Brad moved several shirts and a thick sweater and noticed a bulging cloth bag at the bottom of the drawer. He pulled it out and held it up. "Eddy, take a look at this."

He walked over and dumped the contents onto the bed-spread.

"Hey! Those are my sister's earrings." Eddy said, picking them up. "I bought these for her last Christmas." He looked down at the jewelry. "Hey, wait a minute! That looks like her wedding ring!"

"There's nine...ten... eleven, twelve pieces here." He scooped them back into the bag. "I'll bring them down at dinner, and let's see who recognizes them."

"What a lying, thieving, murderous jerk!" Eddy said, shaking his head. He stepped towards the doorway. "I'm headed to my room. My face is killing me, and I've got a wicked headache."

Brad watched as he walked to the end of the hallway. When he saw Eddy turn the corner, he grabbed the pouch and walked towards April's room. As he approached the door, he stopped and listened. He softly knocked. The door opened and April looked surprised. "Brad! What are you doing here?"

"We just broke down the Reverend's door. You were right. He had scratches on his face."

She motioned for him to enter. "I can't believe he's...such a monster!"

He stepped inside and looked around. "I want to show you something. Is Nicole here?"

"No, she's down with Doctor Hilton. What do you want to show me?"

He turned the pouch upside down over the bed, and the jewelry tumbled out. "We found this in good-old Reverend's room. Looks like he had some sticky fingers."

"There's my ring! And my earrings, too!"

Brad picked them up and handed them to her. April pointed to a necklace. "Nicole's missing a necklace. I bet that's hers."

"I'm taking it all downstairs and showing everyone at dinner."

She picked up her earrings. "How could a man pretending to be a man of faith be so...so awful? I mean, here we are, all trapped in here, and he's roaming around at night stealing things and...and killing people." Tears started running down her cheeks. "Poor Jeremy. He seemed like such a gentle man."

He put his arm around her.

She leaned closer. "This...this is so hard. I just want to go home."

"I know. I'm so sorry for putting you through all of this."

He felt warm. Solid. She continued sobbing.

"It's going to be all right. I would never let anything happen to you."

She nodded and wiped away a tear.

He pulled her closer. He bent down and kissed her. Startled, she tried to push him away. His arms tightened. She hesitated at first and then she pulled him towards her. She reached up and wrapped her arms around him. He laid her down on the bed and kissed her harder, cupping her breast in his hand. For the first time in so long she felt unafraid, wanted, and protected. He reached behind her and slid his hand under her blouse. She froze. He whispered, "It will be okay. We both want this."

She shook her head and pushed herself away. "I...I...can't."

He sat up. "I'm sorry. I shouldn't have...."

"No, don't say that. It's just that...I don't think I'm ready for...."

"I know...I know. I understand." He stood up and tucked in his shirt. "I'd better go. I'll see you downstairs."

She looked up from the bed. "Okay."

As Dennis approached Marquette's city limit, he could see towering snow-banks that ranged from six to twelve feet or more. He slowly drove up South Front Street looking for a motel. He spotted a small mom and pop place and booked a room. After checking in, he rummaged through his pocket for Hank's number. Hank answered on the third ring, and Dennis introduced himself. They talked for a few minutes and worked it out that Hank would come by the next day around nine in the morning.

He turned on the TV and tried to find the news. After running through the channels a few times, he was bored. He wished he had been able to talk Hank into picking him up right away. He put his jacket back on and decided to take a walk.

He left his room, walked down the street for a few blocks, and ducked into the Whitefish Tavern at the corner of South and Main. He sat at the bar and ordered a beer and a perch fish fry. The bartender wasn't very busy because there was only one other person sitting at the end of the long, curved bar. Dennis ordered another beer, and when the bartender brought it to him, he asked, "By any chance, do you know where the Fredericks place is? From what I understand, it's outside of town a ways."

"Wilfred Fredericks place? Yeah, I know where it is. Used to be a fish processing plant out there. The house is way out on Peninsula Point. Why you asking? You one of them movie people?"

Dennis laughed. "No. But, I am trying to get over there."

The bartender shook his head. "It's the only house way out at the end of the point. I hope they have their own plow because it could be days before the county makes it out that far."

"What about a snowmobile? Could I get there with a snowmobile?"

"Oh, yeah. That would do it."

Dennis reached for his new beer. "Okay. Thanks for the information." He finished his lunch and returned to his room. He had turned up the heater when he left, so when he opened the door, he was met with a blast of warm air. The two beers made him sleepy. He pulled off his boots, hung up his coat, and flopped down on the single bed. It didn't take long, and he was sleeping. He was dreaming about Bobby. The same dream he had so many times before. Bobby was moving the chair over to the closet. Dennis was trying to stop him, but he was moving in slow motion. Bobby was reaching up for the gun case. Suddenly, Dennis sat up awake. He was wet with sweat. He thought about the dream and bolted from the bed.

That's it! I know what happened! Now, I have to get over to that Fredericks' place!

It was almost dark when Joe Casperson walked out to his shed and gassed up his snowmobile. He walked back into the house and poured himself a cup of old coffee.

"You taking the snowmobile out at this time of day?" his wife asked.

"Yep. Thought I'd take a little ride."

Madge thought it was a little strange that he would be going out so late, but from past experiences, she knew better than to question him.

"No telling when I'll be back. Probably pretty late."

"Okay, just don't be getting yourself into any trouble."

"Don't worry. I won't." Joe drained his coffee cup and walked out the door. He thought he could catch Trail 14 for part of the way and then head cross-country until he got close to the Fredericks place. He had tied a pair of snow-shoes onto the snowmobile. He planned to stop about a half mile away so nobody could hear the engine as he got near. He'd walk the last part. There was supposed to be a quarter moon. That would be perfect. Light, but not too much. He patted his jacket pocket and felt the familiar feel of his .38 revolver.

As everyone gathered around the table, Claudia rushed over and made sure she sat down next to

Eddy. She turned and smiled at him. He tried to ignore her.

"What's that?" she asked, pointing to the round shiny ball he was rolling between his fingers.

"It's a pellet of iron ore Robert gave me."

She was about to ask him a question about it when Brad walked up to the table and pulled out the pouch he had found upstairs. He dumped the contents out next to his plate. "Come take a look at this. I found all this upstairs in Reverend Bower's room."

Everyone crowded around. "Jewelry?" Robert asked.

"Hey, those rings are mine!" Nicole said. "They disappeared a few days ago."

"He had my earrings, necklace, and wedding ring!" April exclaimed.

Claudia leaned over. "That's my tennis bracelet!"

"You should see what I found!" Eddy said, with a wry smile. "Well, no, you shouldn't see it. I found a bunch of girly magazines in his suitcase." He looked over at Nicole. "Young girls, too." Everyone was so preoccupied about the jewelry that Eddy didn't think anyone even heard him.

Brad looked over and saw a horrified look on Doctor Hilton's face. She wheeled herself over and took a closer look. "I can't believe it. That bracelet is mine!" She picked it up and put it on her wrist. After everyone had picked out what was theirs, there were still two items left on the table. One was an old broach and the other was a small gold ring.

"I wonder who these belong to." Brad said. Just then, Ruth walked by with a pan of fried chicken. "Ruth, come take a look at this." Brad said.

She set the platter down and stepped over. "Where did you get these?" she asked. "That's my mother's broach...and her ring, too!"

"I found them upstairs in Revered Bower's drawer along with a bunch more. Everyone claimed their pieces and these were left over."

Ruth looked shocked. "The preacher? I...I can't believe it. I mean, he did look a little seedy, but a thief?"

"And murderer," Eddy added. "Oh, let's not forget an almost rapist, too!"

After dinner, Brad and Robert took a plate of food into the library. Eddy saw what they were doing and said he didn't want any part of it. Robert untied the Reverend's right hand, and they stepped back and watched him eat. After he was finished, they both walked him back to the bathroom and stood guard at the door. As they marched him back to the room, Ruth stepped into the hallway and handed Robert an old blanket. "Here, let him use this tonight."

As Robert was retying him to the chair, the Reverend said, "Come on now. You got this all wrong. This is crazy and not necessary. Yeah, I grabbed a few pieces of jewelry. I'm sorry! Truth is, I'm flat broke. I thought I could pawn them when I got back home and get me a few nights in a flop house. Look, I wasn't going to do anything to that young girl. Yeah, I snuck a peek when she was in the bathroom. Come on, who wouldn't do that?"

"What about April?" Brad asked. "You about killed her."

"It was an accident. I panicked when she caught me looking at that girl. She started screaming. I...I was just trying to get her to shut up. Really."

"Don't forget about Jeremy," Robert said.

"Hey, I never...."

Robert tossed a blanket over his head. "Sleep tight."

They both walked out and Robert stopped and retied the rope around the door handles.

That evening everyone gravitated to the parlor like before. Eddy knocked on April's door and accompanied her down the stairs. As Nicole walked in with Brad, Claudia was having a hushed conversation with Doctor Hilton. Robert was already in the room, stoking up the fire. With the Reverend captured and incapacitated, the atmosphere seemed much less tense. Ruth brought out some cheese and crackers and set them on a table. Brad stood by the bar. "I'm taking drink orders. Let me know what you want."

Holding an old fashioned, April walked back to the loveseat.

Claudia stood up and said, "I have a question." Everyone turned to her. She continued, "It seems to me that all of the pranks that were happening seemed to stop right after Jeremy was...gone. Did anyone else notice that?"

"I never thought of it before," Doctor Hilton said, "but I guess you're right."

"Are you saying you think he was the one doing all those weird things?" Nicole asked.

"I don't know. I was wondering what you all thought. Could it just be a coincidence?"

"What would he have to gain by doing them?" Brad asked.

"I don't know," Claudia said. "He claimed to have had that retro prerecognition thing. Maybe it has something to do with that."

"It's called retro-cognition," Doctor Hilton corrected.

Claudia chewed on a cracker and held up her finger. "Well, whatever it was, everything stopped when he got...you know."

"I don't know," Eddy said. "I really don't see why he would be behind all of that. But, I guess it could have been him." He turned to Robert. "When do you think the road will be plowed? It seems like the wind died down a few hours ago."

"I'm sure we have a pretty good chance of getting plowed out tomorrow or the next day at the latest."

"What about the damn lights?" Eddy asked.

"Like I already told you. Someone took the battery so we can't start the generator."

Brad's face lit up. "Could we use one from one of our cars?"

Robert thought for a moment. "Maybe. I could give it a try tomorrow morning. Don't want to fool around with that in the dark tonight."

"Well, that would be wonderful," Doctor Hilton said. "Lights and maybe a snow plow tomorrow! Things are definitely looking up." She wheeled herself over to the bar. "Brad, would you mind making me another drink?"

Eddy looked over at Claudia. "Hey, now that things are almost back to normal, maybe you and Fritz can have another session?"

Everyone tried not to laugh. April rolled her eyes and wished she were sitting next to him so she could hit him.

Claudia smiled. "I know you're trying to be funny, Eddy, but I've come to the conclusion that Fritz is just too old for me to do him any good."

Brad laughed. "So, I guess it is true that you can't teach an old dog new tricks!"

Claudia looked back over at Eddy. "Why don't you let me have a session with you?"

Eddy's face got red. "What?"

Claudia got flustered. "You know, ask you a few questions. Ah, maybe my therapy could help you out."

"Probably not!" he replied. "I think I'm more like a cat than a dog."

Claudia's face lit up. "Even better! I seem to have much better success with felines!"

Worried that this conversation was about to take an ugly turn, April piped up, "I wonder what the police are going to think once they get here? We've got a corpse in down the basement, stolen jewels, somebody tied up to a chair. It's probably going to take them a week to check out this whole house."

"Well, I don't plan on hanging around for another week," Eddy said. "I was ready to get out of here the first night we got here."

Doctor Hilton got her drink and turned from the bar. "I'm so sorry our little gathering turned out so disastrous. I imagined, with all of your varied backgrounds, that we were going to be making scientific history this week."

"Speaking of backgrounds, I think you guys should have spent a little more time looking into the Reverend's. If he's a minister, I'll eat my hat." Eddy snickered.

The conversation continued about what kind of criminal record the Reverend had and if he really had ever been a member of the clergy. Some thought he may have been at one time, while others thought it was all a sham right from the start. Shortly after eleven-o'clock everyone started getting tired, and Doctor Hilton agreed it was time to go to bed.

As they headed for the stairs, April said to her brother, "I'm not buying Claudia's notion that Jeremy was behind all of the shenanigans that were going on."

Eddy nodded. "Yeah, that was pretty weak. Who do you think's behind them? I'm sure you don't think it was your darling Brad!"

She stopped at the foot of the stairs. "Stop it, Eddy. Brad's a very nice guy. He's...he's been a good person to talk to. He's really helped me figure some things out."

"Okay, he's a nice guy. Back to my question. Who do you think our little prankster is?"

April thought for a moment. "Ah, I'm not going to say anything just yet, but I don't think it was Jeremy...or Brad."

"Suit yourself," Eddy said. "We all got opinions."

They walked up the stairs in silence. Eddy walked her to her door. He pulled her close and gave her a kiss on the cheek. "Don't be mad at me. See you in the morning." He turned and walked down the hall towards his room.

April pulled the door open and saw Nicole sitting at the end of her bed. She had a big smile on her face. April shut the door, walked over, and sat down next to her. "What's with you? I think this is the first time I've seen you smile in days."

"Oh, my goodness," Nicole said. "I'm not supposed to tell anyone, but I can trust you!"

"What is it?"

"I'm going to Hawaii!"

"Hawaii! That's wonderful, but is this something new? Why so excited now?"

"Because..." Nicole's voice dropped down to a whisper. "Promise you won't say anything?"

April hesitated. "Okay."

"Brad's taking me!"

April felt her cheeks start to flame. "He...he said that?" she asked. She blinked and tried to keep tears away. She pushed herself off the bed. "Ah, excuse me!" She covered her face with her hands and ran towards the bathroom.

Nicole jumped up. "What's wrong? Are you all right?"

From behind the closed door, she heard April say, "Um, yes. Just...just give me a moment."

Joe shivered behind a clump of cedar trees. The damn snow shoes were harder to walk in than he remembered. He waited another half hour and crept closer. He slowly made his way around to the side of the house. The snow banks were up to the bottom of the first floor window sills. He was looking for a room that looked empty or a window that looked like it would be easy to open. As he came around the west side, he noticed there was one window that wasn't covered with a storm window on the outside. He stepped closer and peered inside. It was dark. He couldn't see anything. He pushed up on the window and was surprised to feel it slide open. He pulled his feet out of the snowshoes and stuck them in a snow drift. He pushed the window open farther and quickly climbed inside. He pulled out a small flashlight and panned it around the room.

He jumped back and clicked off his light. *What the hell*! It looked like a blanket was draped over someone sitting on a chair. He switched on the flashlight again and took another look.

From under the blanket, he heard a muffled, "Who's there?"

Joe snapped off the light again and stepped a few steps back from the chair. His heart was racing.

"Robert? Is that you?"

Joe thought for a moment. He couldn't imagine what was going on. He felt for his gun. "Who the hell are you," he whispered.

Reverend Bowers strained to hear in the darkness. That voice didn't sound familiar.

"Who are you?" Joe whispered again.

"I'm Reverend Bowers. Who are you?"

"Why are you sitting under a blanket?"

"I'm tied to a chair."

Joe panned the light around the room to make sure there weren't any more surprises. "Okay. So, why in the hell are you sitting in the middle of a room, tied to a chair, with a damn blanket over you? Has old man Fredericks done that to you?"

The Reverend thought for a moment. "Ah, yes. Yes he did. And Robert, too."

"So, what's going on? Did they catch you trespassing?"

"No...no. Nothing like that. I'm here because...because a young girl from my congregation is being held...in a cult. I tried to save her, but they...they caught me and tied me up."

"A cult?" Joe whispered. "I thought they were making some kind of TV show here."

"No, that was...ah, the cover. To...to explain all the new people coming here. It's...it's...a cult. A devil worship cult. I'm a Reverend. I've got credentials in my wallet. Please...please untie me."

Joe stared at the blanket. *I know Fredericks is a mean son-of-a-bitch, but this sounds ridiculous. Who the hell is this guy?*

Joe cautiously stepped towards him, grabbed one edge of the blanket, and jerked it to the floor. He could see the man had his hands tied securely to the back of the chair.

The Reverend took in a deep breath. "Thank you. God bless you, sir! Now, could you please get me untied from this chair?"

Joe shuffled from one foot to the other. "Ah, I don't know. Usually a man's tied up for some good reason."

"Look, don't believe me. Go down into the basement. There's a body down there. They've already killed someone. A sacrifice...to...the devil. I'm going to be next! Go down there and look for yourself if you don't believe me. But hurry! Please hurry!"

"A body? They killed somebody?"

"Shh. Not so loud! Yes, it's not a lie. Go see for yourself."

"How do you get there?" Joe whispered.

"Turn around and go out...oh shit! They've tied the doors closed. You won't be able to leave this room."

Joe pulled out his flashlight and moved it around the room. "Which doors? These?"

"No! The ones behind you."

He walked over to the doors and pushed on them. They moved about an inch and stopped. Joe pushed harder, and they gave way a little more. He reached into his pocket and pulled out a small penknife. He pushed on the doors again, this time leaning into them with all his weight. A small crack opened up between them. He stuck his knife into the opening and began sawing the ropes. Several minutes later the doors sprang free. He walked back to the Reverend. "Where's the basement?"

"Go out to the foyer. Face the front door and look to the right."

Joe shoved the knife back into his pocket, pulled out the gun from his jacket, and headed to the foyer.

Once in the hallway, he spotted the door. He pulled it open and shined his light down the stairs. He didn't see any body. He carefully negotiated the steep wooden staircase. When he got to the bottom, he stopped and looked around. Sure enough, there it was, just like the guy upstairs had told him. A man was lying on his back, eyes wide open, with a big butcher knife sticking straight out of his chest.

Joe stumbled backwards and muttered, "Oh, shit!" *What the hell have I gotten myself into?* A cold chill went through him. He played the light back and forth around the basement. He stepped back to the stairs and quietly crept back to the library.

He walked up to the Reverend, holding his gun on him the whole time. "You're right. There is a body down there." He backed up towards the window. "Mr., this is way out of my league. I thought I'd just sneak in, grab a few bucks for the sake of my nephew, and hit the road. I don't know what the hell's going on in here, but I ain't staying to find out." He felt behind him and slid the window back open, all the while keeping the gun trained on the Reverend's chest.

"Wait! Just listen, will you! If you leave now, you're going to be responsible for not only my death, but that of a young girl. Do you want that on your conscience?" He didn't wait for an answer. "And…and not only that! Ah, there's fifty-thousand dollars down there. I'll show you where it's at. Fifty-thousand big ones!"

Joe thought for a moment. "How do I know it wasn't you that killed him? You're the guy all tied up in the chair."

"I already told you. I'm a minister. I'm trying to rescue one of my parishioners. Fish out my wallet. You can see my ID." Reverend Bowers stared at the gun. "What about you? You break in here in the middle of the night with a gun. What's your deal?"

"I got a score to settle with old man Fredericks. It's about my nephew. He drowned on Fredericks' boat. Sent them guys out in a bad storm because he's a greedy bastard."

"Hey, there's fifty thousand just waiting to settle the score right now!"

Joe eyed him suspiciously. "How do you know?"

"I saw it. Before they caught on to who I was. It's hidden pretty good, but I know exactly where it is."

Joe slowly slid the window closed "How 'bout this. I untie you. You show me where the dough is, and we split it fifty-fifty."

"You untie me, and the money's all yours. I don't want any of it. You can keep it all. All I want is to get out of here, call the cops, get that girl away from these monsters, and have them all arrested."

Joe walked behind the chair and started untying the ropes. "Okay, then. But, if you try anything funny, I'll blow your ass to pieces."

"Don't worry about that. You get the money, but you have to promise me you'll help me get away from here. If they find out what I've done, they'll kill me for sure."

Joe undid the last knot, and the ropes fell to the floor. "Come on. Show me where that dough is."

Reverend Bowers walked back to the door that led to the basement stairway. Joe was next to him, holding on to his arm, the gun stuck firmly into the Reverend's side. He pulled the door open. "I need the flashlight," the Reverend said.

Joe handed him the light and followed him down the stairs. When they got to the bottom, the Reverend paused and shined the light in a wide semi-circle. Towards the back of the basement was an old coal furnace that had been shut down when Wilfred had installed oil heat.

"Where's the money?" Joe asked.

"Give me a minute, don't rush me. I...I gotta think for a minute. There's a lot of junk down here, and I only saw it once."

Since Reverend Bowers had never been in the basement before, he wanted a little time to scout out the best place to send Joe. "Okay. See that old trunk way over there?" He played his light to a spot in the back of the basement.

Joe peered into the darkness. "You mean over there to the left?"

"Yes. It's that old red trunk. See it?"

"Yeah."

"It's in there."

"Give me the light," Joe said. He slowly made his way towards the trunk. The Reverend pushed several cardboard boxes away, clearing a path to the trunk. As Joe reached down, gun in hand, to lift the lid, Reverend Bowers grabbed an old coal shovel and swung it down hard onto his head.

Joe let out a yell and tried to stumble to his feet. The Reverend swung the shovel again and connected with the side of Joe's face. He fell over the trunk and let out a low moan. After a few seconds, he tried to lift himself up. The Reverend raised the shovel and slammed it down on his head again. Blood spurted out from Joe's nose and splattered against a stack of old wooden soda cases. As Joe groaned, the Reverend bent down, grabbed the gun and shoved it into his pocket.

Upstairs, Wilfred tossed and turned. He had gone to bed two hours before, but he was having trouble falling asleep. By habit, he reached over and switched on the lamp next to his bed. "Damn-it," he muttered to himself. He sat up at the edge of his bed. *Why would someone take the trouble to go down to the basement and disconnect that battery and then hide it?*

He rolled out of bed and slipped on his pants. He grabbed a red flannel shirt from the end of the bed. Fritz lifted his head up from his blanket, looked at Wilfred for a moment, and then lay back down. Wilfred grabbed a kerosene lantern, lit it, and headed down the hallway. *I don't care what Robert said, that battery has to be down there somewhere.*

As he neared the landing at the top of the stairs, he heard someone crying. He held the lantern up and saw a woman sitting on the top step, her head buried in her hands. He walked closer and stopped. "Ma'am. Is something wrong?"

April jumped and looked up. "Oh, I didn't hear you. Something wrong?" She wiped her tears and let out a little laugh. "I guess. Something's wrong with my head. Not only am I stuck in this house, but now I'm a complete idiot, besides." She turned away from Wilfred and started sobbing again.

"Well, there ain't much I can do about those things, but is there something else I can do for you? You want a cup of coffee or something?"

April stood up and wiped her face. "No. I'm sorry. I just had to have a little talk with myself. I think I know what I have to do. But, thank you anyway, Mr. Fredericks." She stood up and headed back to her room.

Wilfred shook his head and walked down the staircase. *Is everyone in this house a complete lunatic?* As he made his way along the hallway, he saw a flicker of light coming from the kitchen. He stepped into the doorway and saw Claudia pressed against the front of the refrigerator. She had a look of terror on her face. When she saw it was Wilfred, she let out a sigh. "Oh, thank God it's you." She grabbed his arm. "Something's going on! I heard voices in the hallway."

Wilfred stepped closer. "Whose voices?"

"I don't know. I couldn't hear exactly what they were saying, but it sounded like two...two guys. I think they went down into the basement."

"Really?" Wilfred said. "I thought Robert gave up on that generator. Okay, let me go have a look."

Claudia grabbed a plate of cookies. "I'm going back to my room."

Wilfred walked past the parlor and saw that the basement door was open. He could feel cold air pouring up from the stairs. *Damn visitors. Don't have a lick of common sense.* He made a mental note to talk to Robert about telling them to make sure that door was always closed.

He held the lantern out in front of him, grabbed the railing, and carefully descended the stairway.

Reverend Bowers spun around. He saw a pool of light illuminating the upper part of the stairs and then watched as Wilfred slowly descended the staircase. He knelt down and ducked behind a rack of old coats.

Wilfred walked over to the generator and swung his lantern around. He didn't see anyone. He cocked his head and listened. *What was that woman talking about?*

He set the lantern down, picked up the two leads to the battery, and looked at them. They had been cut clean off. He glanced around to see if he could see any sign of the battery. There was nothing but old boxes and a pile of old clothes. He stopped. There was a noise. He listened. It sounded like it had come from the back of the basement. He snatched up the lantern and held it in front of him. He listened again. *There it was.* It sounded like...like a low moaning sound.

Wilfred stood up and slowly tried to make his way to the back. He stopped to move a wooden box full of old rusty tools. He took another step and then stopped.

"Ahhhh...help...help me."

He raised the lantern higher and stepped over a pile of junk. In the dim light ahead of him, he saw someone was slumped over a trunk. He stopped. *Was it Robert?* He swung the lantern closer to the body, took a step, bent over and looked. *Holy shit! It's Joe Casperson!*

Wilfred reached out. "Joe! What the hell...."

Suddenly, a rack of clothes toppled over on top of him. Somebody jumped on top of him, hitting him. He fell over. He felt a hard blow to the back of his head. He reached back and tried to cover his head. The room started spinning. It was getting darker. Then, he blacked out.

Reverend Bowers ran back to the stairs. He climbed them two at a time and peeked into the foyer. He shut the basement door and leaned against it, catching his breath. He looked around the hallway, grabbed a chair from the foyer, and jammed it under the basement door handle. He struggled to catch his breath. He crept back to the library, went over to the window, and pushed it open. A bitter blast of cold air rushed in. He shivered and stepped away from the window. *A jacket!* He ran back to the closet in the foyer and pulled out one of Robert's jackets. He put it on and reached for a pair of boots.

He raced back to the library and climbed out the window. Once outside, he followed Joe's tracks through the snow and found where he had parked the snowmobile. His heart sank when he saw there were no keys in the ignition. He panicked.

Snowshoes! He walked back to where he had seen a pair of snowshoes sticking out of a snow-drift. He pulled them out, jammed his feet into them, and started walking towards the woods.

He slowly made his way to the edge of the tree line and stopped. He was out of breath. He grabbed a tree trunk and stood there gasping for air. He was wet with sweat. *This wasn't going to work.* He looked at his watch. It had taken him almost an hour, and he only traveled about a quarter of a mile. It was four-thirty a.m. Ruth would be up in a few hours to start making breakfast. His legs were aching. He turned around and stared at the house. As tired and cold as he was, he wasn't sure he could make it back. The cold was penetrating.

Forty-five minutes later he crawled back through the library window. He stepped into the parlor and listened. He wanted to go back to see if he could find the snowmobile keys in Joe's pocket. *Is Ruth up? Has Wilfred gotten out of the basement?*

He peeked into the foyer. He didn't hear anything. He cautiously stepped out, slipped off the jacket, and was about to put it back into the closet. He stopped. *Wait a minute. If they find out the jacket's missing, they'll think I'm gone.* He slipped it back on. He needed a place to hide; somewhere where he could collect his thoughts and figure out what he was going to do next.

Where? Where to go? He thought back to the first day. The tour Robert and his wife had taken some of them on. The junk room! He remembered the room between Robert's and April and Nicole's room was used for storage. *April! She was the start of all of this. If she hadn't come in when she did, none of this would have ever happened.*

The Reverend climbed the staircase and pressed his ear close to Robert's door. He didn't hear any movement inside. He ran over to the next door and pushed it open. Ruth had called it a junk room, and he could see why. It was full of old furniture covered in sheets, boxes, and trunks. Old dresses and coats hung on clothes racks. He stepped in and shut the door behind him. With the light from Joe's flashlight, he noticed an old couch pushed against the back wall. He made his way over to it, being careful not to knock anything over. He pulled off the borrowed boots, curled up under Robert's jacket, and fell asleep.

An hour later, Ruth shut off her alarm, got dressed, went down to the kitchen, and started setting out flour, eggs, and bacon. She threw some kindling into the woodstove. She poured water into the coffee pot and set it on the stove. As she walked over to the pantry, she stopped. There was a noise. It sounded like pounding. *Is someone pounding on the front door?*

She stepped into the hallway and cocked her head. *There it is again.* She walked down the hallway, and the noise got louder. As she walked into the foyer, she noticed a chair had been moved. She saw that it was wedged under the doorknob of the basement door. Then she heard Wilfred yelling, "Hey! Let me out! Ruth! Ruth! Let me out!"

She ran over, pulled the chair out from under the doorknob, and yanked the door open. Wilfred stepped out. He was holding the back of his head. Dried blood was in his hair and on his hand.

"Good Lord! What happened to you?"

"Joe Casperson! He's dead in the basement!" Wilfred winced in pain. "And...they knocked the hell out of me, too. Run and get Robert." He swayed. "I need to sit down a minute."

Ruth stared at him. "Oh, my God! Are you going to be all right?"

"Yes. Go get Robert!"

Ruth ran up the stairs and rushed into their room. "Wake up! Wake up!

Robert rolled over and tried to see what was going on. Ruth was standing over him. He could see she was upset.

"What is it?"

"It's Wilfred. Someone knocked him on the head and locked him in the basement. I...I heard him pounding on the door."

Robert jumped up from the bed. "Is he okay?"

"There's blood on his head, but he says he's okay."

Robert slipped into his pants. "Damnit. What the hell's going on around here?"

"Oh, there's more."

He grabbed his shirt and spun around. "What?"

"He says Joe Casperson's down there too, dead."

Robert rubbed his eyes. "Casperson? What are you talking about?"

"Just come down as fast as you can."

A few minutes later, Robert rushed into the kitchen and saw Wilfred sitting at the table with a cup of coffee. His hand was shaking. Ruth handed Robert a cup and he sat down next to Wilfred.

"What's this about Casperson?"

Wilfred nodded. "He's in the basement, deader than a door-nail."

Robert looked at his head. "What the hell happened to you?"

"I got up last night because I couldn't sleep. I started thinking about that damn generator and who the hell would take the battery and everything. I got up and thought maybe I could find it down there. When I got to the kitchen, that Claudia woman was sitting at the kitchen table...again. She was scared out of her wits. She said she heard talking. She thought the voices went down to the basement." He took a sip of coffee. "Well, I thought it was you. You and one of the guests going down to try and fix the generator."

Robert looked at him. "What time was this?"

"I don't know. Maybe two-thirty."

He leaned over. "Wait a minute. You actually thought I'd be going down to the basement in the middle of the night to...."

"I know, I know. It was a dumb idea. Anyway, when I get down there, I hear some kinda noise. Sounds like moaning or something. I go look, and sure as hell, I find Joe Casperson laying there with his head all beat in. He was alive, but just barely."

"So, what happened to you?"

"I'm getting there. Then, all of a sudden, someone clobbers me and knocks me out cold. I finally woke up. Not sure how long I was out. I made my way over to the stairs but couldn't get the damn door open."

Ruth's face looked white. She was trembling. "So, when I came down to start breakfast, I heard all this banging from the foyer. I got over there and saw someone's stuck a chair under the doorknob. I pulled it away and Wilfred was standing there. He...he had blood on his face."

Robert looked over to Wilfred. "You say he's dead?"

"Yep. He is now. You want to see?"

"No. One dead body's plenty for me." He picked up his coffee cup. "So, what in the world was Joe Casperson doing in the basement?"

Wilfred tried to shake his head. He winced. "That's a damn good question. Hell if I know."

"And...who killed him?" Robert asked.

"The same guy who knocked me on the head!"

Robert's eyes got big. "Oh, shit!" He slammed his cup down onto the table. "Bowers! I wonder if it was Bowers!" He jumped up and ran out of the kitchen. Wilfred eased himself up, stood there for a moment, and then sat back down. He held his head and glanced over at Ruth. "Damn, I got a little dizzy there." He slowly lifted himself off the kitchen chair. "Okay. That seems a little better."

As Robert ran to the library door, he saw pieces of rope lying on the floor. He stepped into the room and saw an empty chair where the Reverend had been tied up.

Wilfred walked up behind him. "Looks like he got away."

Robert walked over to the window and looked out. It was the first light of dawn, and he could see all kinds of tracks in the snow. "I wonder if Joe broke in here, saw Bowers tied up, and for some reason, let him go."

"Why the hell would Joe break into the house?"

"I don't know. Who knows what that drunk would do?"

Wilfred picked up a piece of rope and felt the smooth edge. "Look. This has been cut with a knife."

"Of course," Robert said. "They couldn't get out of the room. Somehow they were able to push the door open enough to cut the damn rope."

Wilfred felt his head. "You know, none of this is making any sense. Why would Bowers kill the guy who set him free?"

"Good question. And where is he now?" Robert walked back to the window, pushed it open, and stared out. "Looks like the damn fool jumped out. He's probably trying to get as far away from here as possible." He slid the window shut. "He's not going to get very far with all that snow."

"They probably won't find him 'till the spring," Wilfred said. "Remember old man Hankerson? He used to walk down to Jenny's Tavern. Got drunk one night and never made it home. Didn't find him until sometime in March."

Wilfred heard footsteps and turned towards the parlor.

Brad rushed in and looked around. "Where's Bowers? I went to the kitchen for a cup of coffee, and Ruth told me I'd better get over here."

Robert pointed to the window. "He's gone. And now we've got two bodies in the basement."

"Two! Oh, no!" Brad said with a look of panic. "The son-of-a-bitch killed Eddy!"

"No, it's some guy from Marquette. Joe Casperson."

Brad stood there looking befuddled. "Okay, now I'm really confused. How does some guy from Marquette end up dead in your basement?"

"I don't know...I really don't have any idea."

Brad looked down and saw the cut pieces of rope on the floor. "How...how would he even get here? Are the roads plowed?"

"No," Wilfred said, "He's got an old Arctic Cat. He probably come over on that."

"Wait a minute!" Robert yelled. "That's what happened. Bowers killed Joe for his snowmobile! He needed a way out of here!"

Brad held up his hand. "Hold it for a minute, will you. Why would this guy want to break in here in the first place?"

Robert said, "Hell if I know. I had to throw him off the property a few times this fall. He's got a beef with Wilfred. But, break in here? I haven't the faintest idea."

Brad threw up his hands. "When is this going to end? I mean, every time I turn around, it gets worse!"

"You know something?" Wilfred said. "All this shit started when that damn generator battery went missing."

Robert thought for a moment. "I bet that Reverend Bowers must have snuck down there and unhooked it."

"Do you?" Wilfred asked. "Why would he want the electricity to go out like that?"

"Maybe so he could roam around in the middle of the night stealing things, and nobody could turn on the lights and see who he was? I really don't know. He's an odd one, that guy."

Wilfred shrugged his shoulders. "Who the hell knows? All I do know is we got a bunch of strangers running around my house and two dead men in the basement. With all this going on, I'm pretty sure there ain't ever gonna be no TV show, and I bet I never see a dime for all my troubles, either."

Robert grabbed him by the shoulders. "It's been a bad mistake. I know. I'm sorry I talked you into this. I...I really am."

Wilfred turned towards the door, then stopped. "Let's just hope nobody else gets killed before the cops get here. I think you guys better walk around the house and check all the doors and windows, just in case. Me, I'm going back to bed. It's been a hell of a long night." He reached up and gingerly felt his head. "I've got one hell of a throbbing headache."

Dennis was dressed and ready to go at eight o'clock. He tried to watch the morning news, but he couldn't concentrate. He was too anxious to get going. At eight-thirty the phone rang. He grabbed the receiver and heard Hank on the other end. "Um, Dennis. I've...I've got a little problem, and...it looks like it'll be tomorrow before I can get you over to Fredericks' place."

Dennis's heart sank. "What? Tomorrow! No, no, no. Not acceptable! I've got to get over there now...right now!"

"I know. But, yah see, my kid took the machine out this morning. He was going to drive it up on the trailer for me. He was fooling around and hit a stump. Chewed the track up all to hell. It'll take all day to fix, if I can even put it back together. Might need to order some parts, but I won't know for a few hours."

"Look, I'm sorry for your troubles. I really am. But I really need to get over there. Do you know somebody else who can take me?"

"Let me think." Dennis waited. "Well. Maybe I can call my brother-in law. Vern's got a machine, but he's...."

"Okay. Could you please call him and see if he can do it? I'll throw in another fifty bucks."

"Well, sure. I'll give him a call."

"Thank you. Please have him call me either way. If he can't do it, I have to find someone else quickly." He hung up and started pacing the room. He walked over and made another cup of coffee with the little coffee maker that was in his room. He glanced at his watch. *Damn it, man. Call me!*

Half an hour later, the phone rang. Dennis was already sitting next to it with his hand on the receiver. "Hello!"

"Is this Dennis?"

"Yes. Yes, it is."

"I hear you're needing a ride over to the old Fredericks place."

"That's right. Thank you for calling me back. Can you do it?"

"Oh, sure."

Dennis smiled. "Perfect. When can you come and get me?"

There was a long pause. "Well, let's see. I'm at work now. How about I pick you up around four o'clock?"

Dennis's hand tightened on the receiver. "Four o'clock? Look, it's really important that I get over there as soon as possible. Can you do any better that that?"

"Well, I can probably get off a little earlier. How about I pick you up at two?"

Dennis thought about it for a moment. "Well, if that's the best you can do. Okay. I'm at the Breakers Motel on Front Street"

"Okay, buddy. See you at two o'clock."

Robert and Brad checked every door and window on the first floor. Except for the library window, everything else looked okay. They returned to Brad's room, where they spent the next hour trying to make some sense out of all the things that had happened during the night.

They waited until everyone had gathered for breakfast and then Robert stepped to the head of the table. "Can I have your attention, please?" He waited until everyone turned his way. "Ah, I'm afraid I've got some more bad news. Last night it seems that a guy named Joe Casperson, somebody Wilfred and I know, decided to break into the house. We don't know why this happened, but…ah, well…from what we can figure out, we think that, somehow Reverend Bowers got loose and…killed him."

There was a look of horror on everyone's face. After a short silence, everybody started asking questions all at once. Brad raised both hands. "Hold it! Hold it! We can't answer most of those questions; we just don't know. The only thing we can think of is that somehow Bowers found out the man came here on a snowmobile, and he probably wanted to use it to get away from here. Now, how he got loose, we really don't know."

Eddy stood up. "Ruth told me Wilfred got hurt. What's that all about?"

"Yes, that's true," Robert said. "That was the next thing I was going to tell everyone. Bowers knocked Wilfred on the head last night when he went down to see if he could fix the generator. He's going to be all right. He's resting upstairs in his room. He's got a big knot on his head." He looked around the table. "What I wanted to ask you all was, did anybody see or hear anything strange last night?"

Claudia started waving her hand. "I...I was in the kitchen, and I told Wilfred that I heard some guys talking. He...he said he was going to go down to the basement. Oh, I should never have let him go down there!"

"He told me about what you said, Claudia. Please, this sure isn't your fault."

"I've got a question, Robert," April said.

"Okay, what is it?"

"Are we sure the Reverend left? I mean, how do we know he's not in the house someplace?"

"There's a bunch of footprints outside the library window. It looks very clearly like someone opened the window and walked away. Brad and I checked all the doors and windows downstairs this morning," Robert said. "Everything looked normal."

Brad stepped forward. "But, that's why we wanted to ask you all if you saw or heard anything last night. I mean, if the man had a chance to steal a snowmobile and get the hell out of here, I think he'd be an idiot not to do it. It sounds like nobody heard him break into their room last night, so I guess he's probably long gone by now."

Doctor Hilton rubbed her forehead. "So, you...you're telling me now there're two dead people down in the basement?"

Robert nodded. "Yeah."

Nicole buried her face in her hands and started praying.

"Is there anything we can do to get the snow-plows here faster?" Doctor Hilton asked.

"I know!" Eddy yelled. "We can go outside and stomp a big SOS sign in the snow in the driveway. That way, if any plane flies over, they'll know something's wrong."

"Be my guest," Robert said. "We don't get many planes flying over here, but if you think it'll help, go ahead."

"I think we should all stay together today," Doctor Hilton said. "We should play cards, work the puzzles, and play charades...anything to keep our minds off of everything that's happened. Robert assures us the plows will be here soon. Maybe even today. I think we should all try and keep busy. Goodness knows, if I go hibernate in my room with everything that's happened, I'll probably lose my mind!"

Chapter 17

IT SEEMED LIKE an eternity before Vern showed up. Dennis had tried to take a nap, but his head was too busy for that. He had gone for another walk and then, finally, he saw a truck pull up. It was pulling a snow-mobile on a trailer. Dennis grabbed his coat and ran out the door.

As he climbed into the truck, Vern said, "Look, I'm going to have to drop you off and then get right back to work. I thought it would be okay to take off at 2:00, but my crew's behind, and I really better get back there."

"That's okay. I'm just glad you got here." Dennis reached out his hand.

Vern shook it. "I almost cancelled on you, but from the sound of your voice, you sounded kinda desperate."

Dennis looked relieved. "Oh, thank you for not canceling. I don't know what I would have done if that had happened." They drove for twenty minutes, and

258

then Vern pulled over to the side of the road. "This is as close as we can get on a plowed road."

As they got out of the truck, Dennis asked, "Can you drop me off a little ways from the house? I'd rather not have anyone hear us."

Vern stopped and looked at him. "What's that all about?"

He pushed a wad of bills into Vern's hand. "Don't worry, it's nothing bad. I...I just think it will be better that way. You know, I'd like to surprise the wife."

Vern winked. "Gotcha. But you better hope the drifts have crusted over." He glanced down at Dennis's feet. "You won't get very far in them boots if it's a couple of feet of powder."

Vern backed the snowmobile from the trailer, and fifteen minutes later he pulled to a stop. He pointed. "There's the house." He shielded his eyes from the glare of the snow. "Look at that."

"What?"

"Over next to the tree line."

Dennis squinted and looked where Vern was pointing. He didn't see anything. "Yes?"

"Looks like somebody already beat you to it. It's another snowmobile."

"What's it doing over there in the bushes?" Dennis asked.

"Who knows? Looks like they wanted to make a surprise entrance, too. You want to jump off here?"

"Yes, that's perfect. Thanks."

"You need me to pick you up when I get off of work?"

"No. That's okay. Hey, I sure appreciate this."

Dennis watched as Vern turned the machine around and disappeared into the woods. He started walking towards the house. At first the snow crust held him up, but after walking about twenty feet, he fell into a four foot drift. He scrambled out and tried to keep going. Over and over he fell through the drifts. After half an hour, he was wet with sweat and out of breath. He had only made it halfway to the house.

He wished he had tried walking before Vern had taken off. He would have had him drop him off a lot closer, surprise or not. He sat on a drift for another ten minutes, catching his breath, and then started out again. Finally, he walked around the side of the house and stopped. He could see a huge SOS message stomped in the snow in the middle of the driveway.

He panicked and ran up onto the front porch. He yanked off his glove and pounded on the door. As he waited, he tried to think about what he was going to say. Several minutes passed, and he knocked again. The door opened, and he saw the barrel of a rifle poke out of the door. It was pointed directly at his head. Behind the man with the gun, he saw a woman cowering in fear.

Dennis stepped backwards and threw his hands in the air. "Ah, take it easy! I'm Dennis Stoughton, April's husband."

The man lowered the gun. "Oh! We thought you may be Reverend Bowers!"

Dennis gave him a weak smile. "Having a church problem? Not putting enough money in the collection plate?"

Robert didn't smile. "No. Nothing like that."

Dennis asked, "Is April here?"

Robert stepped away from the doorway. "Come in. Yes, she's here. So is her brother, Eddy." He looked around the driveway. "How did you get here?"

"I paid some guy from Marquette to drive me here on his snowmobile. Is everything okay?"

Robert looked around again. "A snowmobile? Funny, I didn't hear anything."

Dennis decided it would probably be better if he didn't mention that he had requested to be dropped off far from the house. As he stepped into the foyer, he asked, "Is April okay?"

Robert opened the closet door and returned the rifle. "Well, under the circumstances, I'd say she is." He glanced around the closet. "Ruth, did you move my jacket...and boots?"

She walked up to him and looked inside. "No, why?"

"Look! They're gone!" He moved some old clothes away. "Bowers! I bet he took them!" He turned back to Dennis. "You didn't see anybody go by you on another snowmobile, did you?"

"No. Nobody was out but us. Um, can I ask you, what's with the SOS sign stamped in the snow?"

"Oh, that. That was Eddy's idea. We've, um, we've had some very unfortunate things happen lately." He saw a worried look on Dennis's face. "But, April's okay. So is Eddy." He stared at Dennis for a moment. "So, you must have wanted to see her pretty bad, renting a snowmobile and everything."

"I did," Dennis said. "Her mother's worried sick about her. She was supposed to get a call when they got here, but she hasn't heard from anyone."

"Our phone's been out for days. We've had one hell of a storm. Electricity's out, too. You didn't happen to see any county plows down at the end of our road, did you?"

Ruth reached out. "I'll take your coat."

"No. There's nothing out there but a huge snowdrift."

"I was afraid of that." He turned to his wife. "I'll stay here with Mr. Stoughton. Could you go tell April that her husband's here?" He turned back to Dennis. "I'm sure she'll be very surprised to see you. She's got a lot to tell you."

A few minutes later Ruth returned with April at her side. April ran up to Dennis and wrapped her arms around him. "I...I can't believe it! Oh, I'm so glad you're here. How...how did you find me?"

Dennis was caught off guard. That wasn't the greeting he was expecting. "Your mother. She told me you and Eddy had come up here. She's worried half to death because she never heard from you."

"I know. I'm sure she's beside herself. We were supposed to call her the night we got here, but we got busy. Then, the phone lines went down, we got snowed in, and there was no way to let her know."

Dennis heard loud footsteps. He looked over and saw Eddy coming towards them. "Dennis! What are you doing here?"

"I'm here checking up on my wife...and you."

"Are you in a truck? You got a four wheeler? Can we finally get the hell out of here?"

"No, I was dropped off by a snowmobile. The roads are still blocked."

Dennis ran to the front door. "Is it still here?"

"No."

He turned back to Dennis. "But, we've got to...."

April held up her hand. "Eddy, calm down! There's a whole lot I want to talk to him about. Please give us some time."

Eddy looked hurt. "I was just trying to see if we could finally...."

April grabbed Dennis by the arm and walked with him into the parlor. She saw Claudia, Doctor Hilton, and Nicole sitting near the fireplace working a jig-saw puzzle together. She pulled open one of the French doors to the library and motioned for Dennis to sit down at one of the oak tables. She sat down next to him, reached over, and held on to his arm. Immediately she started to cry.

"What...what's the matter?"

"It's been...just...just dreadful. Jeremy was killed by Reverend Bowers, and then he attacked me! Now, Robert told us this morning there's somebody else dead down in the basement and...."

Dennis jumped up. "Dead in the basement? Somebody was killed by Reverend Bowers? Are you serious?"

She continued to sob as she nodded her head. "This whole trip has been a nightmare of horrors. She pulled him down next to her and wrapped her arms around him. "I'm...I'm so glad you're here."

He held her tight and kissed her. After a few minutes he loosened his grip and whispered. "I...I missed you so much." He pulled her close again and buried his face into her hair. He kissed her again. After a few minutes, he looked at her and asked, "What happened here? Who's Reverend Bowers? Why...why did he kill someone?"

"I...I don't know. He was just another one of the people Doctor Hilton invited here. I really don't know what happened."

"And he attacked you? Why would he want to go after you?"

"I caught him in our room stealing. It was late. I walked into our room and heard a noise. The next thing I knew, somebody knocked me down and was choking me. My roommate Nicole started hitting him, and I tried to scratch his face to make him let go."

"Wait a minute. You said this guy was a minister?"

"He said he was, but I don't think he was a real one. Turns out he was stealing jewelry from everybody."

"What happened to him?"

"They had him tied up in here, but this morning Robert said somehow he got loose and killed somebody that broke into the house."

Dennis shook his head. "After all this, someone broke into the house?"

"It was somebody they knew."

"What in the hell is going on around here?"

Just as April was about to say something, Brad stuck his head in and said, "We're meeting in the parlor, if you'd like to join us."

April said, "Okay."

Dennis whispered to her, "Wait! I want to tell you about Bobby!"

She stopped and turned around. "No. I forgive you. We don't have to talk about it anymore." She took a few steps towards the door.

"No, it's not that. I think I know…."

She spun around. "Dennis, please…you don't know what I've been through. I love you. I'm sorry for so many things. I just…please, I really can't bear to talk about…."

"Ok. Understood. I'll handle it myself." He took her hand as they both walked into the parlor.

Doctor Hilton wheeled herself over to April who introduced her to Dennis. Doctor Hilton said, "Mr. Stoughton, Ruth told me you were here. I'm quite impressed at the effort you've taken to come all this way to find your wife."

"We were worried. Her mother and I. And, from what April's been telling me, our fears were quite justified. I only wish I had gotten here sooner."

April watched as Nicole walked up and sat down next to Brad. April pointed to her. "That girl over there is Nicole. She's Doctor Hilton's assistant. She's talking to Brad Feldman. He's the producer of the pilot they were shooting here."

"Pilot? A TV show?"

"Yes." She pointed to the person to the left of Brad. "And that woman over there is Claudia. I'll introduce you to them later."

April motioned for Eddy. "Can you go and get Robert and Ruth?"

"What for?"

"I want to ask them something."

"I guess." He pulled her over to the side of the room. "What's with Dennis?"

She looked surprised. "What do you mean?"

"I feel like he gave me the brush-off. I tried to talk to him, and he just…I don't know, he wasn't very friendly."

"That's crazy. I'm the one who pulled him away. I wanted to tell him what's been going on around here."

"I don't know," Eddy said, staring over at Dennis.

She gave him a shove. "Just go get them, will you."

As Eddy got closer to the kitchen, he could hear Ruth talking to Robert. "I don't know what we're going to do if those plows don't get here soon. The food's down to the bottom of the second freezer. It's still keeping things cold, but we've only got a few roasts left and a couple of chickens."

"I was wondering about that. Hell, it's never taken them this long to plow us out. I guess you need to cut back on the portions tonight. And now…we've got another mouth to feed."

Eddy stood in the doorway and let out a discrete cough. "Um, sorry to interrupt, but my sister asked if I could get you both to join us in the parlor."

A few minutes later, Robert and Ruth walked in. Robert looked impatient. "What's this all about? We're in the middle of making dinner."

Eddy walked over to the bar and poured himself a glass of wine.

April said, "I'm sorry. It won't take long. I need to ask you a question, Robert, but I want to make sure everyone's here."

"What is it?"

"Okay," April said, looking around the room. "Please be honest with me. Was it you who was doing all those pranks?"

A look of guilt came over Robert's face. Then, he glanced down at the floor and gave a little cough. "Um, why would you ask me that? I thought we've gone over that a bunch of times."

"We have. But I've been thinking, and it seems to me that, at first, you wanted desperately for Brad to have a good experience so that the pilot would be picked up and everyone could continue this, didn't you."

He looked up at April. "I sure did. If this didn't work out, it was all over for Ruth and me." He turned to Nicole. "I'm sorry I scared you like that. I...I really thought I was doing the right thing."

"The right thing!" Eddy yelled.

Nicole looked surprised. "You wrote that message on my mirror! How did you do it? My door was locked. Did you have another key?"

Robert looked embarrassed. "Um, I...I put those words there in the morning before you got here. It was soap. I knew that whenever someone took a shower, the condensed steam would settle on the mirror and make the words come out. I'm...I'm sorry."

He looked over at Nicole again. "And, I chased you with the violin music."

She glared at him.

"What about the kids voices in my room?" Claudia asked.

Robert looked surprised. "What?"

"One night I heard children talking and singing. It really scared me. How did you do that? Did you pipe in something to my room? Is there some hidden speaker?"

Ruth crossed her arms and stared at him. "Ah, no. I...I didn't have anything to do with that." He glanced over at his wife.

Ruth stepped forward. "Claudia, you're room used to be the twin's nursery. I've told Robert over and over that I've heard kids talking and singing in there, but he's never believed me." She smiled. "Until now!"

Robert scowled at Brad. "I can't believe I let you talk me into doing all that crazy shit. You spouting off to everyone that this had to be all above-board and, then you'd come to me with another stupid idea."

Brad glanced around the room. "Hey, I wanted this to work out for everyone, too. You know, a big payday for us all! But, after Jeremy got...killed, I stopped it all."

Now it was April's turn to look surprised. "I thought it was all Robert's doing because I thought he had the most to gain." She looked at Brad with disgust. "Why am I surprised you were behind it all?"

"I'm sorry. I was only thinking about everyone getting more money if this worked. Don't forget, this was way back before Jeremy. Before Bowers took off on that snowmobile. If I would have known all this was going to happen...."

Dennis looked at April and whispered, "Did he say Bowers took off on a snowmobile?"

"Yes, why?"

"Because I saw one when I got dropped off."

He watched as the color drained from April's face. "What? Oh, no...no, no, no!"

Robert turned. "What's wrong?"

"Tell him, Dennis."

"When I got dropped off, I noticed a snowmobile was parked over by the tree line about a quarter of a mile from here."

"What kind was it? An Arctic Cat?"

"I don't know. It was far away. I didn't even see it at first. I thought it was odd that it would be out there, but I didn't see what kind it was. It looked yellow."

Robert motioned for him to follow. "Come on, show me."

"Goodness!" Doctor Hilton exclaimed. "If that snowmobile's still here, wouldn't that mean...Reverend Bowers is still here?" She looked at April. "Somewhere in the house!"

Eddy stood up. "Let's go take a look!"

Robert grabbed him. "Don't go running off by yourself. Let me check out what Dennis said, first. It may be nothing. Then, if we have to, we'll all go."

Dennis said, "Eddy, when I come back, I was wondering if I could have a word with you."

Eddy spun around so fast, wine from his glass spilled onto April's dress. "Oh, sorry."

He glared at Dennis. "What about?"

She grabbed a napkin and patted the stain. "Eddy! Look what you've done!" She stood up. "I need to change into something else and rinse this out. I'll be right back."

"Wait a minute!" Eddy yelled at her.

"I'll be right back!" she replied.

As she was running up the stairs, her mind was racing. She was still somewhat in shock at seeing Dennis. She was mad at herself for being such a fool. She needed to get back downstairs quickly, before Eddy shot off his mouth, and said something stupid about Brad in front of Dennis.

Reverend Bowers heard footsteps running down the hall. He cracked the door open and peeked out. It was April. *Perfect!* He waited until she was in front of her door fumbling with her key. The junk room door flew open and he sprang out. He pointed Joe's gun at her. "One sound and your dead!"

April turned around and froze.

He grabbed her by the arm and pulled her back into the junk room. He spun her around and covered her mouth with his hand. "Well, look what we've got here! And I was just thinking about you and all the trouble you got me into!"

She struggled to get away, but he held on to her tighter. He grabbed a silk scarf that was hanging from a coat tree and wrapped it around her and over her mouth several times. He found an old belt and tied her hands behind her back. He dragged an old wooden chair over, set it in front of the doorway, and pushed her into it. "We'll just sit here and wait for them to find you. You're going to be my insurance policy out of here." He stood behind her with the revolver pressed tightly against her temple.

When they got outside, Dennis pointed in the direction where he had seen the machine. Robert told him to go back into the house and keep an eye on things. As Dennis returned to the house, Robert slowly made his way through the high snow-drifts. He stopped. He was close enough to see that it was Joe's old Arctic Cat.

Dennis returned to the parlor, and everyone waited for Robert to return. After a few minutes, Eddy walked up to him. "Um, what is it you want to talk to me about?"

Dennis looked around the room. "It's a private matter. We can't discuss it here."

Eddy poured himself another glass of wine.

Dennis glanced at his watch. It had been twenty minutes since April had gone to change her dress. He walked over to Eddy. "Where's April?"

"You know. She's changing clothes."

He walked out to the hallway and looked over at the stairway. *How long can it take to change into another outfit?*

After another five minutes, he walked back over to Eddy. "I want to check on April. Where's her room?"

"Robert said he wants us to wait until...."

Dennis tried to control his anger. "Don't worry about Robert. Where's her room?"

"Okay, okay...it's upstairs. I'll show you." Dennis followed him up the stairs. As they walked down the hallway, Eddy asked, "So, um, what do you want to talk to me about?"

"I'll tell you later. Right now, I want to make sure April's okay."

Eddy stopped in front of her door and knocked. "April, it's us. Me and Dennis." He knocked again and tried the door. It was locked. He yelled a little louder, "April. Open up."

Next door, April heard Eddy calling for her. She struggled in her chair. Reverend Bowers pushed the gun tighter against her head.

"Okay, now I'm worried," Dennis said. "Where else do you think she may have gone?"

"I don't know. This is her room. This is where her clothes are. I can't possibly figure out...." Eddy stopped talking. He heard Robert yelling something up the stairs.

"Hey, Eddy...Dennis...can you get down here, please. We need to talk."

Dennis tried April's door one more time before they returned to the parlor. Robert walked up to them and said, "The snowmobile is Joe's. I...I have a feeling Reverend Bowers is still in the house."

Dennis grabbed him. "And now April's missing!"

Robert stepped back. "Missing? What do you mean? She was just here. How can...."

Eddy interrupted. "I spilled some wine on her dress, and she went up to her room to change.

She...she hasn't come back. Dennis and I just checked her room. It's locked and she's not answering."

Robert turned to Doctor Hilton, "Keep everyone here in the parlor. We'll go back and see if we can find her."

"Wait!" Nicole said. "Here's my key!" She handed it to Robert.

"Thanks. Let's go." Dennis, Brad and Eddy followed him out to the hallway.

When they got to April's room, Eddy knocked and called out once more. After getting no response, Robert slid Nicole's key into the lock and opened the door. The room was empty. Dennis looked around the bed and bathroom for any sign of April's wine-stained dress.

"I don't think she made it in here," he said. "Her dress isn't here."

Robert looked around the room. "All the other bedrooms should be locked. After everything that's happened, that's what everyone's been doing, locking things up tight when they're not around."

"I'll check a few of these other doors," Brad said.

Next door, April heard footsteps in the hall again. She could here Dennis's voice. She knew it was time for her to do something. She pulled her shoulders down, swung her head to the side and pushed the chair back as hard as she could with her feet.

The back of the chair slammed into the Reverend's stomach, and the momentum of the chair with April's weight, pushed him over. As he started to fall, he pulled the trigger and a bullet sailed past

April's head. She rolled to her knees, scrambled over to the door, and started kicking it with her feet.

"What was that?" Eddy asked.

Dennis yelled, "A shot!"

"And it was close!" Robert said. He ran out into the hallway and listened. He heard noises coming from next door. "The junk room!"

As Dennis and Eddy ran out into the hall, they saw Robert reach for the junk room's door-knob. He pushed the door open and saw Reverend Bowers on his knees, a revolver pointed at April's head.

Dennis and Eddy ran up to the doorway.

"Don't make a move! One bad decision and I'll blow this pretty lady's head off!"

A surge of adrenalin shot through Dennis's body, but he held himself back.

The Reverend grabbed April by the collar of her dress, and they both got up. He kept the gun pointed at her head. "Here's the deal. I get out of here and April's just fine. Robert, go down and get that snowmobile key out of whoever it was that broke in here. You come back and give it to me. The young lady and I will walk down the stairs. She'll walk with me to the snowmobile, and I'll drive away by myself. She can wave and throw me a few kisses because she'll be just fine...as long as nobody tries to be a hero. Understand?" His eyes darted back and forth watching everyone who was standing out in the hallway.

"Okay, Bowers. Just take it easy," Robert said. "I'll run down and get the key. There's no need to hurt anybody." He slowly stepped back from the door, turned, and ran back to the stairs.

Brad watched from the hallway.

Dennis saw the fear in April's eyes. He saw the gun pressed next to her head. Eddy was backed up against the hallway wall. He looked like he was about to get sick.

Several minutes later, they heard footsteps coming up the staircase. Robert ran down the hallway holding Joe's keys in his hand.

Dennis was staring at the Reverend's hands.

Robert held out the keys. The instant Reverend Bowers reached for them, Dennis sprang forward. He grabbed the Reverend's wrist with one hand and pushed it aside. The gun went off, and a bullet embedded itself in the wall just inches from Eddy's head.

Dennis drove the palm of his other hand up hard under the Reverend's nose.

Robert heard a cracking sound, and the Reverend flew backwards onto the floor. His head smacked against a metal flowerpot. Blood poured from his face.

Dennis threw himself on top of him and tried to wrestle the gun from the Reverend's hand. He pulled the Reverend's arm up and slammed it down against the floor. The gun went flying out from the Reverend's hand. Brad ran for it and stuck it in his waistband.

The Reverend reached up and grabbed his head. He was screaming in pain. Dennis turned and undid

April's bindings. He looked up at Eddy. "Get her downstairs!"

Robert jumped into the room. "What should we do?"

Dennis got to his feet. "We'll tie him up in a few minutes. He'll be flopping around for a while. I guarantee you; he's never felt pain like this before. He won't have any fight left in him. That is, if he lives."

"If he lives?" Robert repeated.

"Depends how far that cartilage was pushed into his brain."

After twenty minutes, the Reverend had stopped convulsing on the floor, and they were able to tie him to the chair. His shirt was soaked with blood. Robert grabbed a rag from a cardboard box and wiped his face. They shut the door and locked it.

"He should be okay in here for a while," Robert said. "I'm going to drive the snowmobile into Marquette. I should be back here with the cops in a couple of hours."

"Sounds good," Dennis said. "I want to see how April's doing."

April was sitting on a chair holding her head in her hands. Nicole, Claudia and Doctor Hilton were comforting her.

Dennis walked up and knelt in front of her. "Are you okay?"

She looked up and nodded. "You...you saved me."

Dennis grinned. "You never know when that Ranger training's going to come in handy."

Dennis looked over at the other women. "Robert's taking the snowmobile into town. The police should be here in a few hours. I think everyone's nightmare is finally over."

Claudia jumped from her chair. "Oh, thank goodness!"

Doctor Hilton shook her head. "It seems impossible. Everything that's gone on here." She looked over at Brad. "First, we had those nasty tricks that scared everyone. Then poor Jeremy. Our missing jewelry and what happened to April. The poor man in the basement. I swear. I don't know where the police are even going to start with this mess!"

Dennis took a step towards Eddy. "So, while we're reviewing everything that's been going on, I just want you to know that I know what really happened."

Eddy looked surprised. "What do you mean?"

"Come on, Eddy. Don't you have something to tell your sister?" He looked over at April. "Now is the time."

Eddy took a step backwards. "Um, how...how could you know? You weren't even here."

April turned to Dennis. "What are you talking about? What happened?"

Dennis took another step towards Eddy. "Tell your sister what happened, Eddy. Go on, tell her!"

Eddy broke into a sweat and started shaking. He threw up his hands. "Don't pull any of that commando shit on me!"

Dennis stepped closer. "Tell your sister, Eddy."

Brad stepped next to Eddy so he couldn't run out of the room.

"He...he knew...the son-of a bitch just knew. He knew about the Ouija board. He told me it was never the desk."

Dennis stared at him with a confused look."

Eddy spun around and glared at April. "And, I know you didn't tell him because we never told anyone about that damn board." Tears started running down his face and he started trembling. "So, I knew he knew about B...B...Bobby, too. I didn't want him to tell you. I...told him to shut up but he wouldn't stop talking about the damn Ouija board. I gave him a push and he turned and knocked me down. I jumped up and grabbed the knife." He buried his face in his hands. "I think he knew about Bobby and...I...I didn't want you to stop loving me."

"Bobby? What about Bobby?" April asked.

He pulled his hands away from his face and started at her. He screamed, "The gun! I left the gun out!"

"What gun, Bobby?" April asked.

He turned and pointed at Dennis. "His gun. I...I was so upset after that stupid Joel came over. He kept yapping on and on about his new job in the Loop, his fancy car, all his money he was making! I was sick of it. Sick of everything. Sick of going to the doctors, sick of living with Mother. When he finally left, I went to the closet and got the gun. I wanted to blow my head off, but...I couldn't...I...I was too scared. I left the gun on the coffee table and went into my room. I took a pill and fell asleep. The next thing I knew was when I heard the shot! It was all my fault about Bobby!" He burst into tears.

April jumped up and reached for him, but he pushed her back.

Tears were streaming down her face. "You...you...didn't mean...."

Dennis stepped closer. "Come on, Eddy. It's all over now. Come...."

Eddy jerked away and screamed, "No!" He turned to Brad, yanked the gun out of his waistband, and put it to his head.

'Eddy!" Dennis yelled.

"I'll do it!" Eddy said. The gun was quivering in his hand.

"Give me that!" Brad said. He lunged at Bobby and tried to wrestle the gun from Eddy's grasp. The gun went off, and a bullet took off the end of Brad's little finger. He screamed out in pain, clutched his hand, and dropped to his knees.

Eddy turned and ran out of the parlor. As he made his way down the hallway, he grabbed a chair and tossed it behind him. He bounded up the staircase. When he got to the top of the landing, he saw Wilfred standing in front of his door pointing a deer rifle at him.

"Put the gun down, son."

Eddy stopped. He stared at Wilfred for a few moments.

"Put it down!"

Eddy relaxed his fingers, and the gun fell to the floor.

"Good. That's good," Wilfred said.

Dennis ran up behind Eddy and grabbed the revolver. "Come on, Eddy."

Wilfred walked over holding the rifle loosely in front of him. "What the hell's going on? I heard a shot, so I grabbed my gun. I waited for a while and then heard a bunch of yelling downstairs. Then, there's another shot and this guy comes running up and...."

Eddy gave Dennis a shove, then reached over and pulled the rifle from Wilfred's hands. He turned and clubbed Dennis in the head with the butt. Dennis collapsed onto the floor. Eddy pushed past Wilfred, ran into the old man's bedroom, and slammed the door.

Fritz leaped from his bed and started growling, his long fangs bared. The hairs on his back were standing straight up. His lips were curled.

Eddy pointed the rifle at him and moved to the spiral staircase. He ran up the steps and pushed open the door to the widow's walk.

Dennis sat up. His head was throbbing.

"Are you okay?" Wilfred asked, staring down at him. Dennis clambered to his feet. "Where is he?"

Wilfred pointed to his bedroom. "He's in there!"

Dennis ran into the room. Fritz stood in his bed and barked a few times. Wilfred walked in. "Easy, Fritz! Easy! It's okay."

Dennis looked around the room and didn't see Eddy. He felt a blast of cold air shoot down the iron stairs.

Wilfred pointed. "The widow's walk!"

Dennis ran up the staircase. The door was open. Eddy stared at him with a wild look. His back was pressed against the railing. He was holding the rifle.

"Come on, Eddy," Dennis said, holding out his hand. "Let's get you back downstairs."

"No...no...no. I'm sorry. I'm so sorry. Bobby...It's all my fault!"

"Eddy, it was a mistake. A tragic mistake." He stepped closer, arms outstretched. "Come on. Nobody blames you."

Eddy turned, threw down the rifle, and vaulted over the railing. Dennis ran to the edge of the walk and looked down. He saw him lying on top of a snow-drift. An ominous red ring of color was growing around his head. Dennis stepped back. Eddy's neck was impaled on one of the ornamental metal spikes of the fence.

April appeared in the doorway. "Are you okay?" She looked around. "Where's Eddy?"

Dennis stopped her from getting any closer. "He jumped. Don't look! He's...he's gone."

She collapsed in his arms.

Two and a half hours later, the sound of snowmobiles broke the silence as Robert returned with several Michigan State Police troopers. Two county snow plows were not far behind them.

The house was designated as a crime scene for the next seven days. Everyone was put up in a hotel in Marquette, and they were all questioned multiple times before the authorities were satisfied they had all of the answers. The national media had a field day once the particulars of the events leaked out. One newspaper headline printed "FREDERICKS HOUSE OF HORRORS!" in capital letters and then everybody else picked up on it.

Chapter 18

REVEREND BOWERS WAS found guilty of murder, attempted murder, theft, and a multitude of other lesser charges. He was sentenced to life with no chance of parole.

Wilfred, Robert, and Ruth sold their stories to several national entertainment shows for an undisclosed sum of money and the back taxes were paid off.

Nicole never made it to Hawaii. Brad Feldman returned to California after being detained by the authorities for another few weeks. He was served with divorce papers two days after he returned. Because of all of the negative publicity his TV pilot had generated, he was terminated from the cable channel. He hooked up with Tiffany Torrance, and they moved to Hawaii where he got a job renting out beachside chairs and canopies at the Ala Moana Resort on the Big Island.

Doctor Hilton burned all of her ESP files from Duke University the day after she got home. She finished out her year at Western Michigan University and then retired.

Claudia returned to California where she quickly got over her initial trauma. She capitalized on her stay at the Fredericks place by joining a speaker's circuit where she traveled around the country giving speeches about her experience.

Eddy's death took a terrible toll on their mother. April could see that both her mother's health and spirit were declining fast. Dennis agreed that they should sell the apartment in Chicago, and Margaret was happy when he moved in with them.

Unfortunately, Dennis's experience with violence at the Frederick's house, sent him into a tailspin. Several weeks after they had sold their apartment, Dennis spent a month at the VA clinic in Milwaukee. He felt much better when he returned, but he was shocked to see how far Margaret had deteriorated.

Margaret surrounded herself with pictures of Eddy, and she would spend long hours in her room, crying to herself. She blamed herself for allowing him to travel up to that house in Upper Michigan. She knew his condition was too delicate for something like that.

April tried everything she could think of to stop the decline in her mother's condition, but on May 12th, Margaret passed away. She weighed only eighty-seven pounds.

The night after the funeral, April cried herself to sleep cuddled next to Dennis. As the first light of dawn illuminated her room, April rolled over in bed and let out a loud gasp. Dennis jerked awake. "What is it?" he asked.

April's eyes were wide. She covered her mouth with one hand and pointed to a small, round, shiny ball on the nightstand. "It's...it's Eddy's iron ore pellet!"

ACKNOWLEDGEMENTS

This book would not have been possible without the dedicated assistance of Gordon Anderson, Julie Beam. Duncan Hebbard, and Dave Hohenstern.

Books by James R. Nelson

The Maze at Four Chimneys
The Black Orchid Mystery
The Pilot

The Stephen Moorehouse Mystery Collection

The Butterfly Conspiracy
The Peacock Prophecy
Menagerie of Broken Dreams

Made in the USA
Columbia, SC
30 November 2019

Welcome to
HOLSOM
POPULATION: WEIRD

03 · *Part One*
"DISCERNMENT!"

·

15 · *Part Two*
"EYEWITNESSES!"

·

27 · *Part Three*
"DELIVERANCE!"

·

39 · *Part Four*
'CRY WOLF!"

·

51 · *Part Five*
"LAW & DISORDER"

·

63 · *Part Six*
"FEAR FACTORS!"

MERE MOMENTS AGO, A *GIANT ROBOT* (NICK-NAMED *ROVER*) BLASTED THROUGH THE CEILING OF A 40-YEAR OLD SCIENTIFIC COMPOUND *HIDDEN* BENEATH THE OLD *HOLSOM* BARN. AN INSTANT LATER, THE BARN'S ROOF FARED NO BETTER, AS ROVER--WITH MOUSE AND JORGE IN TOW--*SMASHED* HIS WAY THROUGH TO *FREEDOM.*

UNFORTUNATELY, MR. SIMMONS HAS ARRIVED SCANT SECONDS *TOO LATE* TO SEE WHATEVER LEFT A TELLTALE *VAPOR TRAIL* ACROSS THE FADING AUTUMN SKY...

WHAT IS GOING ON HERE?

DISCERNMENT!

WRITTEN & LETTERED BY: CRAIG W. SCHUTT   PENCILED BY: GORDON PURCELL   INKED BY: JEFF ALBRECHT

COLORED BY: CRAIG & MARSHA SCHUTT   EDITED BY: SINDA S. ZINN

I'M OUTTA HERE!

THIS PLACE IS COMIN' APART!

LADIES FIRST!

YOU'RE NO LADY, MISS VILE, SO BACK OFF!

OOOOFFFHH!

YOU'D DO GOOD TA REMEMBAH WHO'S BUTTERIN' YOUR BREAD THESE DAYS, MY BOY.

IF AH GO UP IN SMOKE DOWN HERE, SO DOES YOUR HOPES OF A BETTAH LIFE, YA HEAR?

LOUD AND CLEAR, BOSS...

MOUSE!

JORGE!

ROVER!

ANYBODY!

I'M DOWN HERE!

NO!...

"THE-THE LORD (SOB) IS MY SHEPHERD, I SHALL NOT WANT. ...HE-HE LEADETH ME BESIDE THE STILL WATERS..."

"YEA, THOUGH I WALK THROUGH (SOB) THE VALLEY OF THE-THE SHADOW OF-OF D-DEATH, I WILL FEAR NO EVIL..."

"...F-FOR THOU ART... WITH...ME..."

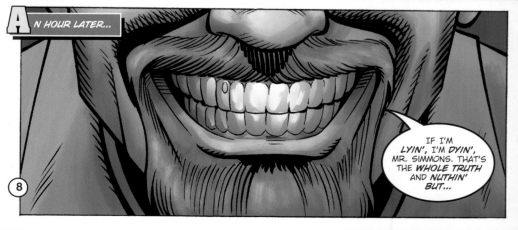

AN HOUR LATER...

IF I'M LYIN', I'M DYIN', MR. SIMMONS. THAT'S THE WHOLE TRUTH AND NUTHIN' BUT...

...BUT WHAT ABOUT *LUCY*, SHERIFF?

JUST *CALM DOWN*, MR. SIMMONS...

LET ME GET THIS *STRAIGHT*, MR. RAYE: YOU AND MISS VILE DROVE OUT TO THE OLD HOLSOM BARN BECAUSE YOU WERE INTERESTED IN *PURCHASING* THAT LAND, RIGHT?

SO WHEN YOU GOT THERE, YOU *CAUGHT* JAKE AND SOME OF HIS BUDDIES COOKING UP SOMETHING *ILLEGAL* IN THE BARN AND CONFRONTED THEM.

THE OTHER KIDS GOT AWAY, BUT IN THE *CONFUSION* SOME OF THEIR "EQUIPMENT" GOT KNOCKED OVER AND THE OLD BARN WENT UP IN SECONDS.

BUT YOU MANAGED TO *CATCH* JAKE AND GET OUT OF THE BARN JUST BEFORE IT *BLEW UP*.

IS THAT THE WAY IT *WENT DOWN*, JAKE?

Y-YESSIR... JUST LIKE MR. RAYE SAID, SIR.

B-BUT *PLEASE*...DON'T TELL MY AUNT, SHERIFF. H-HER *HEART*...

WE'LL KEEP YOU *TONIGHT*, JAKE, BUT I WON'T LET YOUR AUNT KNOW ABOUT THIS UNTIL I'VE HAD A *FORENSICS TEAM* FROM THE CITY LOOK AT THE SITE TOMORROW.

SHERIFF, THIS IS ALL *BOGUS* AND YOU *KNOW IT!*

WHAT *IF* LUCY WAS OUT THERE? HER PARENTS SAY SHE *STILL* HASN'T MADE IT HOME...THEY'RE ON THEIR WAY HERE...

9

I **APPRECIATE** YOUR CONCERN, MR. SIMMONS, I REALLY DO.

BUT THERE'S NO **REAL EVIDENCE** THAT PLACES LUCY AT THE BARN TONIGHT, OR ANY REASON TO BELIEVE SHE'S BEEN ABDUCTED.

AT THIS TIME, I CAN'T **LEGALLY** FILE A MISSING PERSON REPORT OR SEND OUT AN **AMBER** ALERT...

GOT A RIGHT **ACTIVE** IMAGINATION THERE, DON'T YA, MR. SIMMONS?

SOME OF US ARE NEITHER **IMPRESSED** NOR **INTIMIDATED** BY YOUR MONEY, MR. RAYE. THE SHERIFF'S A **GOOD MAN**-- HE'LL GET TO THE **BOTTOM** OF THIS.

MAKE **SURE** THAT FORENSICS TEAM FINDS ALL THE **RIGHT EVIDENCE**, MISS VILE. THEN BRING IN A COUPLE OF **"SPECIALISTS"** TO TRACK DOWN THAT **ROBOT** BEFORE SOMEONE ELSE GETS A LOOK AT IT.

CONSIDER IT **DONE**, JD. BUT WHAT ABOUT **JAKE?**

PROMISE HIM THE **MOON** FOR NOW. KEEP HIM **HAPPY.** KEEP HIM **QUIET.**

UNFORTUNATELY, WE NEED THAT BOY TA STAY ON **OUR SIDE** --'LEAST UNTIL I GET WHAT'S **MINE...**

10

MEANWHILE, ABOUT 15 MILES NORTHWEST OF HOLSOM...

YOU THINK THIS IS *FUNNY*, JORGE?

OH, *YEAH*, EINSTEIN... *HILARIOUS*...

YOU REALLY GET YOUR *KICKS* SEEING OTHER PEOPLE *SUFFER*, DON'T YOU?

DON'T GO ALL *"PSYCHO-ANALYST"* ON ME JUST BECAUSE I COULD JUMP THE CREEK AND YOU *COULDN'T*.

NOT MY FAULT YOU'RE A PHYS ED *FAILURE*.

YOU WANNA TALK ABOUT *FAILURES*? LOOK IN THE *MIRROR*, JORGE.

SHELBY, LUCY, AND I WERE THE CLOSEST THING YOU HAD TO *DECENT FRIENDS*, AND YOU SOLD US OUT TO JD RAYE.

DID YOU THINK YOU COULD JUST *RUN OFF* WITH ROVER AND LIVE HAPPILY-EVER-AFTER? THAT NO ONE WOULD *MISS YOU* OR COME LOOKING FOR YOU?

WHO WOULD MISS *ME*?

YOU? MY *DAD*, MAYBE?

IT'LL BE DAYS--MAYBE EVEN *WEEKS* BEFORE HE NOTICES I'M NOT AROUND...

13

A LITTLE OVER 24 HOURS AGO, THE INFAMOUS *OLD HOLSOM BARN* SAT IN THIS CLEARING. NOW ALL THAT *REMAINS* IS CHARRED WOOD AND RUBBLE...

LET ME GET THIS *STRAIGHT*, LIEUTENANT--EVERYTHING MR. RAYE SAID *CHECKS OUT?*

I'D STAKE MY *REPUTATION* ON IT, SHERIFF.

OF COURSE, WE'LL SEND ALL THE DOCUMENTATION TO YOUR --AH--*"OFFICE"* ONCE OUR PEOPLE FINISH THEIR REPORTS, BUT I'VE WORKED THIS REGION LONG ENOUGH TO *RECOGNIZE* A BLOWN ALCOHOL STILL WHEN I SEE IT.

SO WHAT ABOUT...*YOU KNOW*...

EV-10-BD1

THE *"SECRET, UNDERGROUND MAD-SCIENTIST LABORATORY?"*

WELL... YEAH...

"EYEWITNESSES!"

Script & Lettering: Craig W. Schutt
Pencils: Steven Butler • Inks: Jeff Albrecht
Color: Craig & Marsha Schutt
Editing: Sinda S. Zinn

15

THERE IS SOME INDICATION THAT A SMALL STORM CELLAR EXISTED BELOW THE SILO, BUT I *DOUBT* IT WAS MORE THAN TEN FEET DEEP. MOST LIKELY THE KIDS USED IT TO *STORE* THEIR "PRODUCT." THAT WOULD *EXPLAIN* THE EXPLOSIONS.

PLEASE.

YOU'RE *SURE* ABOUT THIS?

I'M *GOOD* AT MY JOB, SHERIFF. I'M NOT ABOUT TO SIGN A WORK ORDER FOR HEAVY MACHINERY AND SOUNDING EQUIPMENT JUST SO YOU CAN GO ON SOME *WILD-GOOSE CHASE.*

I WANT MY *CHECK* DELIVERED *TOMORROW,* UNDERSTOOD?

WHY, *GOOD MORNING* TO Y'ALL, TOO, MA'AM.

THAT ONE'S *ALL BUSINESS,* SHERIFF-- ALL BUSINESS.

ARE YOU *AWARE* THAT YOU JUST TROMPED ACROSS A *CRIME SCENE,* MR. RAYE?

16

HUH? OH, YEAH...*SORRY* 'BOUT THAT, CHIEF. GUESS I WAS TOO *ANXIOUS* TA HEAR WHAT THESE CITY FOLK FOUND OUT.

I HAVE A *FEELING* YOU ALREADY KNOW THE *ANSWER* TO THAT, MR. RAYE...

UH... **HEY**, TABBY. H-HOW'RE YOU DOIN'?

'KAY.

SO... **UMMM**... WHATYA READIN'?

YOU WOULDN'T UNDERSTAND.

IS THAT AN **ASTRONOMY** BOOK? I'M ACTUALLY PRETTY **INTERESTED** IN ASTRONOMY.

LET THE STARS BE YOUR GUIDE

YOU WOULDN'T BE INTERESTED IN **THIS**, BELIEVE ME.

REALLY? HOW DO YOU KNOW?

YOUR DAD'S A **PREACHER**, RIGHT?

WELL... **YEAH**...

THIS IS **ASTROLOGY**, OKAY?

IT'S ABOUT HOW YOU CAN TELL THE **FUTURE** BY WATCHING THE STARS AND STUFF AND HOW YOU CAN **COMMUNE** WITH THE EARTH...

...ALL KINDS OF THINGS I'M SURE DADDY WOULDN'T **APPROVE** OF.

OH...

WELL... **OKAY**, M-MAYBE WE DON'T **AGREE** ABOUT SOME THINGS. THAT DOESN'T MEAN WE COULDN'T BE **FRIENDS**, DOES IT?

WHY? YOU'VE GOT *PLENTY* OF FRIENDS. I *WATCH PEOPLE*, JORDAN, AND I *LISTEN*. THERE'S BEEN TALK AROUND THAT YOU HAD SOME KIND OF *"RELIGIOUS EXPERIENCE"* OR SOMETHING WHEN YOU ALMOST *DROWNED* THE OTHER NIGHT.

SO LET ME *GUESS*, YOU'RE TRYING TO *PROVE* YOU'RE A *"GOOD CHRISTIAN"* NOW BY MAKING FRIENDS WITH A *FREAK* LIKE ME, *RIGHT?*

TABBY--I-I... ...I THINK YOU MAY BE RIGHT...AT LEAST A LITTLE...

??!

I DON'T THINK I'VE LOOKED AT YOU *TWICE* SINCE 4TH GRADE. IT'S NOT LIKE I'VE *IGNORED* YOU, TABBY-- IT'S *WORSE* THAN THAT. YOU JUST DIDN'T *MATTER* TO ME.

I-I DON'T HAVE ANY *RIGHT* TO BOTHER YOU NOW...

JORDAN, *WAIT A MINUTE...*

JORDAN!

NOAH'S SISTER DIDN'T *COME HOME* LAST NIGHT! AND THEY HAVEN'T HEARD FROM HER *ALL DAY!*

WHAT? LUCY'S *GONE?*

THEY THINK SHE WAS *HANGING OUT* AT THE OLD HOLSOM BARN WITH THAT JAKE THE SNAKE GUY. AND *GET THIS--* THE BARN *BLEW UP* LAST NIGHT!

THEY'VE EVEN GOT COPS DOWN FROM THE CITY LOOKIN' INTO IT--SOMETHIN' ABOUT *ILLEGAL MOONSHINE* AN' STUFF. CAN YA *BELIEVE* IT?

I'VE GOTTA SEE *NOAH*...HE MUST BE ABOUT TO *LOSE IT...*

YEAH... NOAH AND LUCY *WERE*--I MEAN *ARE*--PRETTY CLOSE...

THANK YOU, *GOD*, FOR HELPING ME FIND THIS CABLE. I JUST *PRAY* IT LEADS TO SOMETHING... *ANYTHING*...

HOW *LONG* HAVE I BEEN DOWN HERE? MY MOM AND DAD ARE GONNA BE SO *SCARED*. AND NOAH... HE'LL BE *WORRIED*, TOO.

WHAT'S *THIS*? SOME KIND OF *MACHINE*? MAYBE...*PLEASE* LET IT BE A CONTROL PANEL OR SOMETHIN'...

I KNOW THERE ARE LIGHTS DOWN HERE...I JUST NEED TO FIND THE *RIGHT SWITCH*...

20

CLICK

YES!

WE HAVE LIGHT!

21

HOW MANY TIMES DO I HAVE TO *TELL YOU*, SHERIFF? LUCY WAS OUT THERE WITH THE REST OF US WHEN MR. RAYE SHOWED UP-- JUST *ASK* HIM OR MS. VILE-- THEY'LL TELL YOU THE *SAME THING*.

ALL THEY'VE SAID WAS THAT THERE *MIGHT* HAVE BEEN A YOUNGER GIRL WITH YOU. THEY'RE NOT *SURE*...

...BESIDES, YESTERDAY YOU TOLD MR. SIMMONS THAT LUCY *WASN'T* WITH YOU AT THE BARN. IN FACT, MR. SIMMONS SAID YOU WERE *ADAMANT* ABOUT THAT.

HOLSOM POLICE

WHY *CHANGE* YOUR STORY NOW?

LIKE I *SAID*--AT FIRST I DIDN'T WANT LUCY TO GET IN TROUBLE. W-WE *LIKED* HER.

SHE WAS KINDA LIKE OUR *SIDEKICK*, YA KNOW? AND A HECK OF A *GOOD* SPY.

BUT THEN I REALIZED...SHE WAS ALWAYS IN THE WAY, *KNOCKIN'* STUFF OVER... THE LITTLE TWERP PROBABLY *CAUSED* THE FIRE WHEN SHE TOOK OFF...

SAVE IT.

I KNOW *ALL ABOUT* YOU, JAKE HARDIGAN. I KNOW ABOUT THE VERY *MESSY DIVORCE* YOUR MOM AND DAD WENT THROUGH LAST YEAR, AND HOW NEITHER ONE OF THEM WANTED CUSTODY.

HOW NEITHER ONE OF THEM WANTED THE *BAGGAGE* OF A TEENAGE SON--EVEN ONE AS *WELL BEHAVED* AS YOU. SO YOUR AUNT TOOK YOU IN.

SHUT UP!

SHUT UP! YOU DON'T KNOW NUTHIN'! YOU DON'T KNOW NUTHIN' ABOUT ME!!

I KNOW YOUR WHOLE LIFE HAS BEEN NOTHING BUT A *LIE* SINCE YOU MOVED TO HOLSOM.

YOU'VE BEEN LIVING A *DOUBLE LIFE*--ACTING LIKE SOME KIND OF BIG-CITY *HOODLUM* AT SCHOOL, BUT CONVINCING YOUR AUNT YOU WERE A *PREPPY*, CITIZENSHIP-AWARD WINNER HEADED FOR LAW SCHOOL.

SHERIFF, YOU *CAN'T* TELL AUNT MYRTLE ABOUT ME. SHE TOOK ME IN WHEN *NO ONE* WANTED ME...I'VE ALREADY CAUSED HER ENOUGH *PROBLEMS* WITH THAT *GIANT RO*--I-I MEAN...

YOU WERE GOING TO SAY *"GIANT ROBOT,"* WEREN'T YOU, JAKE?

I DUNNO WHAT YOU'RE TALKING ABOUT.

RRRIGHT.

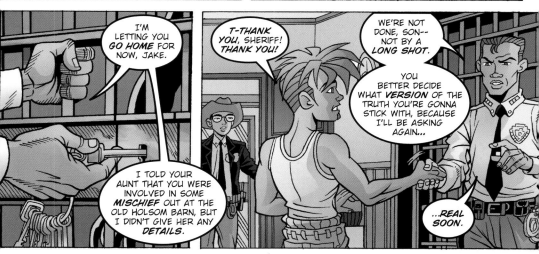

I'M LETTING YOU *GO HOME* FOR NOW, JAKE.

I TOLD YOUR AUNT THAT YOU WERE INVOLVED IN SOME *MISCHIEF* OUT AT THE OLD HOLSOM BARN, BUT I DIDN'T GIVE HER ANY *DETAILS.*

T-THANK YOU, SHERIFF! THANK YOU!

WE'RE NOT DONE, SON-- NOT BY A *LONG SHOT.*

YOU BETTER DECIDE WHAT *VERSION* OF THE TRUTH YOU'RE GONNA STICK WITH, BECAUSE I'LL BE ASKING AGAIN...

...REAL SOON.

YOU'RE NOT GONNA JUST LET HIM *GO,* ARE YA?

FOR NOW. HE WASN'T DOING *ANYONE* ANY GOOD SITTING IN A CELL...

I DON'T KNOW *EXACTLY* WHAT'S GOING ON AROUND HERE, BUT THAT BOY'S UP TO HIS *NECK* IN WHATEVER IT IS.

AND THIS *NEW GUY,* THIS JD RAYE FELLOW? HE'S GOT US ALL *DANCING* AROUND LIKE A BUNCH OF *PUPPETS.*

AND I *DON'T LIKE IT* ONE BIT...

ATTENNNTTION!!

koff koff koff

AFTER--AHEM--*EXTENSIVE* RESEARCH, IT SEEMS THAT YOU TWO --ER--*MEN*--ARE SUPPOSEDLY THE *BEST HUNTERS* IN THE FOUR-COUNTY AREA, RIGHT?

YES'M.

THAT'S ACCORDIN' TA OUR *THIRD COUSIN,* OTTO, MA'AM.

I AM *NOT* YER COUSIN, RALPH.

WELL, 'COURSE I KNOW *THAT*--I'M RALPH --*YOU'RE* OTTO, SILLY...

YER AN *IDJIT,* YA KNOW THAT?

WHOP!

MOMMA ALWAYS SAID OTTO HERE WUZ OUR *FOURTH* COUSIN, ONCE REMOVED...

REMOVED FROM *WHERE,* RUBEN?

GROANNN...

24

...YOU KNOW YOU'RE TOO *VALUABLE* TO OUR EFFORT TO PLACE IN *HARM'S WAY* LIKE THAT. WHY, UP UNTIL A DAY AGO, YOU WERE PROBABLY THE *ONLY LIVING EYEWITNESS* TO HORATIO HOLSOM'S METAL MONSTROSITY.

WE *NEED* YOU HERE, HELPING US WITH OUR *STRATEGY*...

WELL...WHEN YOU PUT IT LIKE *THAT*... I JUS' WANNA SEE THEM KIDS BACK HOME *SAFE* N'SOUND.

AS DO WE *ALL*, MR. FARLESS. AS DO WE *ALL*.

JUST REMEMBER...*GENTLEMEN*... IF YOU FIND THE ROBOT OR THE BOYS, DO *NOT* APPROACH THEM. I'VE GIVEN YOU BOTH *GPS** TRACKING DEVICES THAT YOU CAN USE TO *SIGNAL* US WHEN YOU'VE FOUND SOMETHING.

THEN WE'LL MOVE A TEAM IN TO *"CLEAN UP."* UNDERSTOOD...?

*GLOBAL POSITIONING SYSTEM--EDITOR

SEVERAL MINUTES LATER...

NEVER *SHOT* ME NO *ROBOT* BEFORE, RUBEN. KINDA LOOKIN' FEWARD TO IT.

NOW DIDN'T YA'LL *HEAR* WHAT MISS VILE SAID ABOUT *NOT* KILLIN' IT?

AWWW, RUBEN, DON'T YA'LL KNOW NUTHIN'? YA CAN'T REALLY *KILL* A ROBOT--IT'S JUS' A *MACHINE*...

26

CRAIG W. SCHUTT~STORY & LETTERS   GORDON PURCELL~PENCILS
JEFF ALBRECHT~INKS   DANIEL BURTON~COLORS   SINDA S. ZINN~EDITS

"DELIVERANCE!"

"Now Moses was tending the flock of Jethro his father-in-law, the priest of Midian, and he led the flock to the far side of the desert and came to Horeb, the mountain of God. There the angel of the LORD appeared to him in flames of fire from within a bush.

Moses saw that though the bush was on fire it did not burn up. So Moses thought, "I will go over and see this strange sight—why the bush does not burn up."

"When the LORD saw that he had gone over to look, God called to him from within the bush, 'Moses! Moses!'

And Moses said, 'Here I am.'"*

*SEE EXODUS 3:1-4!
--EDITOR

RRRIIGHT. A BUSH THAT'S ON *FIRE*, BUT DOESN'T *BURN UP*. LIKE THAT *REALLY* HAPPENED.

WE ASKED FOR A *CAMPFIRE* STORY, ROVER--*NOT* SOME SUNDAY SCHOOL LESSON.

I thought it appropriate for our current situation.

HOW'S THAT?

We are undoubtably pursued by entities of unknown origin and number who intend to deliver this unit and Horatio Holsom's journal into the hands of JD Raye, a person of dubious purpose.

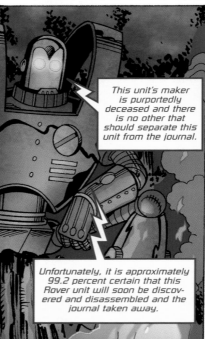

This unit's maker is purportedly deceased and there is no other that should separate this unit from the journal.

Unfortunately, it is approximately 99.2 percent certain that this Rover unit will soon be discovered and disassembled and the journal taken away.

SO TELL US SOMETHING WE DON'T *ALREADY* KNOW. AND I STILL DON'T SEE HOW THIS HAS *ANYTHING* TO DO THAT MOSES STORY...

I **GET IT**. IT'S THE .8 PERCENT FACTOR OF UNCERTAINTLY, RIGHT?

Yes. We require a deliverer.

THINK WE CAN ROUND UP ENOUGH **FROGS** FOR A PLAGUE? SOUNDS LIKE OUR ROBOT'S DEVELOPIN' A SENSE OF **FAITH** OR SOMETHIN', EINSTEIN...

HA!

SHUTTUP, JORGE.

ROVER MEANS THAT IT'LL TAKE A **MIRACLE** OF SO-CALLED "BIBLICAL PROPORTIONS" TO GET US OUT OF THIS MESS.

This unit is incapable of faith. This unit can only process information and react appropriately.

When all probable outcomes have been assessed, there always remains unforseeable potentials, no matter how remote.

DID HE JUST SAY WHAT I **THINK** HE JUST SAID?

YEAH, I THINK HE **DID**. "THERE'S ALWAYS **HOPE**," RIGHT, ROVER?

Affirmative.

29

ALRIGHT, THEN!

GROUP "A," SWING YER MEN TA THE NORTH-WEST O' HERE. GROUP "B," FOLLOW THE CREEK DIRECTLY WEST. "C" GROUP, SWEEP SOUTH AN' SOUTHWEST TOWARDS TOWN...

WHO PUT YOU IN CHARGE, RAYE?

YOU'VE GOT A LOT OF GALL EVEN SHOWING UP HERE, SEEING AS HOW YOU'VE ACCUSED LUCY OF HELPING BURN THIS OLD BARN DOWN BEFORE RUNNING AWAY!

G-GENTLEMEN, PLEASE...I NEVAH ACCUSED LITTLE MISS LUCY OF ANYTHIN'!

IT WAS THAT SCOUNDREL, JAKE "THE SNAKE" THAT MADE SUCH INFLAMMA-TORY--AND NO DOUBT ERRONEOUS-- REMARKS.

AH AM HERE TA HELP!

MR. LANCASTER, MR. SIMMONS. THIS WON'T HELP US FIND LUCY.

EVERYONE'S UNDERSTANDABLY ON EDGE.

BUT I THINK WE WOULD WELCOME ANY ABLE-BODIED HELP WE COULD GET, AND MR. RAYE HAS BROUGHT SOME MUCH NEEDED EQUIPMENT AND MANPOWER WITH HIM...

...EVERYONE IS ANXIOUS TO HELP, MR. LANCASTER. HALF THE TOWN HAS TURNED OUT HERE ON A SATURDAY MORNING TO HELP LOOK FOR LUCY. IF SHE'S LOST IN THE VICINITY, WE'LL FIND HER, OKAY?

J-JUST A *LITTLE BIT* FARTHER...

M-MADE IT.

I-I MADE IT...

C-C-COLD... SO *COLD*...

SWEET TEXAS!

IT'S HER!

HEY! EVERYBODY!! I FOUND HER!!

THERE THERE, LITTLE MISSY. EVERYTHIN'S GONNA BE *ALRIGHT.*

C-COLD. C-COLD...

OF COURSE YOUR COLD-- YER *DRENCHED,* GIRL...

N-NO. THEIR *SKIN*...COLD *METAL* SKIN... SO *COLD*...

METAL *WHAT?*

CRY WOLF!"

SCRIPT & LETTERS: CRAIG W. SCHUTT
PENCILS: STEVEN BUTLER
INKS: AL MILGROM
COLOR: CRAIG & MARSHA SCHUTT
EDITS: SINDA S. ZINN

SO...**WHAT** IS IT? A MOUNTAIN LION, MAYBE?

IT **CAN'T** BE...

YOU'RE GETTIN' THAT "I KNOW **SOMETHING** YOU DON'T KNOW" LOOK, EINSTEIN-- **WHAT'S UP?**

THE GOOD NEWS IS...I THINK I KNOW **WHERE** WE'RE AT.

I'D SAY THAT WAS **GREAT** NEWS, CONSIDERING ROVER'S GLOBAL POSITIONING WHATCHAMA-CALLIT GOT **BUSTED** WHEN WE **BROKE OUT** OF HORATIO'S HIDEOUT.

YEAH...BUT THE **BAD NEWS** IS, I THINK WE'RE NEAR **BARN HOL-LOW**--A LITTLE TOWN 'BOUT 40-45 MILES NORTHWEST OF HOLSOM.

I THINK THAT RIDGE WE JUST CAME DOWN FROM IS CALLED **BARTON HILL** 'ROUND HERE.

WHY DOES THAT SOUND **FAMILIAR?** SOME KINDA **LEGEND** 'BOUT A **HAIRY** BLUE MAN WITH GLOWIN' EYES...

IT'S AN **OLD** STORY-- GOES BACK TO THE DAYS WHEN **INDIANS** LIVED IN THESE PARTS.

DETAILS VARY, LIKE IN ALL **URBAN LEGENDS**, BUT...**HEY**--WHAT'S THAT **SOUND?**

ROVER!

WHERE'S HE GOIN'?

SOMEONE'S COMING!

I HEAR **SCREAMS!**

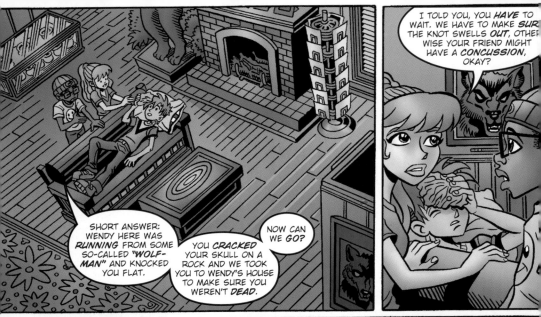

I TOLD YOU, YOU *HAVE* TO WAIT. WE HAVE TO MAKE *SURE* THE KNOT SWELLS *OUT*, OTHERWISE YOUR FRIEND MIGHT HAVE A *CONCUSSION*, OKAY?

SHORT ANSWER: WENDY HERE WAS *RUNNING* FROM SOME SO-CALLED *"WOLFMAN"* AND KNOCKED YOU FLAT.

YOU *CRACKED* YOUR SKULL ON A ROCK AND WE TOOK YOU TO WENDY'S HOUSE TO MAKE SURE YOU WEREN'T *DEAD*.

NOW CAN WE *GO*?

B-BUT...

NO ARGUMENTS.

I'LL GO WARM UP SOME POTATO SOUP I MADE EARLIER. YOU BOTH LOOK LIKE YOU COULD USE A *HOT MEAL.*

FEEL FREE TO *BROWSE* AROUND MY DAD'S *"BLUE WOLF"* MUSEUM...

SOUP SOUNDS *GREAT* TO ME. HAVEN'T HAD A HOT MEAL IN OVER A DAY...

WE'RE TRYING TO *HIDE*, REMEMBER? GIANT ROBOT, JD RAYE, HORATIO HOLSOM? DOES ANY OF THAT *RING* A BELL?

HEY--WHERE *IS* ROVER, ANYWAY?

HE *FOLLOWED* US HERE AT A SAFE DISTANCE. HE'S PROBABLY *WATCHING* US FROM THE WOODS...

HEH...HOPE HE DOESN'T RUN INTO THIS *"BLUE WOLF"* DUDE...

ARROOOOO

AAARRR-- EH?

CUT THE *THEATRICS*, LONNIE AND GET BACK TO THE HOUSE *RIGHT NOW!*

AWWW, DAD...IT'S STILL EARLY...

FOR SOME *INSANE* REASON, YOUR SISTER JUST BROUGHT *TWO KIDS* INTO THE MUSEUM. IT'S TOO *RISKY* FOR YOU TO STAY OUT ANY LONGER TONIGHT.

DID YOU *HEAR ME,* LONNIE? I SAID *RIGHT NOW!*

UBABUBBABABBA...

...LONNIE?

43

AAAAAIIIIIEEEE!

THANKS, WENDY.

NO PROB. YOU'D THINK YOU GUYS HADN'T EATEN IN *DAYS*. I GUESS "LIVING OFF THE LAND" ISN'T VERY *FILLING*, EH?

SAY *WHAT?*

BLUE WOLF MUSEUM

OH...UMM...I-I TOLD WENDY ALL ABOUT OUR *"SCOUTING EXCUR-SION"*...H-HOW WE HAVE TO *ROUGH IT* FOR A COUPLE OF DAYS TO EARN OUR--ER...

..."BACKWOODS *HONOR BADGE* CERTIFICATES?"

"BACKWOODS HONOR BADGE?" *HEHE*--WENDY, YOU DIDN'T *BUY* ANY OF THAT *LAME-O* STORY, DID YOU?

NOT FOR A MINUTE.

LOOK. *TRUTH IS*, WE BOTH *RAN AWAY* FROM HOME. MY DAD'S A DRUNKEN *BUM* AND MOUSE'S PARENTS TOTALLY *IGNORE* HIM. SO WE JUST TOOK OFF--WE DON'T KNOW *WHERE* WE'RE GOIN' OR HOW *LONG* IT'LL TAKE TO GET THERE.

WE JUST DON'T WANT TO GO *BACK*, YOU KNOW?

MAN, I'D BE TOO *SCARED* TO EVER RUN AWAY... IF MY DAD GOT *MAD*...

WENDY!

YIPES!

HEY!

I... NOTICED YOU HAD...*COMPANY*, WENDY.

MY FRIEND GOT A PRETTY BAD *BUMP* ON HIS HEAD, SIR, AND WENDY WAS KIND ENOUGH TO *HELP* US OUT.

HE'LL BE FINE.

WE WERE *CHASED* BY THE BLUE WOLF, DADDY... AND I *RAN INTO* JORGE AND KNOCKED HIM CLEAN *OUT COLD*...

HOW MANY *TIMES* DO I HAVE TO TELL YOU GIRL? DO *NOT* VENTURE TOWARD BARTON HILL *AFTER DARK!*

YES, DADDY...

SO...WHAT DO YOU BOYS *THINK* OF MY MUSEUM? I'VE BEEN *STUDYING* THE BLUE WOLF OF BARN HOLLOW FOR ALMOST TEN YEARS--COLLECTED EVERY ARTICLE WRITTEN ABOUT THE *VARMIT*, AND BROUGHT TOGETHER A GOOD AMOUNT OF *EVIDENCE*, AS WELL.

I'M ALMOST *FINISHED* WRITING A *BOOK* ABOUT THE LEGEND.

THE *CRITTER'S* BEEN UNUSUALLY *ACTIVE* LATELY. I'M HOPING I CAN AT LEAST GET A *PHOTO* OF IT--THAT WOULD PROBABLY BE GOOD FOR ANOTHER *200,000* BOOKS SOLD, DON'T YA--

DAD! DAD!

DAD, YOU'RE NOT GONNA *BELIEVE* IT! I-IT'S *REAL!*

AT LEAST 10 FEET TALL WITH *GLOWING* EYES-- *METAL* FROM HEAD TO TOE...

METAL?

Y-YES, DADDY...

WENDY--YOU MAKE SURE THESE BOYS FIND THEIR WAY *HOME*. AND THEN *STAY* IN THE HOUSE, YOU *HEAR?*

YOU DID *WHAT?!*

I-I GUESS I *DROPPED* MY MASK WHEN I *TOOK OFF...*

I THINK YOU'RE LETTING THESE *CRAZY* BLUE-WOLF LEGENDS GET TO YOU, SON. MAYBE *I'LL* WEAR THE *COSTUME* FROM NOW ON...

YOU KNOW, I KIND OF *WISH* I COULD GO WITH YOU GUYS.

MY DAD'S NOT A *BAD* GUY, BUT HE'S ALWAYS COMIN' UP WITH THE NEXT *CRAZY* GET-RICH-QUICK SCHEME. TENDS TO GET HIM IN *TROUBLE...*

SOUNDS LIKE SOMEONE *I* KNOW...

MY DAD IS SO *GOOD* AT *LYING,* I DON'T EVEN KNOW IF HE REALIZES WHAT THE *TRUTH* IS ANYMORE.

Y-YEAH... THAT'S *ROUGH...*

SCARY THING IS...LONNIE'S STARTING TO *ACT* A LOT LIKE DADDY, AND I'M *AFRAID* I'LL END UP LIKE *THEM,* YOU KNOW?

I ALWAYS THOUGHT *MOM* WAS THE STABLE ONE. SHE TOOK US TO *CHURCH*--DID ALL THE RIGHT THINGS, YOU KNOW? THEN ONE MORNING WE WAKE UP AND SHE'S *GONE.*

TURNS OUT SHE HAD BEEN *LIVING A LIE* FOR A LONG TIME.

I CAN *RELATE.* MY DAD LOST HIS JOB, STARTED DRINKIN'...THAT WAS BAD ENOUGH. BUT MOM JUST *GAVE UP* ON HIM AND TOOK OFF.

BOOM!

WHAT WAS *THAT?*

BETTER STOP YER *SHOOTIN'*, RALPH--WHATEVER'S OUT THAR SURE AIN'T NO *RO-BOT.* AIN'T NO *WOLF MAN,* NEITHER...

MAYBE *NOT,* RUBEN--BUT CALL ME A CROSS-EYED COONDOG IF'N THERE AIN'T *SOMETHIN'* HIDIN' IN THE WOODS HERE...

YA *AIN'T WRONG,* BROTHER. IF I SMELLS RIGHTLY, I B'LIEVE THERE'S *TWO FELLERS* CROUCHED DOWN IN THEM BUSHES OVER THAR.

EARL'S WELDING

BUBBA'S GAS MAKE 'S GO

WH-WHAT ARE WE GONNA *DO,* DAD?

GIVE ME A *MOMENT* TO THINK...

WHAT IF THEY *FOUND* ROVER?

WHO'S *ROVER?*

UMM...HE'S ANOTHER...ER...*KID* THAT RAN AWAY WITH US...

KLANG!

SSSHHHH!

IT'S *OKAY!* IT'S *OKAY!*

HE'S WITH *US!*

BUTBUTBUTBUT...

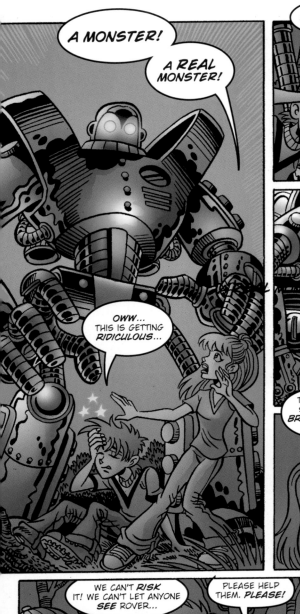

A MONSTER!

A REAL MONSTER!

OWW... THIS IS GETTING *RIDICULOUS...*

Situation analysis: Distance: 400 yards north-by-north-west. Two men, one armed, appear to have trapped two other men, one wearing some form of wolf facsimile costume...The weapon has been discharged...

OH, NO!

THE GUY IN THE WOLF SUIT'S GOT TO BE MY *BROTHER,* LONNIE! WE'VE GOTTA *HELP* THEM!

WE CAN'T *RISK* IT! WE CAN'T LET ANYONE *SEE* ROVER...

PLEASE HELP THEM. *PLEASE!*

AWWW, *MANNN...*

WE'LL HELP THEM, OKAY?

I *PROMISE...*

NOW THIS'LL GO A HEAP *EASIER* FOR YOU'NS IF'N YA JUST COME OUT NOW.

BROTHER RALPH HERE HAS A MIGHTY *ITCHY* TRIGGER FINGER...

BUBBA'S GAS

EARL'S WELDING

DAD, WE *GOTTA* GIVE OURSELVES UP!

AND THEN EVERYONE WILL KNOW THE *TRUTH* ABOUT THE BLUE WOLF!

NO *BOOK DEAL!* NO *MONEY!*

IS THAT WHAT YOU *WANT?*

WHAT I WANT IS TO *NOT* GET SHOT!

WHUMP

YOU'VE GOTTA BE *KIDDIN'* ME...

49

50

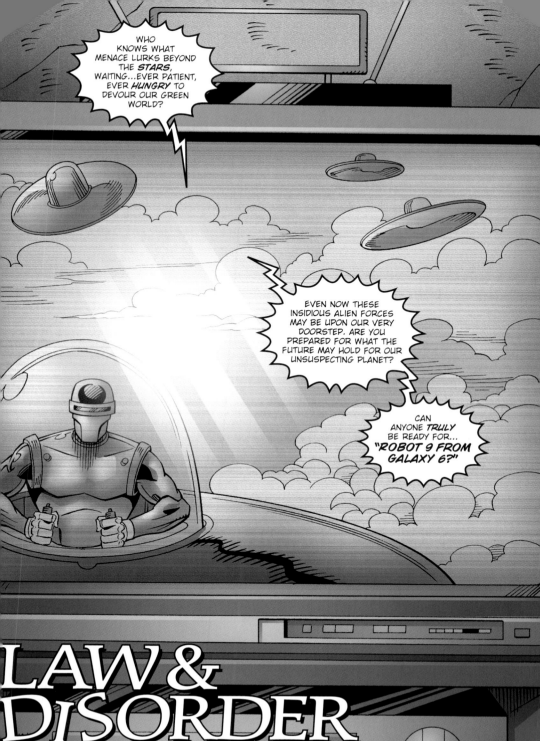

LAW & DISORDER

SCRIPT & LETTERS: CRAIG W. SCHUTT • PENCILS: GORDON PURCELL
INKS: JEFF ALBRECHT • COLOR: CRAIG & MARSHA SCHUTT
EDITS: SINDA S. ZINN

I moved to Holsom from the city, hoping to get away from the craziness and nutcases. So much for that plan.

Even though it looks insane when I type the words, I can't just ignore the evidence. Somewhere...I think not too far away...two kids are running around the countryside with a (and I can hardly bring myself to admit it)...a giant robot...

Best just to go over the facts again.

Item one: About 40 years ago, a reclusive old scientist named Horatio Holsom (they named the town after his family) lived around here and suddenly disappeared.

Item two: Sometime shortly before Horatio vanished, a backwoods kid named Otto Farless, who lived near the old Holsom barn, said he stumbled into a nest of "giant, metal men" who he thought were invaders from outer space or something...everybody around here thinks he's a kook...

53

Item three: Earlier this month, a gang of bank robbers crashed their getaway plane near here. The pilot kept saying he had to dodge some kind of "flying giant robot."

Item four: Several days ago, during a storm that almost wiped the town off the map, a few crazy kids were miraculously saved from drowning in a flooded creek.

One of them described seeing eyes as "bright and big as headlights."

Item five: According to at least three eyewitnesses, that same night some kind of giant metal man attacked Jake "the Snake" and frightened his aunt so badly she needed medical attention.

Good ol' Otto was there—said he had tracked the thing and finally had photos of "the monster."

Item six: The very next morning a Texas real estate magnate named JD Raye flies into town in his private Lear Jet and begins to throw money around and offers to rebuild the town.

But he seems to have a special interest in Horatio Holsom's old property and immediately begins to pull strings to purchase the land...

Item seven: I had confiscated Otto's camera and taken the so-called photos to be developed, but the local photo lab said the film in the camera was too old.

Conveniently, none of the pictures could be developed...

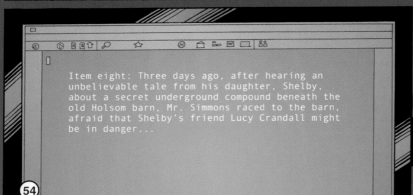

Item eight: Three days ago, after hearing an unbelievable tale from his daughter, Shelby, about a secret underground compound beneath the old Holsom barn, Mr. Simmons raced to the barn, afraid that Shelby's friend Lucy Crandall might be in danger...

He arrived just in time to see a strange vapor trail coming from the blazing roof of the barn and vanishing into the western sky...

Item nine: It just so happens that JD Raye and his lawyer flunky, Constance Vile, were at the barn when it blew up. According to them, they were inspecting the property and discovered Jake and some other kids had an illegal still of some kind set up in the barn, which accidently exploded while they were there.

Item ten: Jake takes the fall and alleges Lucy was not only involved in their scheme, she actually caused the explosion. Meanwhile, JD Raye makes sure that Jake's aunt's medical bills are completly covered and her house repaired...

Item eleven: The crime lab team from the city does a very brief inspection of the scene and verifies JD and Jake's stories.

KLICK!

But after disappearing for over a day, Lucy reappears near the old barn site, insisting she had escaped the underground compound by finding her way through a maze of caverns, where she was chased by two "evil robots."

Item twelve: According to Lucy, two boys— Theodore "Mouse" Johnson and Jorge Martinez, both narrowly escaped JD Raye by hitching a ride with their friend, "Rover," evidently a "good" robot. It was their escape route through the compound's ceiling and the barn that actually destroyed the site...

Final item: Neither Theodore nor Jorge have been in school this week, and their parents had no idea they were missing.

So, as impossible as it seems, I've got two missing kids running around with a giant robot, and a very crafty, very powerful Texas businessman somehow knee-deep in this mess.

I can't bring anyone else into this—they'd take my badge and probably lock me away—and I'm not sure I'd blame them.

Guess I've got no choice but to try to find those boys on my own. Then I'm moving back to the city, where things are a lot more normal...

Can't wait to get out of this backwater hole and get back to the city where things are a lot more normal...

I never asked for this assignment. But when the great JD Raye says jump, you don't even ask how high...you just jump.

But if JD can pull this one off—and I'm beginning to think that's a big "if."—I'll be set for life—I won't owe Mr. Raye any more favors. And with everything I know about his connection to old Horatio Holsom and his crazy Cold War robots, JD will have to let me go.

Trouble is, JD's obsession with Horatio's artificial intelligence programming has made him careless. Just hope his money can cover up his mistakes. That's always worked for him in the past...

I'm too scared to sleep.

Every time I close my eyes I see those horrible robots coming after me. How could Horatio have created such awful things?

Are Shelby and Noah right about Rover? Is he dangerous too?

Pastor Jenkins and my mom and dad keep saying how thankful we should be to God for saving me from those things in the caves, and I am thankful—there's no way I could have got away without God's help.

I always try to do the right thing. So why has everything turned out so rotten? Jake "the Snake" is telling these awful lies about me. I'm afraid those robots are coming to get me. I'm worried about what will happen to Mouse...and even Jorge.

The truth is...I know it's not God's fault that we're in this mess. We were stupid to get involved with all that Horatio Holsom stuff.

Pastor Jenkins and my mom and dad keep saying how they should be to God for saving me from those things in the caves, and I am thankful—there's no way I could have got away without God's help.

God didn't give up on me and I'm not gonna give up on Him...

God didn't give up on me, and I'm not gonna give up on Him...

Horatio's Journal: I fear the end is near. I may finally have to give up on my plans. No one understands that what I am doing is for the good of mankind. Even my former partners have turned against me...

Horatio's Journal: Only I was willing to do what had to be done. Only I dreamed of a new utopia far beneath the surface world, where I could protect the survivors of the coming nuclear holocaust and insure that the human race would endure...

Horatio's Journal: Others would take my work from me and use it for dire purposes, as weapons to hurl against "the enemy." This cannot be.

I have exhausted the last of my family's fortune to plant false clues, to build several other compounds that would seem much more likely to house my genius than this unlikely location.

Sadly, I must go away, probably never to return...

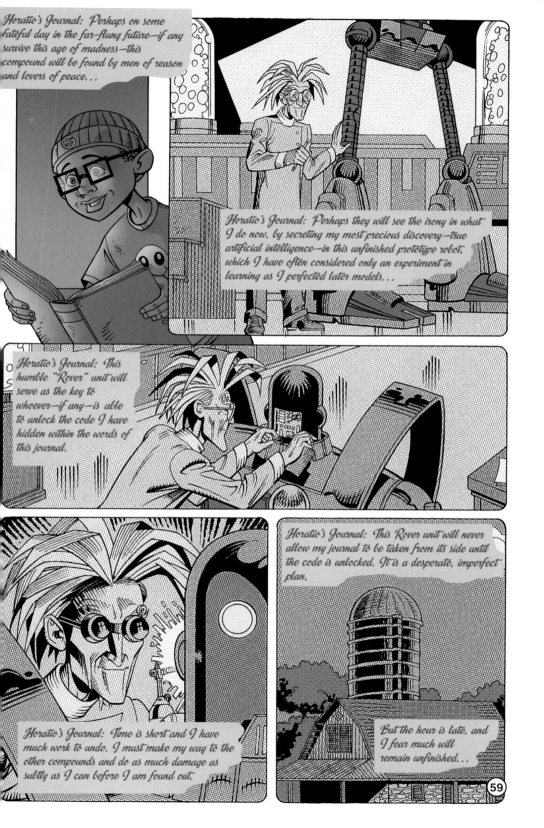

WOWSERS. SO THE CODE IS IN THE JOURNAL, AND ROVER'S THE **KEY** TO THE CODE...

W-WHATYASAY?

NOTHIN'. I DIDN'T SAY **NOTHIN'**.

HUH. MUST'VE BEEN **DREAMIN'**.

THAT CRAZY BLUE WOLF THING WAS AFTER US, AND THOSE HILLBILLY HUNTERS WUZ WITH HIM...HEY-- THAT WENDY WARREN GIRL WAS REAL **NICE** TO NOT TELL HER DAD ABOUT US, HUH?

THAT'S WHAT **I'D** HAVE DONE TOO, IF A 12-FOOT TALL **ROBOT** WAS GLARIN' DOWN AT ME...

In the deep woods where a man can walk miles still today without seeing another human being, the old legends stubbornly persist...

~~Blue Wolf of Barn Hollow~~
The Metal Man from Barton Hill
An investigation by Wesley Warren

Even in the deep woods of the American Midwest, the old legends fade as technology brings the light of reason to even the darkest corners. But sometimes that same technology can create the stuff of new legends. Such is the case with the "Metal Man from Barton Hill," a relative newcomer to these hills I call home. It is this strange visitor, which some claim resembles a "giant robot" straight out of an old, low-budget film from the fifties, that I now turn my attention to...

62

"FEAR FACTORS!"

Story & Lettering: Craig W. Schutt   Penciling: Steven Butler

Inking: Jeff Albrecht Coloring: Craig & Marsha Schutt

Editing: Sinda S. Zinn

"YEEEE"

LUCY!

ARE YOU ALRIGHT?

WE'RE *HERE*, HONEY!

IT WAS JUST ANOTHER *NIGHTMARE*, LUCY--YOU'RE *SAFE*--I *PROMISE*.

I-IT WAS THAT *HORRIBLE* ROBOT THING AGAIN. LIKE SOME BIG, METAL *BUG*. I-IT WAS IN MY *CL-CLOSET* AND-AND THEN...

IT'S *OKAY*, HONEY. THERE'S *NOTHING* THERE, REMEMBER?

I KNOW, MOM. I CAN'T *HELP* IT...THEY'RE STILL *DOWN* THERE, UNDER THE OLD BARN. WHAT IF THEY COME *AFTER* ME?

GIVE IT *TIME*, DEAR--IT'S ONLY BEEN A COUPLE OF DAYS SINCE YOU GOT OUT OF THAT HORRIBLE CAVE. *GOD* KEPT YOU SAFE THEN, AND BROUGHT YOU *BACK* SAFELY TO US.

HE'LL *KEEP* YOU SAFE NOW, TOO, OKAY?

MY-MY *HEART* WANTS TO *BELIEVE* THAT, MOM. BUT MY *HEAD* SAYS THIS ISN'T OVER YET...

65

EDGAR ALLAN POE
"THE RAVEN" Deep into that darkness Peering, long I st there wondering, fearing doubting

SO...**POE** HAS BUILT UP A LOT OF **SUSPENSE** BY THIS PART OF THE POEM. HAS ANYONE HERE EVER BEEN **AFRAID?**

YOU MEAN LIKE BEING AFRAID OF THE **DARK?** NOT **ME,** NOSIREE.

BESIDES, IT'S JUST SOME **STUPID BIRD** IN THE POEM... I DON'T KNOW WHY THE DUDE'S SO **CREEPED** OUT ANYWAY.

TABITHA, CAN YOU TELL ME **WHY**--AS DILLON SO **ELOQUENTLY** PUT IT--"THE **DUDE**" IN THE POEM WAS SO "CREEPED OUT?"

WELL, YEAH...IT'S LIKE THIS GUY'S WIFE OR GIRLFRIEND HAD **DIED** AND THE BIRD IN THE DARKNESS WAS LIKE **DEATH** OR A MESSENGER FROM DEATH OR SOMETHIN' **COOL** LIKE THAT.

VERY **GOOD,** TABITHA. SO YOU THINK THE RAVEN IS "**COOL?**" IT DOESN'T **SCARE** YOU?

WELL...**NO.** WHY **SHOULD** IT?

I THINK THE DARK IS **BEAUTIFUL**-- YOU KNOW, **MYSTERIOUS,** EXCITING...NOT SO **ORDINARY,** I GUESS.

AND I THINK MR. EDGAR ALLAN POE WOULD HAVE **AGREED** WITH YOU, TABITHA, SO YOU'RE IN **GOOD COMPANY**...

66

..."GOOD COMPANY," EH? DIDN'T THAT POE GUY END UP BROKE, DRUNK, AND DEAD?

HMMM? YEAH...I THINK SO.

NOAH--BUDDY--WHAT'S WITH THE ZOMBIE ROUTINE? YOU FEELIN' OKAY?

YEAH...JUST A LITTLE TIRED, IS ALL.

LUCY WAS UP AGAIN WITH NIGHTMARES, WASN'T SHE? IT'S ALL SO UNBELIEVABLE-- MAD SCIENTISTS AND GIANT ROBOTS--AND NOW MOUSE AND THAT JORGE KID ARE MISSING TOO. IT'S ENOUGH TO GIVE ANYONE NIGHTMARES.

I THINK EVERYONE NEEDS TO GET A GRIP. I MEAN, C'MON...WHAT IS THIS--A COMIC BOOK OR SOMETHIN'? SO OL' HORATIO WAS A LITTLE STRANGE...SO HE BUILT SOME WEIRD TOYS IN HIS BASEMENT...NO BIG DEAL.

THAT OTTO FARLESS IS PLENTY STRANGE TOO, AN' WE LET HIM IN CHURCH LAST WEEK! AND I BET THOSE TWO "MISSING" KIDS JUST RAN AWAY FROM HOME. FROM WHAT I HEAR ABOUT JORGE'S DAD, THAT'S WHAT I'D DO...

AND I'M SURPRISED ANYONE'S NOTICED THAT MOUSE GEEK IS MISSING.

I MEAN, I DIDN'T EVEN REALIZE HE STILL WENT TO SCHOOL HERE!

AT LEAST HE HAD SOME FRIENDS--YOU KNOW, FELLOW GEEK-STERS--TO HANG OUT WITH.

IF "ASTROLOGY GIRL" BACK THERE WENT AWAY, WHO WOULD EVEN NOTICE?

YOU KNOW *WHAT*, DILLON?

I WOULD.

I WOULD NOTICE.

WHAT WAS *THAT* ALL ABOUT? JORDAN HASN'T BEEN ACTING LIKE HER *OLD SELF* SINCE THAT NIGHT WE ALMOST *DROWNED.*

YOU THINK MAYBE SHE GOT *WHACKED* ON THE HEAD TOO *HARD* OR SOMETHIN'?

YOU JUST *DON'T GET IT*, DO YOU, DILLON?

YOU ALMOST *DIED* IN COLD SPRING CREEK TOO. DIDN'T THAT MAKE YOU *WONDER* ABOUT WHERE YOU *STAND* WITH *GOD?*

HEY-- I'M AS *GOOD* AS THE NEXT GUY. BETTER 'N *MOST,* IN FACT.

I GO TO *CHURCH* EVERY SUNDAY.

I ATTEND THE *YOUTH ACTIVITIES,* DON'T I?

HAVE YOU EVER ACTUALLY *LISTENED* TO A *SINGLE MESSAGE* THE PASTOR HAS *PREACHED,* DILLON?

I *WORRY* ABOUT YOU...

I *SWEAR,* EVERYONE IN THIS *WHOLE TOWN* IS GOIN' *CRAZY...*

68

I'M *TELLIN' YA*, THE MAN'S *CRAZY* IF HE THINKS WE CAN GET THROUGH HERE!

SSSHHHHHH!

HE MIGHT *HEAR* YOU...

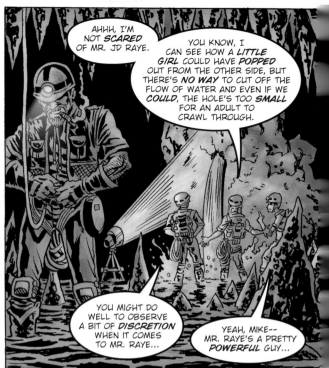

AHHH, I'M NOT *SCARED* OF MR. JD RAYE.

YOU KNOW, I CAN SEE HOW A *LITTLE GIRL* COULD HAVE *POPPED* OUT FROM THE OTHER SIDE, BUT THERE'S *NO WAY* TO CUT OFF THE FLOW OF WATER AND EVEN IF WE *COULD*, THE HOLE'S TOO *SMALL* FOR AN ADULT TO CRAWL THROUGH.

YOU MIGHT DO WELL TO OBSERVE A BIT OF *DISCRETION* WHEN IT COMES TO MR. RAYE...

YEAH, MIKE-- MR. RAYE'S A PRETTY *POWERFUL* GUY...

LISTEN TO YOU GUYS, *SHAKIN'* IN YOUR SNEAKERS.

JD RAYE PUTS HIS PANTS ON ONE LEG AT A TIME, JUST LIKE THE *REST* OF US...

ACTUALLY...

...AH *PAY* SOMEONE A *LARGE* AMOUNT OF MONEY TA *SELECT* MY PANTS EACH AND EVERY DAY O' THE YEAR. THEY ALSO *POLISH* MY $10,000 COWBOY BOOTS AND *WAX* MY FIVE $140,000 HUMMERS.

UNTIL ABOUT *THIRTY SECONDS AGO*, AH WAS ALSO PAYIN' YOU A *COMFORTABLE SALARY...*

...YOU'RE FIRED!

KERSPLASH

AH JUST NEVAH GET *TIRED* O' SAYIN' THAT...

WHAT IS *WRONG WITH YOU?* WHAT DID SHE EVER *DO TO YOU?*

*HEY--*IT'S JUST PART OF THE *GAME,* JENKINS. AND WE *BOTH KNOW* SHE WAS NEVER A PLAYER TO BEGIN WITH. WATCH IT OR YOU MIGHT BE *NEXT...*

IS THERE A *PROBLEM* HERE, GIRLS?

NO MA'AM.

YOU'RE GONNA HAVE QUITE A *SHINER,* MISS TALON. JORDAN, GO WITH TABBY TO THE NURSE'S OFFICE.

O-OKAY...

TABBY-- ASHLEY'S *WRONG--* I DO *NOT* THINK YOU'RE A LOSER.

OH, C'MON, JORDAN--YOU REALLY KINDA *DO.*

BUT YOU KNOW-- I THINK YOU MIGHT ACTUALLY CONSIDER ME *WORTH* "SAVING." ASHLEY COULDN'T *CARE LESS.*

I GUESS THAT *COUNTS* FOR SOMETHIN'...

NURSES OFFICE

72

Caution. Unidentified small human unit approaching 20 degrees south-by-southwest at approximately .09 miles per hour...

WHAT IF IT'S ONE OF JD RAYE'S *GOONS*?

DIDN'T YOU *LISTEN*? ROVER SAID IT WAS A *SMALL* PERSON. AND YOU'RE LOOKING *NORTHWEST*, JORGE... I THOUGHT YOU SAID YOUR DAD USED TO TAKE YOU CAMPING.

HE *DID*. HE ALSO SAID I WAS LIKE MY *MOM*: "ABSOLUTELY *NO* SENSE OF DIRECTION."

Affirmitive.

ROVER--SEE IF YOU CAN'T *GRAB* WHOEVER'S COMING. BUT, BE *CAREFUL*...

STILL GIVIN' METALHEAD HIS MARCHIN' *ORDERS*, EH, EINSTEIN? I THINK THAT GOT US INTO THIS *MESS* IN THE FIRST--

SSSSHHHH!

I THINK HE'S *FOUND* SOMEONE...

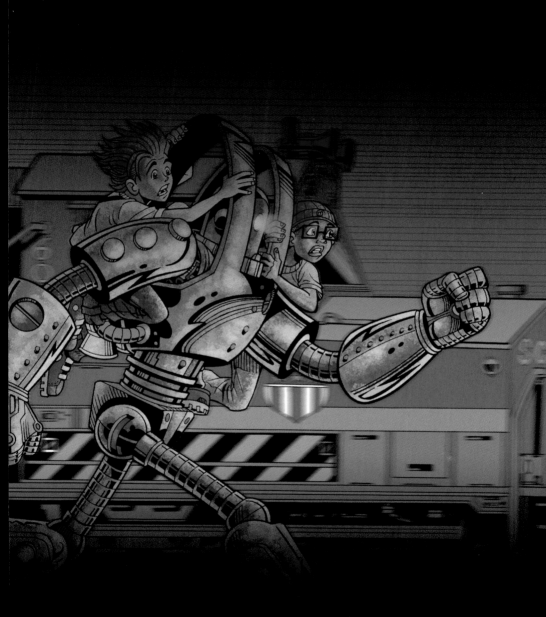

TO BE CONTINUED IN VOLUME 4...

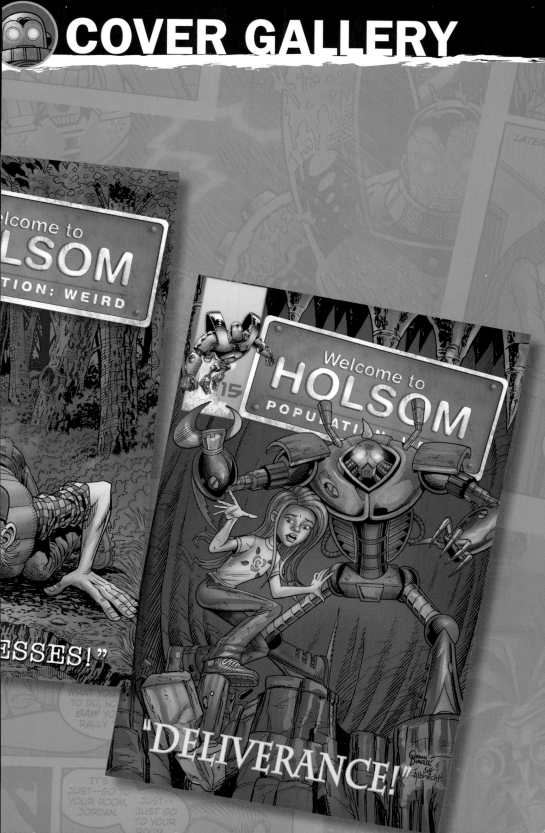